WHEN MIST AND BRINE TOUCH

ISABEL TUTAINE

GOLDEN BRIDGES PUBLISHING

CONTENTS

I'm not afraid of storms for I'm learning how to sail my ship.
Louisa May Alcott, Little Women, 1880

CHAPTER ONE

HEADING HOME

Port Hansweert, Holland, 1894

Captain Littledove shoved his way through the Port Hansweert harbor office that always stank of fish and bureaucracy. Except for cheese and beer, he didn't see any reason for a place like Hansweert to exist, seeing that the sun was so low to the ground everywhere, even mid-day was dull as dusk.

He wove his way to the largest desk on the floor, where he swung one leg over the back of the chair in front of it and sat, legs apart, one palm pressed against each knee. Bouncing one foot, he glared at the man behind the desk.

Heroditus Kraken, the harbormaster, looked up, suffered a spasm at seeing him, and shoved his chair as far as the wall behind him allowed. His hand flew over his nose, now lumpy from a punch Littledove once delivered after discovering the harbormaster arranged for stevedores to skim part of his cargo.

Littledove narrowed his eyes, and Kraken began slapping forms in front of him like a maniac. Without a hint of hurry, Littledove inspected each sheet front and back to ensure Kraken had not slipped an exemption clause into standard terms that would later make his life a hell. With Kraken, he had to double check everything. He smirked at the harbormaster and began signing the forms.

Kraken shifted his eyes from side to side, leaned forward ... ventured a whisper. "Stranded passengers scheduled for the *Andrea* are looking for passage to America—a doctor, his wife, two daughters. Very nice-looking daughters, I'll say. It can be profitable for you!"

"I don't run a hen frigate," snapped Littledove without looking up. He knew Kraken took substantial bribes to find passages for stranded people.

"Look." Kraken rattled a piece of paper with the amounts the passengers were offering to pay for passage. "Do these people a favor."

A bit of curiosity leached out of Littledove when he saw the figures. He sat up. "That's first-class passage money on a first-class ship. I run a cargo ship."

"They'll pay the same to be on your ship. They're desperate! Desperate, I tell you! You'll make good money. Just come and take a look at them."

Littledove wrinkled his nose at the hefty sums scribbled on the scrap of paper and resumed signing without speaking.

Kraken continued in low tones. "Heard the *Black Death* sunk the *Andrea*. They say she's a red galleon with black sails! Sinks every ship she crosses."

Littledove stuck out his chin and snorted. Pirates seldom sank ships, because destruction required funds and effort. They preferred to sneak up on their prey looking like any other ship rather than declare themselves from afar with fancy red hulls and black sails and give a prey a chance to flee. The *Andrea* might have sunk, but not because of pirates. He shoved the signed papers across the desk and stood, hands on hips.

He rarely took on passengers, but for no other reason than to raise Kraken's hopes, he said, "I'll 'ave that look now."

Never one to miss a financial opportunity, Kraken bolted to his feet and waved for Littledove to follow. They crossed the hall, and the harbor master gestured for Littledove to take a look through a window where the word WACHTRUIMTE (WAITING LOUNGE) arched across the glass. Littledove peeked between the T and the E of the gold letters.

An older gentleman sat on one side of the room, hand draped over a black leather medical bag. A matronly wife and two daughters huddled close by, heads bowed in conversation. The women's dresses had a quality he seldom saw in his walk of life. Nothing flashy. Everything was understated but smacked of opulence. Two of the women were so pale and thin they reminded him of chopsticks from the Orient. The third, shorter and pleasantly plump, had hair the color of Belgium chocolate. The women were very fine. Very fine.

Littledove capped his thoughts and turned to the harbormaster. "No. Women like them need luxuries I don't have."

He waited smugly for Kraken's disappointed frown, but Kraken swung open the door to the waiting lounge and said, more to the waiting passengers than to him, "Just talk to them."

The doctor sprang to his feet and began walking to the door with his medical bag, as if ready to board. The seated women startled into a stand, and Littledove immediately saw one was on the verge of womanhood but was still very much a child. She grinned coquettishly at him. A look like that, even from a child-woman, on a ship full of sailors could cause problems. He didn't need that.

He wondered if the pleasantly round woman was on ice skates when she glided to the window with a fluidity that did not even disturb the tiny pleats of her skirt. By the window, she rotated slowly and deliberately to face him while sunlight spiraled around her bosom, waist, and hips through the silk strands of her dress. She was the finest by far. Not stiff. Not timid. Not giggly. Not as fine boned as the other two, but still very, very fine.

Her sight rose up his body, studying every inch of him, before settling on his face. He couldn't read her expression.

On a good day, he'd feel privileged to indulge in fantasies about a woman like her. A fantasy was about as close as he would likely get to someone with that amount of presence.

"Good afternoon!" said the harbormaster. "This is Captain Littledove of the *Bessie*. He's heading out to America. He's interested in taking on passengers."

"I said no," Littledove snapped, ready to strangle Kraken.

Kraken smiled obsequiously before he slithered away. The passengers continued staring at Littledove as if he were some kind of savior—except for the daughter by the window. Littledove recalculated. Perhaps she was the wife. Lucky doctor.

The doctor spoke. "Are you heading to the east coast of America? Preferably north. Massachusetts? New York? I can make my way elsewhere from there."

"I's heading to Edith's Bay in Maine. On a cargo ship. Windjammer. No luxuries. Very rough at sea."

"I am not prone to sea sickness," said the doctor. He looked at his companions.

The chopstick matron and the woman by the window exchanged looks. They arrived at a consensus in some silent, cryptic way Littledove could not decipher. Observing the interaction, the chopstick girl smiled in preparation to giggle, but the matron put her hand on her shoulder to stop her.

"You bunk with the mates," Littledove said to the doctor, even if he had not completely shed his reluctance. The money was easy, after all. And a doctor on board was always good to have. The women he could do without, but they were part of the package. "Your wife and daughters sleep together in separate quarters—" He stopped speaking when confusion infused the passengers' expressions and they began looking at each other, bewildered.

The little coquettish one released her suppressed giggle and piped, "We are not married! None of us are! We are sisters!"

Littledove closed his eyes and stopped himself from cursing out loud. Kraken lied about the most inane things. He was incapable of being honest long enough to wipe his own ass.

Littledove continued speaking as if he were not mortified at having assumed a bunch of strangers were married. "Then the arrangements'll suit you. Three meals a day. Fare's reduced by a third because there're no luxuries. Make sure you understand that. No luxuries. No tea at three. No cabin boys. No servants. Basic meals. Ship's rough at sea, not dainty like a clipper. Wear clothes that don't rip easy. Recommend wool because it's always cold. Also, I don't allow fraternizing with the sailors. Anyone distracting them spends the voyage locked in their quarters."

The woman by the window squinted tightly as if to control a sudden urge to laugh. Her body contracted from her repose, and she ever so delicately rested one finger on her upper lip so the rest almost hid her smile.

Littledove stepped toward her. "Got problems with that?"

The woman made an effort to straighten her smile into a serious line. "Of course not, Captain. That is a most reasonable request. I was just wondering what sort of sailors you employ that we might want to fraternize with them."

"Men get imagination after time at sea. I don't tolerate misunderstandings of that kind on my ship."

"Of course, Captain." She straightened her lips again, but her eyes indicated her amusement had yet to pass.

The little one began speaking, her voice high pitched with excited indiscretion. "We were supposed to travel on the *Andrea*, but Black Death pirates sank it and—"

Littledove cut the girl short by addressing the matron. "Put what you need for the voyage in one trunk for each. There's no access to the other ones until we dock. Show up at pier fourteen tomorrow at six a.m. with passage in hand."

He walked away, leaving them to sort themselves. Perhaps taking on a club of hatchet murderers was safer than taking on a flock of fancy hens. To women who carried themselves with such majesty, seamen with their uncouth ways were no more than ridiculous creatures. But to those seamen, these women would be as appealing as French bonbons filled with liquor.

Before committing to traveling on the *Bessie* with Sarah and Jelly, Eliza inquired about Captain Littledove, who struck her as suffering from pernicious annoyance with everything. When she mentioned his name, those who had heard of him raised their eyebrows and nodded with respect. One man claimed the wind called Littledove by name and spoke to him directly. Another said he could identify hidden water currents by the way a ship creaked.

Eliza was not the least bit comforted by the tall tales and minimally comforted that no one had said anything overtly unflattering about him. The *Bessie*, despite a fresh coat of paint on the hull, reminded her of the tubs servants used to soak bed sheets on wash days. That some of the sails were patched did not inspire her confidence either.

Nonetheless, the next day she boarded the *Bessie* with her sisters because they needed to have passages on the same ship, and the ship was going directly to Edith's Bay, where they lived. And Dr. Aves seemed like a proper gentleman who might mitigate any issues that might arise with cargo ship sailors who lacked the polish of the staff on the clipper ship.

For the most part, Eliza kept herself and her sisters at a distance from Captain Littledove, whose vocabulary could sometimes turn milk rancid and was causing Jelly to ask what some of the words meant. Eliza didn't know what many of the vile words meant, but at least she had the sense not to ask. Jelly was too full of indiscretion. Sarah simply assumed everything the captain said had vile connotations and kept away from him. Eliza was grateful he seldom spoke to them directly, even if he always seemed to know exactly where on his ship they were.

Two weeks into the voyage, Eliza grew nervous when Littledove began roaming the decks with the listlessness of a mad man. He stared at the water with unusual frequency, listened to the sails when they flapped, and sniffed the air like a hound. Sailors kept an eye on him, mostly to stay out of his way as he stomped across the deck, one arm folded behind his back while swinging his other arm. But when Littledove pulled his spyglass out of his coat, all sailors raised their heads in attention.

Within the hour of giving commands to swap out the lighter sails for sturdier, unpatched ones, the wind picked up dramatically. The ship began veering, and a mess of seawater rose over the bulwark and crashed on the deck with a force that threatened to wash men overboard.

By this time, Eliza and her sisters were restricted to their quarters, where Sarah soon became queasy while Jelly giggled her way across the ocean, riding the ship's sudden jerks as if on a roller coaster. Eliza was trying to quiet Jelly for Sarah's sake when a lurch sent her rolling out of her bunk. Jelly laughed herself inside out as Eliza picked herself up from the floor. Fed up, she gathered her hair into a bun.

Jelly cut her giggles short as she climbed out of her bunk. "Where are you going? Take me with you!"

"I shall be right back. Stay here and look after Sarah, like a good sister."

Before Jelly could insist, Eliza slipped into the passage, where walking was almost impossible as the ship careened side to side and up and down. She bounced between the passage walls until the passage floor disappeared under her feet. Airborne, she slammed into the floor again. She would have gone back to the room but heard Sarah retching and Jelly shouting at Sarah to stop.

In a moment of honesty, she felt she would rather try her luck at taming sea dragons than return to her sisters. She picked herself up and continued teeter-tottering toward the light at the end of the passage until she found herself peering into a large, dimly lit room full of unoccupied bunks and swinging hammocks. Ah, the forecastle, where the sailors slept. She had read about it in a book.

Dr. Aves and a few sailors were huddling by a small stove at one end of a table that was bolted to the floor along with the long benches on either side of it. Dr. Aves' medicine chest was securely wedged between a bench and a table leg. On closer look, Eliza saw each seated sailor was nursing an injury. She was on the verge of backing out of the room after realizing she was the only woman there, but Dr. Aves looked up.

"Miss Strauss, please give us a hand. We need to expedite treatment so these men can get back to work."

As if in cahoots with the doctor, a sea swell sent her scrambling across the room and into the table. With as much poise as she could muster, she slipped onto the bench next to Dr. Aves and looked over the five sailors. All the teeth among them could not form a complete set for one. She wasn't sure what she was getting herself into, but she would much prefer anything over cleaning up after Sarah.

"Hand me a splint, Miss Strauss. Top of lid. On the left. Small ones are in the jar. We prefer curved ones for fingers," Dr. Aves said, which was just enough information for Eliza to pull out a curved splint about the length of a sailor's swollen index finger.

The line of patients continued growing as men waited with frightening slashes, bruises, sprains, head knocks, lungs full of sea water, red eye, new coughs and old ones that had gotten worse in a matter of hours. Some came in so wet and cold their lips were lavender and they could barely speak. Frostbite began appearing on fingers and toes and one sailor's nose as the storm raged on.

Eliza took a while to realize the man who was wandering around the forecastle picking up wet clothes and dirty bandages was the cook. She watched him for a while before suggesting, "If I may impose upon you, can you please make something hot for the men to drink?"

"Tha's jus' a bitty stove, Miss."

"Then may I suggest you make a bitty amount of something. A little is better than none. These men do not have the luxury of being sheltered here as you and I are."

"Ee pot'll go fly off and burn everyone! It'll set the ship on fire. Then you'll be dealin' wi' Cap'n Littledove, who real good dun like fires."

"That shall never happen, Mr. Cook, for I am certain you are very capable."

The men around the table sniggered at her flattery and egged on the cook by muttering that he had benefits they did not. He grumbled vividly as he stomped to the stove, where he whipped up a small pot of undercooked oatmeal that the men devoured as if it were steak with gravy.

Ruddy from the influx of approval, the cook took possession of the task and called to a sailor who was not too injured, "Put sum water in ee bucket with ee oats so it'll cook more quick!"

Small amounts of cooked oatmeal began materializing at a faster pace. The cook chose well because oatmeal stayed in the pot, whereas a liquid would have spilled everywhere. The oatmeal was more pan fried than boiled to reduce moisture. Sailors hailed the cook as a hero because even a half cup of lukewarm, undercooked oatmeal in the belly made a difference when a man went back to the deck to slosh in icy waters against a bitter wind.

Eliza had no idea how much time passed before the ship began to level out of its erratic moves and she could walk across the forecastle without stumbling like a drunkard. Most of the sailors who hobbled into the forecastle now stayed and fell asleep in hammocks and bunks. She had no sense of what time it was because sailors slept in four-hour shifts, day and night, but she felt tired enough to think she'd been up all night.

Her thoughts floated to Sarah and Jelly, lingered on them for a moment, then dissipated as she concluded they had to be safe in their room. Otherwise, Jelly would have sought her out. Eliza arched the sourness out of her back, taking in the recent lack of urgency in the forecastle.

Then Captain Littledove staggered in. His usual loose-limbed, rolling gait that accommodated the ship's constant shifts was reduced to a stiff sway. His rubber boots came up over his knees, although she imagined they were full of water because his thighs were soaked. A wide-brimmed oilskin hat obscured his face, and a loose oilskin coat made him look much wider than he was. Only his height kept him recognizable to Eliza, who looked away when he leaned against a wall to scan the room, now full of snoring sailors.

Dr. Aves wound his way around the clothes and bandages strewn on the floor to look after Littledove. From the corner of her eye, Eliza watched him remove Littledove's oilskin coat with a gentleness that implied the body in it was brittle and might snap from any sudden movement. He guided Littledove to the end of a long table, away from the other sailors. Eliza sensed she came up in the conversation when Littledove began shooting vexed glances in her direction while Dr. Aves spoke.

"Miss Strauss," said Dr. Aves as he came up behind her. "Please tend to Captain Littledove. He can't feel his hands, so be careful."

Eliza was tempted to encourage Littledove to come closer to the woodstove, but he was hunkered as if he might never again move. His cheeks and eyelids were burned from wind and salt water, and his lips were chapped. A drip was forming at the end of his intricately veined nose. He looked miserable as an occasional shiver made his teeth knock.

She draped a blanket around his shoulders as she had done with many of the other sailors and hesitated before pulling out his ponytail, which she knew was dripping cold water down his back. He stared at her with an arched eyebrow that made her feel she had intruded on his person.

"May I ask whether you can move your fingers, please?" Eliza asked.

Dr. Aves taught her to test for frostbite and broken fingers to determine how best to remove gloves. Cutting off gloves was to be avoided because some sailors had only the pair they wore. Littledove set his jaw and slowly stretched his fingers.

"If I may inquire, do you think anything is broken?" she asked.

Littledove shook his head.

"Then let us remove these gloves." *Let us*, not *May I*, Dr. Aves instructed her to say, so she gave the impression of being in command, causing the men to be more likely to follow her instructions while in discomfort. Eliza liberated Littledove's hands from the gloves, by now too wet to protect his skin, revealing calloused fingers that were raw and red and icy cold. She checked his hands for frostbite before wrapping them in wool cloth. His look softened as she tucked the corners around his wrists.

"If I may ask, how long were you out there?" asked Eliza.

"Eight watches straight."

She was relieved to finally hear him speak, although she had no idea what his answer meant. Eliza smiled graciously and said, "I trust we did not come close to sinking."

Littledove glowered at her. "That's what the captain's for. To keep the ship from sinking."

Aware she offended him with what she thought was small talk, Eliza retreated. "I shall get something warm for you to eat."

Littledove's eyes shifted at the mention of something to eat. He looked at the cook, who stood by the stove, holding a tiny pot with a giant leather hearth glove while joking with some men. Then Littledove tugged the blanket over his shoulders and shivered into a sulk.

Eliza placed a cup half full of oatmeal and a mug of water before him. He pushed aside the mug, gingerly scooped a bit of oatmeal onto his tongue, and swallowed. Then in four spoonfuls, he emptied the cup just as Dr. Aves placed another mug on the table.

"Captain's tea. Good for aches," said Dr. Aves, although Eliza could smell the rum from where she sat. "Recommend you drink the water first if you want to be able to walk to your quarters."

The moment Dr. Aves walked away, Littledove reached for the rum. Eliza slipped her hand over his wrist. "Dr. Aves asked you to drink the water first."

Littledove flashed his eyes at her as if she had been assigned to annoy him, but he did not defy her touch against his wrist. He pulled the water mug toward himself and emptied it in a few gulps. Then he downed the rum in one, slamming the mug on the table as he tucked his chin to swallow it. The rum sent a bit of color into his cheeks.

"Report on my men, Miss Strauss."

"Report?"

"Yes, report. How'd you find them?"

"Perhaps Dr. Aves would be better—"

"I'm asking you, not Aves. Report on the men." He paused, stricken with concentration. "Please." The word did not come easily to him.

Eliza folded her hands on the table and composed herself. "Several have broken fingers. Almost all have rope burns. Someone has a cracked bone in his wrist. I believe someone has a cracked rib. One had a nasty head bump. Many bruises and sprains. Oh—someone lost a tooth. Dr. Aves put in a few stitches on a few men, but nothing looked serious. Some frostbite here and there, but no lost fingers or toes. Many are complaining of sore throats."

"What's the cook doing?"

As if he does not know, thought Eliza, remembering the cook told her that Littledove did not permit cooking during storms. But did making oatmeal constitute cooking? Eliza braced herself. "I asked him to make something hot for the men."

Littledove's sight flickered over the empty cup before him that once held oatmeal. "Cooking's not allowed in storms."

"He used a small pot and held it to ensure it would not slip off the stove."

"Still not allowed."

"I take full responsibility. I asked him to make something hot for the men."

"Just because you volunteer responsibility doesn't mean he should've done it."

Eliza looked the captain over. Surely, he couldn't be upset over such a small thing. "Captain Littledove, if I may, the stove was already lit and watched. Absolutely no harm was done, and even you have benefited. You may try to deny that, if you wish."

Littledove stared hard at her before tacking. "The other ladies also loose on the ship doing good?"

"They are resting," Eliza answered curtly, offended that Littledove spoke about her sisters as if they were goats that occasionally got loose.

"You didn't stay in your quarters. You disobeyed my orders."

Eliza straightened her back. The captain was beginning to annoy her. "I cannot wait for your permission to be of help when help is needed. For all I know, you might have fallen overboard."

Littledove turned gray with indignation at her suggestion that he might have fallen off his ship. They stared at one another, neither looking away until Eliza's eyes dried out and she blinked. Littledove looked into his mug, probably wishing it still had rum, and said more gently, "Going against orders is real dangerous on a ship in storm."

"May I ask if you have yet scolded Dr. Aves, Captain Littledove? Or is he next in line because you were taught ladies always go first?"

Littledove stretched himself as if he had not heard her and explored the regained flexibility of his body. He put his forearms on the table and began to slide a mug from one hand to the other.

"Captain, you look exhausted. Please stop picking fights and get some rest." Eliza began to stand.

Littledove shot to his feet. "Stay seated, Miss Strauss. I'm coming back."

His look nailed her to the bench. She remained seated, unable to fathom why he needed her to stay. Littledove strode to the men around the stove with his shoulders angled to made clear he was determined not to look at her. The men fell silent as he approached and entered another mood.

"Good work. Real good work. All o' you," said Littledove. "I's proud."

The men beamed. They nodded and nudged one another after he wandered away. Eliza took note. The captain's praise was valuable.

He made his way back to her. "Let me walk you to your quarters, Miss Strauss."

"If Dr. Aves does not need me—"

"We're done here." He hesitated, then repeated as if asking permission, "If you don't mind, I can walk you to your quarters."

Eliza responded by heading out of the forecastle without saying another word. Their silence pursued them as they walked down the passage and pressed more tiredness into her.

She suspected Littledove was escorting her back to enforce his order that he wanted all passengers in their quarters, and she grew incensed at being treated like a misbehaving child. Outside of the room, she waited on the verge of snapping for Littledove to deliver his final mandate of the night.

"Understand I'm tired, Miss Strauss. And I'm cold. Second mate has the watch. He's cold and tired too, so stay in your quarters so he gets less to worry about."

"Well, I have not been warm since I boarded your boat. And I am not complaining."

When her words finished tumbling out of her mouth, Littledove looked as if she had slapped him. Eliza froze as she realized she was unjustly furious at imagined offenses he had not committed. The man had almost frozen on the deck guiding the ship through a storm. He had earned his grumpiness.

Before she could regroup and apologize, Littledove made an about-face and walked away, occasionally touching a wall to steady himself. Embarrassed at having spoken to him with such disregard, Eliza opened the door and slipped into her quarters, where her sisters were now asleep.

Chapter Two

GREETING THE UNWELCOMED

Littledove made his way around the deck, miffed that Eliza continued to herd her sisters to the opposite side of the deck from where he stood. He'd cut down on his swearing and forbidden the men from singing lewd shanties when the women were on deck, but she persisted on guiding them to the farthest place on board from where he was.

Just how superior did she think herself? He was surprised she'd even thought that the sailors needed something hot to eat during the storm. He marveled at how such inviting softness of body could harbor such aloof disdain. Showed him what he knew about women.

Occasionally, he considered himself fortunate that the ladies were across the deck when the giggles of the little coquettish one gathered to almost hysterical levels, as if a pandemonium of parrots lived in her mouth. He was convinced ninety percent of the girl's brain was devoted to giggling. Why girls were not taught to laugh so a man's teeth didn't hurt was beyond him.

From his peripheral vision, he watched the sisters make their way to the foredeck as he headed to the aft deck, where he pulled out his spyglass. The pale, thin thread of gray clouds hovering on the horizon pushed their slights out of his thoughts.

Another storm. Its distance and thinness neither alarmed nor deceived him. 'Twas the season of storms, after all. He only hoped the storm would not be as fierce as the previous one that almost took out several of his men and left him sore and depleted for days. He made his way to the foredeck to take a look at the conditions in the direction they were heading. He never counted on outrunning a storm, but sometimes he got lucky.

The passengers' voices floated over the deck. He set his jaw when he realized the sisters were trapped in a conversation with Dr. Aves and could not walk away to avoid him.

Littledove gave his lapels a quick brush to look his best for no apparent reason and trotted up the steps to the foredeck. As he acknowledged the passengers with a nod, he found himself wishing his sails had the quality and amplitude of the ladies' skirts. Very fine skirts.

Don't get imagination, he warned himself. *Women like that're used to things you don't even know about, never mind afford.*

He was about to look through the spyglass when a chuckle and a burst of titters prompted him to look at the passengers again. Everyone was engaged in the conversation and laughing. Except Eliza. She was studying him. Openly. Caught off guard, he snapped his spyglass to its full length and jerked his head in a nod.

She tipped her head to one side and looked at the spyglass. Then at him, taking in his face. Then back to the spyglass in his hands.

He lowered the spyglass, unsure how to proceed. He had forbidden fraternizing. However, his duties as a captain included talking to passengers. He could not possibly spend an entire voyage without speaking to them because they were ... fine women. Very fine women.

He held out the spyglass to see what Eliza would do. To his surprise, she began walking toward him. He stifled a grin with a serious expression to hide the chill of thrill and silently handed her the spyglass when she was by his side. Then he fixed his sight on the horizon.

"Where do you recommend I look, Captain?"

"Northwesterly. Where we're heading." He kept his sight on the horizon.

Eliza pressed her eye to the spyglass and swept the horizon, tipping Littledove that she couldn't tell northwest from her elbow. When she lowered the spyglass, she clenched the bulwark and swayed as if combatting a bout of dizziness. He forbade himself from reaching out to steady her.

"May I ask if you are aiming to get to that island?" she asked when she opened her eyes.

"There's no islands out here."

Eliza frowned and looked through the spyglass again. "Then what, may I ask, is that?"

"Pod of whales, pro'bly."

He took the spyglass from her and looked in the general direction she pointed. He firmed his grip around the spyglass when he spotted what she had probably seen. Something cone-shaped. Whatever it was bobbed like a ship but was not one. Not land, either. Did not look like part of the sea. Was too consistent on the surface to be a breaching whale. Might be an illusion, but it did not fade or waver. A buoy? Not in a place too deep to anchor.

"Windle!" Littledove shouted and walked away from Eliza.

The first mate came running, and Littledove instructed, "Look northwest."

Windle squinted in the direction. Exasperated, Littledove thrust the spyglass against Windle's chest. He had not meant for the mate to look with a naked eye. Windle plugged his eye into the eyepiece and took his time adjusting the focus and scanning the ocean.

He lowered the spy glass, shook his head, and shrugged. "Dunno, Captain."

"Find out what the hell that is," said Littledove. "We're heading toward it."

Windle sent a sailor with the spyglass to the crow's nest with twenty warnings that the spyglass was the captain's and not to drop it. Close to ten minutes passed, during which Littledove occasionally rolled his shoulders and shook out his arms to release tension. He hated not knowing. Sometimes he squinted at the crow's nest, imagining the sailor found mermaids and was taking time to enjoy them before letting on.

Then the call came. "Ship! Ship ahoy!"

Littledove squinted with naked eyes at the thing. Whatever it was still did not look like a ship. He half-sprinted across the deck and was at the base of the mast before the sailor finished climbing down.

"Report," he demanded.

"A strange one, Cap'n. Like she be in mournin'—"

Littledove had no patience for blither. He grabbed the spyglass from the sailor, looked and focused, looked and focused until his mouth fell open. He pulled the glass from his eye to rub the eyepiece clean and looked again.

"All hands on deck!" he shouted, and in preparation to reverse the ship's direction, added, "Ready about! Windle!"

"Aye, sir!"

"Take the passengers under. Put them all in the ladies' quarters—"

"Dr. Aves too?"

"Yes! Aves too. Tell them to keep the door locked. Put their trunks against it. No one's to leave the room, no matter what. No one's to make any sound, especially not the ladies. No talking. No lights. Give Aves a pistol and tell him to shoot anyone who tries to get in."

Littledove kept the *Bessie*'s sails so full of wind for speed they were straining, and the men on deck struggled to shift them. He had no time to change the light sails for heavier ones and was praying out loud into the wind that a sail would not blow out and slow them down. He had never sailed the *Bessie* this fast in his life, not even under a wager because no wager was ever large enough to cover the cost of a ripped sail.

Now he could clearly see the ship. The hull was a dull gray, but the sails were so black he could hardly tell them apart. No wonder they looked solid from a distance. She was, undeniably, the *Black Death*. And she was faster than the *Bessie*, who was too flat-bottomed for speed. The *Black Death* covered so much distance in such a short time the ship seemed propelled by magic.

Littledove sailed hard and recklessly until one of his lower sails blew out with a loud rip that made his skin crawl, even if he was not surprised. They had no chance now. Not that their chances had ever been good because a brigantine was always faster than a windjammer loaded with cargo, but now he could no longer deceive himself that the *Bessie* might be fast enough. He was doing everything he could do, and it was not going to be enough.

Littledove looked at the *Black Death* through his spyglass again. Someone wearing a bright yellow vest was gesticulating and seemed to be in charge of the men loading the deck cannons. Littledove scanned downward. The cannon ports were being opened. Each port ominously filled the eyepiece on his spyglass.

He looked over his men. All eyes were on him, and all eyes were afraid. By now they had seen the black sails, and those who did not already know what they signified had been informed. Only he could pull them out of this predicament, just as he pulled them through storms.

In desperation, Littledove listened to the wind. He checked the messages the weather deities were scribbling in the waves for him. He gave the helmsman a new course into the storm that no one had yet sensed was lurking. He ordered the helmsman to stay the course at all costs.

He told the mates to keep the course too and to keep all the sails full of wind, something he rarely did when heading into a storm because unpredictable shifts in winds made a ship difficult to handle. But he knew no one could board a ship in a storm, especially one whose sails were full.

Black Death pirates did more that steal. They killed.

Littledove urged the storm to come upon them, but the *Black Death* was faster, and it was almost upon the *Bessie*. He looked through the spyglass and saw the man in the yellow vest giving orders to aim the deck cannons. Littledove called his first mate, instructed him to surrender without a struggle when the pirates boarded, and to let them take the cargo. The goal was to survive. Dead men had no use for cargo. Then he went below deck.

In the static of the unexplained danger, Eliza was glad Jelly slipped into her bunk so Dr. Aves would have a place to rest with the least amount of self-consciousness about sharing dark quarters with three young women. Sarah curled up in her own bunk, wide-eyed with fear, her pallor almost illuminating the darkness.

Eliza patted Jelly on the back. Even Jelly had the sense to stay quiet. Perhaps Jelly's fear would last until the situation passed so she would not get bored and start making demands.

The banging on the door almost made Eliza yip in a startle. In one motion, Sarah drew her knees up to her chin. Jelly was about to scream, but Eliza slapped her hand over her mouth and stared her into silence. Dr. Aves pointed the pistol at the door, but his hands were shaking so hard Eliza doubted he could hit the door.

"Open up! It's Littledove! Goddamn it, open up! Littledove here!"

"Oh, please do not shoot!" Eliza whispered, suddenly glad Dr. Aves could not bring himself to use a pistol.

She leapt out of the bed over Jelly, not caring that her petticoats were showing. With strength she did not know she had, she began to pull the trunks away from the door. Sarah and Dr. Aves joined her.

Littledove was trying to shove the door open with his shoulder. "It's Littledove! Littledove! Open the goddamn door!"

The door was barely halfway open when Littledove reached in and grabbed Eliza's wrist. He pulled her between Sarah and Dr. Aves into the hallway and said to everyone still in the quarters, "Close up. Nothing's changed."

On Jelly's voice, he slammed the door shut. "Eliza! Where are you taking Miss Eliza?"

Littledove pulled Eliza by the wrist as he ran down the passage. Several explosions went off on the deck. A mast cracked and squeaked as it splintered and fell with a force that shook the ship like an earthquake shakes land.

Littledove opened the door to his quarters and pulled her inside. He reached over his head to press something that caused part of the wall to swing open like a door.

"Pirates. Don't leave this place until you don't hear anything or I come get you. Don't get out for anyone that's not me." He shoved her onto a bench in the compartment behind the panel. "And don't make noise."

"My sisters—"

Littledove slammed the panel shut. Almost immediately, Eliza heard more explosions, more yelling, more shouting. The rapid pops of gunfire surprised her because she had never seen any of the sailors with firearms. Then footsteps of a thousand men rumbled down the stairs and through the passage. She went from breathing hard through her mouth to holding her breath.

"Lookie here! It's Cap'n Littledick! Lord of the watering can."

A tiny slice of light was parting the darkness in the compartment, and she peeked through the crack in the panel, worrying all the time that someone would notice her eye. She could see the room in less than one-eighth-inch slivers.

A sliver of Littledove backed into her view with the glint of a knife in his hand. She had never seen Littledove without that knife on his belt. He used it to cut everything from jerky to ropes. Another man had to be standing in front of Littledove, but she could not see him.

"Hoorst, you bastard," growled Littledove. "You dropped even lower."

More men stampeded into the room, but she could not see them. Littledove was outnumbered. Eliza stuffed her skirt into her mouth to keep from making any sound. The compartment closed in on her like a coffin. The more she tried to see, the more the darkness pressed against her eyes.

"Bastard's mine!" shouted Hoorst.

The new men chortled. One said with slick sweetness, "All for you? Not sharin'?"

After the rhetorical question, they left in a thunderous huddle, wishing Hoorst much pleasure. Eliza heard the latch catch when they slammed the door behind them and became part of the cacophony in the passage.

"Gonna make me a flyswatter out o' you pigtail, Littledove. Gonna use it to kill flies all o'er the world."

Through the crack in the panel, Eliza saw glints of knives and slivers of colors as Littledove and Hoorst went back and forth across the room, tipping chairs in front of one another, knocking things off shelves, flinging things that shattered wherever they landed. Several objects smashed against the panel of the compartment, and each time Eliza almost levitated from the bench with fright and shoved more of her skirt into her mouth.

She went cold when, above the racket of footsteps and crashing things, she heard Jelly screaming. She listened for Sarah but knew Sarah would become all eyes and never make a sound. But Jelly's shrieks continued to come down the hallway.

Eliza had never heard such terror in a scream. Dr. Aves was pleading for the pirates to leave the girls alone. Jelly's screams combined with sobs when she passed by the door to

Littledove's quarters. Eliza heard her for a little longer, but when they took her on the deck, not at all. Sarah never emerged from her silence.

Now sick with fright, Eliza listened to an unbelievable amount of gunfire coming from the deck and prayed no bullet would strike Sarah or Jelly. More than the gunfire, her inability to do something—*anything*—terrified her. With hordes of armed pirates storming the ship, she could not expect to save Sarah and Jelly by pummeling her fists against pirates' chests and kicking them in the shins. She didn't even have a knife, much less a pistol.

Her helplessness grew as she realized what little she could do was only enough to put herself in her sister's predicament without a good outcome for anyone. Still, the notion of doing something would not abandon her.

Something metallic rattled in the room, and Eliza looked through the crack. *Littledove.* Littledove could help her rescue her sisters. He had the strength. He would know what to do.

Through the crack, she could see Littledove's sleeve and ... and ... no knife in his hand. Was that the hand he used to hold his knife? She could not remember. A second sliver of cloth was entwined with Littledove's clothes. She made out that Littledove and Hoorst were rotating slowly, as if dancing.

A moment later, Littledove shoved Hoorst away. Hoorst swayed, making a gurgling sound as his blood spurted all over Littledove. One of Hoorst's knees buckled, and he spiraled to the floor as the other knee buckled. He finished falling face down in slow motion, spasmed with a kick, and then was still. The handle of Littledove's knife stuck out of his neck.

Littledove stood with unusual stillness for a man who always seemed to be in motion. Eliza could see strips of his face, now almost colorless. Eliza looked up and down the crack when he tipped and grabbed the bedpost, leaving a streak of red on the wood. Hoorst's blood?

She looked as best she could all over the room, an exercise that was like inspecting the Grand Canyon through a reed. She listened to the racket outside the room, in the passage where she had last heard Jelly screaming and felt Sarah disappearing into silence. She needed Littledove to help her rescue Sarah and Jelly. Littledove would be her weapon.

Eliza ran her hands along the edge of the panel and found the latch over her head. Her hands were shaking so much she could barely release it. All of her was shaking. She opened the panel a crack, prepared to snap it back shut at a moment's notice.

Her being splintered with fright and her senses took over, each one emerging solitarily as it was needed. Her sight spotted the latch that locked the door protruding as if under a magnifying glass. Her hearing registered Littledove's breaths as if they were church bells.

Her sight resumed, seeing the room as if its space was a solid object. Her skin dissolved in the compartment and rematerialized outside of it.

Littledove's breathing faded as her heartbeat deafened her, pounding as rapidly it sounded like running footsteps. The sweeping winds she heard turned out to be her breaths. Her sight took over again. A hilt was sticking out of Littledove's side, and he was dripping his own blood as he clung to the bedpost.

Go back! she saw him mouth but could not hear him.

Her voice spoke. "Come with me."

Littledove shook his head. *Go!*

"I am going to pull it out." Hands like hers wrapped around the hilt and pulled. The knife came out with a sound like a slurp, and a moment later, she was splattered with blood. Littledove gagged and doubled over.

The door shook as someone tried to open it. "Hoorst! You finish him?"

Her senses reconvened into Eliza. She grabbed a pillow from the bed and pressed it over Littledove's wound. "Come."

She slipped her shoulder under his arm. Together, in an intense, unearthly calm so contrary to the chaos around them, they floated into the compartment while the cabin door rattled as pirates tried to get into the room.

"Hoorst! You there? You better have yee knife stickin' up 'is arse by now. We needs you on deck."

Eliza sat Littledove on the bench in the compartment and straddled his legs to fit herself into the tiny space. The rattling of the door grew louder with the possibility that it might break open at any second and pirates would spill into the room.

Chapter Three

BANDAGING THE WOUNDED

The cabin door latch snapped with a metallic clang, and the door banged open just as the latch on the compartment's panel door caught. Several men tumbled into the room and began to swear about Hoorst's body. One man slipped on the blood and released a blast of curses. Someone else called for a manhunt to find Littledove. Only one man wondered aloud how Littledove left the locked room, but his thought was overtaken by commotion.

Eliza began to shake uncontrollably as the men, in a tsunami of destruction, ransacked drawers, broke glass, knocked books off shelves, and more. Even her internal organs were shaking, and she felt a warm trickle of urine roll down her leg. She could not even bring herself to look through the little crack because she was afraid they would see her if she looked. Nothing outside the compartment was still, and the sound of the motion accumulated around her like solid mass. She began to cry silently, not even daring to sniffle.

Littledove was rocking in pain. Eliza could see his face when he tipped forward into the sliver of light. He was gasping, and she stuffed cloth from her skirt into his mouth to prevent him from making sound. She pulled him to herself and clung to him, as much to comfort herself as to prevent him from rocking. His bloody shirt stuck against her bodice.

The ransacking continued without any hint of ever ending until it terminated as abruptly as it began. The room cleared out, although she could still hear commotion in the passage. Someone yelled to get Hoorst, and a few men came back into Littledove's quarters. She saw their shadows flit across the crack as they removed the body. More footsteps moved up to the deck. None descended. She realized the gunshots stopped a while ago.

Sarah? Jelly? Where are Sarah and Jelly?

By the light of the crack, Eliza saw Littledove's eyes were clenched as he now rocked his forehead side to side against her shoulder. He was drawing air in shallow, abbreviated breaths, as if even breathing hurt. Without commotion, anyone might hear them now.

"No sound. No sound," Eliza whispered in Littledove's ear. The mandate to keep silent trumped everything, even pain and fear.

The noises of people on the ship became lighter and irregular. The ship listed and began to sway more distinctly. Littledove swung backward during a lurch, and Eliza put her hand on the back of his head just in time to stop him from banging his skull against a stud. She pulled him forward against her shoulder again.

"No sound. Rest against me."

She stroked his back. His entire weight was against her body, and she was grateful to be able to lean against the studs behind her. Sometimes his body clenched and spasmed. He was trying to swallow, but the gag made that small comfort difficult. Eliza feared he would moan without the gag. The pillow she had used to cover Littledove's wound was now saturated with blood and transferring its wetness past her skirt to her petticoat.

"Shhh," she whispered. "Very quiet. Shhh." The difference between life and death was the ability to remain silent and a half-inch panel of wood that any hatchet could hack apart in minutes. "Very quiet. Shhh."

Eliza stroked his forehead to comfort him. She did not know what she would do if Littledove bled to death in her arms in a compartment the size of a broom closet. That was as unimaginable as Sarah and Jelly being carried off by pirates. And that had already happened.

Time had a way of remaining undefined in the compartment. The light from the crack stopped cutting the darkness, which Eliza wanted to interpret as nightfall, but the ship was rolling more than usual, an indication that it was in a storm. Storms traveled with their own darkness that did not preclude the possibility that night had not yet fallen. The natural creaks and groans of the ship rendered Eliza unable to hear anyone else who might be on board.

The risk of leaving the compartment felt so overwhelming that Eliza stayed in it until her legs lost feeling and her skirt grew heavy with Littledove's blood. By then, the ship's rolling was not as pronounced. Littledove rested heavily against her, perhaps asleep, perhaps unconscious. At least he was alive.

She rubbed her fingers together, and dry blood flaked off them. Slowly, she cracked the panel open and peeked out. Fear augmented her hearing, and despite the moaning and creaking of the ship, she determined no one was in the room. The passage outside the room sounded empty. She leaned Littledove against the studs and pulled her skirt out of his mouth. Littledove's eyes opened in slits.

She put her hand against his forehead. "I think everyone has left. Stay here while I take a look outside."

Littledove mumbled incoherently.

Between heartbeats, Eliza inched the panel open, all the time expecting someone to pounce into the room. With no feeling in her legs, she tumbled out and landed on the floor, astonished at how much noise a falling body could make. She crouched, forcing herself to ignore the slick of blood on which she landed, and stayed as still as she could while listening for indications that others were on the ship. Her legs tingled unpleasantly and did not want to move.

When no one appeared, she looked around. The room looked nothing like the one she had entered. The floor was covered with everything that had once been in a cabinet or drawer, and almost everything was broken. Everything was smeared with blood, Littledove's or Hoorst's or someone else's.

Feeling she had fallen out of a closet into a nightmare, Eliza crawled to the door, trying not to make any sound, which was impossible while crawling across a bed of debris. She heard water trickling. When she opened the door, water rolled across the floor toward her and mixed with the clotted blood on the floor.

Still unable to stand and not willing to back into the blood again, she crawled on all fours into the thin layer of water in the passage. She looked up. The hatches were not battened. She knew from previous storms that battening hatches was one of the first things Littledove ordered before storms, and sometimes they were battened before he issued the order. A new brand of fear—that the ship would fill with water and sink—displaced her fear of being found.

From where she was on the floor, she could see a few links of a chain hanging from the iron grid of the closest hatch. Perhaps she could use the chain to pull the battens over the hatch. Sailors always fiddled with chains when they battened the hatches.

Eliza stood and stumbled across the hall on legs she could barely feel. She jumped twice to reach the chain before the ship rolled and the chain rattled down through the holes in the iron grid. Link by link, each thumped on her head and shoulders like rocks. She cried out until she slipped on the water and fell.

She was struggling to get the chain off her when she froze mid-motion. Pirates might be on the deck. Perhaps they heard the chain rattle. And she cried out like a fool when the links landed on her. Eliza listened. No footsteps. If pirates were on deck, they would have come for her by now. Hatches did not shriek in pain when battened.

Tingling with fear, she crawled up the steps and approached the door to the deck. Littledove always chased everyone off the deck until no more than the necessary people remained during a storm because people might be washed overboard. He claimed even experienced sailors were sometimes overtaken by waves.

Eliza calculated her chances while listening with an intensity that made her head ache—or perhaps it had been aching all along and she only just noticed. The exaggerated rolling of the ship had not quite ceased, but the water coming through the open hatches dripped, not poured. She might be safe if she just cracked open the door and peeked without stepping onto the deck.

Eliza glanced at the hatch. Someone would have heard her by now. No one was coming for her. After a moment of considering options, she unlatched and cracked open the door to the deck.

A slap across her face sent her rolling on her knees and breasts to the bottom of the steps. High strung with fright, she yipped each time the door bashed open and closed in the wind. At the bottom of the steps, she recognized the white cape in the doorway was a flapping sail from a fallen yardarm. Eliza coughed to keep herself from vomiting from the fright.

Desperate to find Sarah and Jelly, she crawled up the steps on her hands and knees, pausing at each step to listen and sometimes to rub her scraped shins. She pushed the sail aside just enough to look at the deck from the level of the threshold. The rain was lighter than the shifting of the ship suggested it would be. No one was on the deck that she could see. Perhaps everyone had been taken to the pirate ship. Or had been thrown into the ocean.

"Sarah? Jelly?" she called in a whisper. Then, realizing no one could hear a whisper on deck, she called louder, "Sarah! Jelly!" and frightened herself into slamming shut the door.

She held her breath as she waited for pirates to come and throw her into the ocean. No one appeared. Not pirates. Not Sarah. Not Jelly. Eliza opened the door again and stuck out her head. Not one person was on the part of the deck she could see. The ship felt deserted.

She closed the door and sat with her back to it, feeling lightheaded. Then she remembered Littledove. There were only so many places Sarah and Jelly could hide in a place as limited as a ship. She hurried back to the captain's quarters.

Littledove was sprawled on the floor, either having fallen out of the compartment or having tried to leave it on his own. He was barely conscious. When Eliza put her hand over his, he startled and formed fists.

"Be still. Be still. Just be still. Shhh. It is I, Miss Strauss." Eliza struggled to hold his wrists. "Shhh. Be still. I am going to take care of you. Shhh." When Littledove stopped struggling at the sound of her voice, she added, "I think we are the only ones on board. I think we are safe."

On her knees, Eliza undid his tie and unbuttoned his shirt. He was a long pen stroke of a man. Not broad-shouldered in the least. Hardly any fat over ribs and sinew. She looked at the stab wound, a gash that stretched open like a red mouth. Eliza rolled into a seated position and hugged her knees. In one moment, everything shifted from terrifying to daunting.

Bandages. Ointment. Boiling water. Eliza abandoned Littledove and ran through the wet hallways to the mate's bunk, where Dr. Aves kept his medicine chest. Even in the chaos of the ransacked room, she could see the chest was not there. Creeping swiftly, she headed to the forecastle, now eerily deserted. No medicine chest there either. Eliza proceeded to the kitchen, listening at doors along the passage to check whether anyone—Sarah? Jelly?—was behind them and eventually opening each door. Even the emptiness in each room made her eyes tear with fear.

In the kitchen, she opened every drawer and cabinet, looking for whatever might be useful. Kitchen towels would have to do for bandages, if she found any. In the next cabinet she opened she found not towels but starched aprons that had never been worn, at least not by the cook. Good enough.

The stove was still warm, and she shifted the logs in it to resuscitate the flames as she had seen servants at home do. She filled a dented pot with drinking water from a barrel and hoped the stove would generate enough heat to boil it.

She was not sure what she would do with the boiling water, but at home, doctors were always asking for boiled water. She could not possibly pour it on Littledove's wound to cleanse it. Eliza looked at an apron. Boil it? No. She needed dry bandages immediately. She left the pot on the stove until she could think about the purpose of boiled water.

Stitches. Where to get stitches? She sat on a broken crate and began to unravel the lace from one of her petticoats. When the water hissed to a boil and overflowed from the pot, she threw the thread into the rolling water without thinking. That's what the boiling water was for, she remembered from a time a stable boy required stitches. She should have remembered that sooner. Her head was not working right.

Thoughts clicked through her mind at incredible speed as she opened cabinets and drawers, looking for solutions to problems as she became aware of them. She ransacked the utensils in a drawer where she found a fowl trussing kit, complete with a curved needle that she added to the pot of boiling water.

The smell ... the smell ... She had not smelled it before, but now it seemed everywhere. A distinctly unpleasant smell of something rotting. Eliza sniffed around. The thought of a dead person in the hull revolted her. She sniffed again. Herself?

Her skirt. Her skirt was rigid with putrefying blood. One observation from her bloody skirt would last her entire life: Death smelled terrible. She had often heard people speak romantically of death as the release of the soul onto the benevolence of deities and afterlives. Now she realized it was the first step of putrefaction. People who went to funerals and complained about the intensity of the incense were unaware that putrefaction stank.

Eliza took off the skirt and the petticoat under it that was also soaked in blood and threw them aside with disgust. The bloody bodice went as well. For modesty, she tied an apron on herself. She hesitated before she slipped off her underwear. The rest of her petticoats would keep her modest. She counted on Littledove being in too poor condition to notice what she was—or, rather, was *not*—wearing.

In apron and petticoats, Eliza began her search for rum, which she heard from a friend of her father's had been used on wounds during wars. Dr. Aves and Littledove often indulged in a bit of rum. Surely there had to be at least one bottle left on the ship. She continued to open cabinets until she found a case of tall bottles. Rum!

Eliza pulled out a green bottle and made out the words molded into the glass: Whiplash's Tonic. She stood still, feeling compelled to listen for sounds made by anyone else. Hearing no one, she unscrewed the bottle cap and almost fell over from the acrid, medicinal smell. She remembered Dr. Aves cleaned a sailor's gash with the tonic, and the sailor almost burst into tears from the sting.

That the pirates left an entire case behind was not a good endorsement for the substance because they had not left much of anything else. She considered looking for another tonic, but time was of essence, and she suspected pirates would never leave behind anything like rum. Pirates could probably smell rum even when it was sealed in a bottle.

She capped the bottle and slipped it into the apron pocket. She grabbed the pot with the thread and trussing needle and hurried back to Littledove, her feet sloshing through the wet passage. She listened for Sarah and Jelly.

Eliza entered Littledove's quarters already looking around. Littledove might not cooperate, she knew, even if he was only half conscious.

The bed would hold in place. Like all the other furniture except one chair, it was built into the room so it would not slide when the ship rocked. The studs in the secret compartment would probably hold as well. And Littledove was between the two.

She cut four lengths of rope from one she found. She hesitated before taking off Littledove's boots and looping a piece of rope around each ankle. Then she tied the other ends to studs in the compartment.

The other two lengths, she looped around his wrists. Littledove mumbled a protest when she raised his arms over his head and tied each rope to a bedpost, taking out as much slack as possible until he was spread-eagle. He was still struggling half-consciously to lower his arms when Eliza drew the same emotionless expression she had seen on Dr. Aves when he poured Whiplash's Tonic over the sailor's arm. Dr. Aves explained that the tonic burned because it cauterized, which meant it stopped bleeding. She allowed the expression to work its way into her before she tipped the bottle over Littledove's open wound.

Littledove arched his back and shrieked when the tonic hit his flesh. He opened his eyes wide as if to give the pain an exit from his body, and when that failed to work, he shut them tightly as if to keep more pain from entering. Neither tactic worked. He shrieked again.

He writhed as Eliza pierced the trussing needle through his skin across the wound as if she were sewing a hem while she listened to more swear words than she thought existed. She persisted with determination, heart hardened to his agony because otherwise she would simply collapse. At least she had the sense to bandage the wound before she cut the ropes that held him because afterward, he curled into a fetal position and rocked.

"Try not to move. It hurts less if you do not move," she whispered, recalling something Dr. Aves had said to the sailor. Like a mantra, she recited, "Move less, hurt less. Try, try. Please try."

But Littledove bucked and rocked and rolled while she tried to restrain him until he shuddered from the pain's severity. His arms fell away from his chest. Eliza bolted upright. She killed him! In a panic, she shook his shoulders so hard his head banged against the floor.

"Captain Littledove! Captain Littledove! Sir!" she shouted until she was shrieking.

Littledove slowly spasmed into consciousness and rolled his head from one side to the other. Exhausted from the relief of knowing he was still alive, Eliza curled into a little ball and sat beside him. If no one came forth after his cry, then no one was on the ship—although Sarah and Jelly might hide even more after hearing a cry that sounded as if it came from a tortured beast.

A little while later, Littledove slid his hand across the floor. Eliza touched his wrist, and he grasped her hand so tightly she thought he would break her fingers.

Whatever he needs, she thought. *Whatever he needs to get through this, I shall give to him.*

An hour later, just as he began to exhaust himself into sleep, Eliza folded a blanket and slid it under his head as a pillow. She covered him with several more blankets, noting the room was getting cold because the fire in the tiny woodstove had died.

For another hour she sat by him before she crawled into his bed, afraid to leave him alone. She could now admit Littledove had seen more than one man die. He had just killed a man, even if in self-defense. Now understanding clearly how such an experience would weigh a person's soul, Eliza despaired to think she might now have the experience of seeing Captain Littledove die on the floor of his own quarters.

Chapter Four

PUMPING THE BILGE

Eliza spent the night whispering to Littledove "I am sorry you hurt so much" and "Shhh. Be still. Move less, hurt less."

Each time he moved, even in his sleep, he jolted as if from unexpected pain and moaned. She tried to give him water. Sometimes she stroked his forehead. If he raised his hand, she took it and held it. But really, nothing she did eased his pain.

As the sun rose, Eliza decided a sick man could not remain dirty. Lack of cleanliness would only cause more illness. She began stroking away the grit, the sweat, and her fingerprints in dried blood on his face with a moist cloth. He barely opened his eyes. Methodically, she made her way across his shoulders and down his arms.

When she got to his abdomen, he pushed her hand away and clutched the blanket. Eliza put down the moist cloth to fold her hands over his.

"I shall be very gentle. Nothing I do shall hurt as much as what you felt last night."

Littledove did not relinquish the blankets when she tried again to pull them out of his hands. By now she knew he was fully awake because his eyes were clamped. He looked gray and queasy.

"I must clean the wound so it will not get infected and hurt more. I promise to be very gentle. Very gentle."

Eliza stroked his fingers, hoping to create a little oasis of comforting sensations. The next time she tried to pull the blankets out of his grip, he did not resist.

She proceeded delicately, starting on the side that did not have the stab wound and moved toward it. Littledove jerked when she hit the first sore edge of the area around the wound. She paused while he took a few deep breaths, then continued, barely touching his skin. Sometimes he held up his hand as if to stop a carriage at a crossroad, and she took his quivering hand to comfort him. She had never seen anyone in such intense pain.

From his abdomen, she proceeded to his feet and legs, leaving the pelvic area for last while she thought about what to do. She considered skipping the region altogether but knew blood had poured over it. While she washed his legs, she made herself brave and proceeded with the attitude that she would deal with whatever was there the same way mothers dealt with changing babies.

Her courage allowed her to proceed but did not overrule her embarrassment when she actually began cleaning the distinctly male regions. She felt herself blushing furiously as she wiped, torn between being too embarrassed to look and wanting to inspect what she had never seen close up: the parts of men that were perilous to unmarried women. Their mother had told her and her sisters that a woman who so much as looked at the area would have a difficult time getting married because a man would know. And here she was.

She counted that Littledove would not have enough blood in him to inflate those parts, the way her older, married sister once described how the mechanism worked. She took comfort that Littledove had not expressed lechery when he had been well.

Littledove kept his eyes closed, probably because of the pain, possibly in embarrassment, a gesture Eliza took as a token of untapped gentility. If he opened his eyes, she would be mortified.

When she finished the task, she covered him with several more blankets. The temperature in the room had plummeted during the night. As an afterthought, she slid a few blankets under him with much shifting and tugging.

Eliza made her way to the kitchen—the only place that was still relatively warm—but even there, the fire in the stove was dying. She fed the stove as many things as she could to keep it going, including her bloody clothes, but most of the things burned quickly and did not sustain the heat as well as logs, which she could not find.

To take advantage of what was left of the heat, she placed a pot of water on the stove. From a brick of salted beef the pirates dropped in the haste the storm inspired, she chipped meat and dropped it into the pot. She added rice she scooped from a spill on the kitchen floor. Perhaps the water and its contents would turn into soup.

With kitchen staff to prepare all meals at home, Eliza had never cooked anything. For that matter, she had never even boiled water.

The next time she looked at the water, the meat looked like brown mop strings floating in yellow water. The rice was barely discernible. She tasted the concoction, frowned at the crunchy rice and at the overpowering taste of salt. The beef probably needed to be soaked before being cooked, but she did not know if they had enough drinking water for such finesse.

Why she bothered to taste the concoction, she did not know. It would have to do, no matter how it tasted. Before she left, she warmed herself by the stove while she stuffed spoons and two tin mugs into the pocket of her apron. With soup pot in hand, she made her way back to Littledove's quarters.

Littledove struggled for a few minutes to sit up. She had to let him rest before she handed him a spoon and mug, but his hands shook so much the soup dribbled down his arm. He pushed the mug away. Without dispute, she wiped his arm and took the mug to the table, where she separated the solids from the broth.

When she turned back, she held out the tin. "Come, take this. I shall steady your hand."

Littledove hesitated. His eyes seemed to be going in and out of focus.

"Come, now. A little compromise is in order when you are bruised. Take the mug. There is no shame in having a little help."

Littledove slapped his hand on the mug, having no control in his gestures anymore. Eliza doubted he could judge distance. She circled his hand with hers before guiding the mug to his mouth. Probably unable to control his lips, Littledove slurped noisily.

When he drained the broth, Eliza patted his mouth clean and retrieved the other mug with the strands of meat from the table. Intuiting Littledove was too proud to be fed, she slapped a fork handle in his palm and bent his fingers around it. With his hand, she plunged the fork into the mug to spear bits of the meat. Patiently, she waited until he lifted the fork, then helped guide it to his mouth. Littledove pulled the meat from the fork with his teeth and chewed slowly.

When he finally looked up, Eliza said with far more confidence than she felt, "Captain Littledove, you are not alone. I shall do my best to care for you."

When Littledove next awoke after sixteen hours of restless sleep, he had trouble identifying the new sensation he was feeling. It was all encompassing and not altogether unpleasant. Was he dead?

No. He was warm. That was the sensation. Warmth. Downright toasty warm. He tugged the blankets off his nose and cheeks. The cold in the room immediately registered on him. He tucked his nose back under the blankets.

One, two, three, four, five blankets, he counted by fingering the edges, and several more under him to protect him from the cold of the floor that could leach warmth out of a body with irredeemable rapidity. He felt the itch of wool against his forehead. A knitted cap was pulled down to his eyebrows and over his ears. Between the cap and the blankets, he imagined only his eyes were visible.

He shifted. Pain startled him the moment he moved. During the night, pain sometimes pierced him awake. The burn of Whiplash's Tonic, always unmistakably distinct in its potency, made the coexisting, pulsating throb of the stab almost desirable by contrast. He shifted again in search of relief and bumped his elbow against something hard.

With his fingers, he explored the object—a ceramic jug wrapped in a cloth. A jug of hot water? How ingenious. In all his life of sleeping in cold beds at sea, he never once thought of pouring hot water into a jug and using it to heat the space around him under the blankets.

"May I ask how you are feeling, Captain Littledove?"

He waited for his eyes to focus on Eliza and wondered long had she been sitting in his chair, tightly curled into a nugget with several blankets pulled around her. But she did not look the least bit warm. The room was freezing. He closed his eyes and nodded as an answer.

Eliza slid off the chair. She poured a mug of icy water that reflected the temperature in the room and lifted his head so he could drink, then sat by him on the floor.

"Would you like a report about the *Bessie*, Captain?"

Littledove wondered if she was mocking him by offering to report. He considered, curious about the state of his ship. The mizzenmast snapped during the attack, and he suspected more things broke during the storm. He did not want to contemplate the state of the *Bessie*'s interior after she had been ransacked and looted, if his quarters were a representation.

He looked around. The floor was clear of trash. The blood was gone. He caught sight of Eliza's exquisitely manicured hands, now raw and chapped.

"Aye. Report," he said. He always needed to know about the state of everything on his ship. When Eliza hesitated, he waved her on impatiently.

"The *Bessie* is in good shape except for two downed masts. All the sails seem to be in good condition except for some of the lower ones that must have been on fire. I believe the storm snuffed that out just in time to prevent more damage. I think one big sail is torn but not all of them. I know they all have names, but I do not know them. I am in the process of taking inventory of what we have to eat. So far, I have found a reasonable amount of salted meat and peas and water, although the livestock is gone. They also took Dr. Aves' medicine chest, so we shall have to make do with what we have to make you better. I have been boiling linens in the kitchen for bandages."

Littledove blinked. That was the most optimistic report of a wrecked ship he had ever heard. The effort to keep his eyes open was overwhelming him.

"... Crew?"

"I think the storm washed them overboard. Perhaps some were taken to the pirate ship. I gave a sea burial to two men who were caught on some ropes. Unfortunately, I do not know their names."

"Burial?" mumbled Littledove, too familiar with the effort it took to wrap a body and slide it into the ocean. He could not imagine Eliza having the strength to perform a sea burial.

"Well ... I just—just cut some ropes—the ones that are tied into squares? They were tangled in them, and they fell into the ocean. That was the best I could do. I also said a prayer for them. I am sorry I could not do better."

The bodies, caught on ratlines and exposed to salt water for several days, were probably so bloated they were barely recognizable as human. They might not have survived being moved without ripping apart. The memory of blue-gray skin and eyes filled with larvae made him swallow to settle his dry heaves. That Eliza had even gone near them spoke volumes—of what, he wasn't sure.

The ship tipped sharply, and he became fully alert. He attempted to sit up but almost passed out when he raised his head. Bringing up his knees, he rolled on his side with a groan.

"Ship's taken water. She needs to be pumped." Littledove raised his head again, but his body would not follow.

"Captain, please. You cannot get up."

"If she takes on water, she'll sink, and we'll go down with her."

Eliza stopped short. "We are sinking? Is not the purpose of a boat to travel across water without getting occupants wet?"

"She takes on water in storms," mumbled Littledove, rocking after a failed attempt to prop himself on an elbow. He coughed and gasped. The pain was overwhelming, with stinging sensations coming out in rays from the stab wound to all parts of his body.

"She takes on— Because the pirates left the hatches open? Can we get the water off the ship? Do we have a bucket?"

"Bilge pump." Littledove drew a breath in preparation to try to sit again.

"Captain, you cannot move in your condition."

"Won't lie down and sink!" With his scorn went his last bit of energy. He felt his body unravel into a sprawl under the blankets. He couldn't even bring his arms together.

"Where is this ... this pump?" asked Eliza.

"Pump room," muttered Littledove. Flecks of color were appearing against the inside of his eyelids. He did not know a person could begin to pass out while lying down.

Eliza grabbed his shoulders. "Where. Is. The. Pump. Room."

"Two decks down. On ... right." He opened his eyes and saw Eliza's face behind gray blotches. "You can't do it."

"Captain Littledove. From now on, we employ common sense, not impractical heroics. I may not be a seafarer of your caliber, but at least I can sit up and walk. You cannot. I shall see what I can do."

She rose from his side and blinded him with a swirl of her hems when she turned. When he stopped feeling the hems against his eyelids, she was gone, having transformed into quick, pitty-patty footsteps as she ran down the passage. Littledove closed his eyes and finished passing out.

Eliza's first attempt to descend to a lower deck made her rush back to the upper deck to get a candle. The lower decks were terrifyingly dark without much light surviving the journey through the hatches. In the candlelight that splashed up the passage walls as she walked, she found a door inauspiciously labeled with a small sign: PUMP. She had never been so deep into the hull, and this particular deck smelled so much like a cesspool that Eliza began to wonder if the pirates left dead bodies on it.

Opening the narrow door of the pump room, she peered into the equally narrow room she doubted would accommodate a person and a candle. In the hallway, she anchored the candle with a dab of wax on the floor. Tentatively, she stepped into the chamber, jumping when she brushed several saws and axes that hung on one wall and made them clank against one another. The teeth of a saw snatched and ripped her sleeve and scratched her shoulder.

The windowless, claustrophobia-inspiring room came with an intense stench that made her gag. She took a small comfort that the brass pump was polished to full brightness and reflected some of the candlelight. Leaving the door open, she stepped in and followed the line of the extraordinarily long wooden handle to the darkest corner of the room. Fully determined, she grabbed the handle and pulled it down with all her weight, almost swinging from it. It didn't budge.

The pump was broken! The pirates broke the pump so the ship would sink! That's how they sank the *Andrea*!

She imagined the waters rising deck by deck. Littledove would drown first because he could not crawl to the top deck, and she could not carry him. She could not even lift him onto the bed. The thought of his body floating lifeless in his quarters like a dead goldfish in a bowl almost made her scream, but she knew if she screamed, her mind would fly out of her mouth and be gone forever.

The ship listed with a creak, and the door to the little room slammed shut, finally making her scream because she now stood in a darkness dense enough to feel like liquid. She slapped her hands on the wall to feel her way to the door. The axes and saws swung against one another, making high-pitched scraping sounds. Something sliced her hand, sending a whip of pain up her arm. She jerked her foot when something fell to the floor, barely missing her toes. Eliza jumped back and knocked her head against the pump handle.

She grabbed the handle and clung to it ... The handle ... The handle. Was connected. To the brass thing. The pump. Across the door. The pump was across the door.

Hand over hand, she followed the handle, knowing if she let it go she would lose her bearings and be forever lost in a room the size of a matchbox. The skinny door was directly opposite the pump. If she reached the pump, she could find the door.

The ship listed again, making the little door open and close quickly and reveal the dim light of the candle as its outline. Eliza abandoned the pump handle and lunged toward the light. More blades fell from the wall as she crashed shoulder-first against the door. Her weight sprang it open without resistance.

Out of the chamber she tumbled into the passage, unwittingly stepping over the candle and almost setting her skirts on fire. When her hands slapped against a wall, she slid to the floor in tears. Then she gathered her limbs and sat in the passage, trying not to lose the rest of her mind in another scream. She grabbed the candle and held it tightly as her hands shook, not knowing what she would do if it went out. She was not convinced she could find her way back to the top decks in such darkness.

The door bounced against its frame again, taunting her to go back in. If she had to go into the little room again, she would die. She surely would. She tried to calm herself by looking at the candle.

Do not drop the candle. It cannot go out.

She drew a breath. If she did not go back into the pump room, the ship would sink. And if they drowned, the darkness would be eternal. She had to go back in. She would go back in. She would. She really would. She would go in. She would go in. Now.

From the floor, Eliza pulled open the door. The feeble light from the candle eased into the little chamber and stood at attention as a reflection on the polished brass pump. Next to the reflection, a chain caught her attention.

She stretched out to keep the door open with her foot while she fingered the chain. The candlelight revealed a pin at the end of the chain. The pin connected to a brass rod that connected to the wooden handle. The chain kept the pin from being lost when it was out of its holder.

She looked around. The axes and saws looked gruesome now that her eyes were adjusted to the dark. Still holding the door open with one foot, she grabbed an ax that had fallen and wedged it under the door as a doorstop. Again, she anchored the candle with a dab of wax on the floor beside the door, this time in a place she would not trip over it and snuff it out.

Fortified by the bit of dimness she now considered light, Eliza eased herself forward and pulled the pin out of the holder. The handle lowered itself on its own by a few inches, with a creak that made her skin pucker. She grabbed the handle and began to pump with all her strength and sense of life.

Almost immediately, she heard a muted gush of water. She had heard this sound before. So. Pumping was done regularly on a ship, which meant it regularly took on water. Eliza swore she would never again set foot on a ship.

Terrified that the ship would sink if she ever stopped pumping, she willed herself into a trance and pumped through her aches and fear. By now she could not tell whether she had become part of the stench or had stopped smelling it.

She did not trust the moment when the gush of water in the pipe began to lessen and the pipe began sounding hollow. She gave the pump one last pull before she bolted from the chamber. Although she listened carefully, she could not hear any change in the sounds of the ship. Whatever sent Littledove into such a panic that he almost stood up and walked was beyond her comprehension, but she was certain pulling the handle again would not yield a dryer ship. Now she noticed her entire body ached.

From the hallway, Eliza stretched herself into the chamber and replaced the pin. She removed the ax and closed the door to lock the darkness in the little chamber so it could not spill out and swallow the entire world. Ready to leave, she loosened the candle from the floor and froze when she saw by the flickering light several plump rats scurrying past her. One took a moment to sit on its haunches and serenely groom its whiskers while inspecting her.

Eliza grabbed the ax and backed away from the rat until it scampered away. Balancing the ax while she protected the flame on the candle with one hand, she made her way back to the captain's quarters, where Littledove was now sound asleep. Eliza rested the ax by the bed where she sat and within moments fell as asleep as he was. She did not even take off her shoes.

CHAPTER FIVE

COMING TO TERMS

Dusk had infiltrated the room, and Littledove was studying what he could see of Eliza's skirts spilling over his mattress. She sat up, dulled with sleep, but leapt off the mattress when she realized he was looking at her.

"You could have told me there was a pin," she said, as if they were in the middle of a conversation.

"Pin?" mumbled Littledove.

"On the pump. You did not tell me there was a pin that needed to be removed. I thought the thing was broken and we were going to drown!" Her voice rose to a shout.

Littledove shifted his body to face her as best he could from his position on the floor. Eliza began stomping around him in a froth of skirts, the way ocean waves frothed around the *Bessie* during storms.

"Do you think things are not sufficiently difficult that you can leave out such an important piece of information? First, you tell me we are going to drown if the boat is not pumped. But you do not tell me the one thing I need to know. And that was about the pin! The pin that locks the handle in place! I thought the pump was broken! I thought the ship was going to sink! I thought we were going to die!"

She switched to a controlled whisper of a shout after taking a breath to refuel herself. "For better or worse, Captain Littledove, you may still be the captain of this leaky tub, but I am now your crew. Your *entire* crew! And I would greatly appreciate if you provided me with the information I need to keep us both alive!"

Eliza turned away and rested her head in her hands. Her shoulders rolled up and down with a sob.

Littledove's amazement momentarily superseded his pain. He was not used to raging women. Not that he had never experienced them. He just never got used to them in such a state. They were downright intimidating when they got in those states.

He was barely used to women of any kind, except the ones he used to occasionally enjoy superficially at ports. He never imagined that women with Eliza's exquisiteness were capable of such anger. They always presented themselves far above the fray, emitting occasional warmth not exceeding the level of mild affection for a cat.

He was used to giving orders to men who already knew how to do the jobs he commanded them to do. If they did the wrong, he cursed at them, and the next time, they did it right. Such an approach would not work for his new crew of one. His new crew required patience and gentility, qualities he had not exactly cultivated.

Littledove cleared his throat. "Miss Strauss, can you sit by me? Please." He broke the seal of warmth around himself by pulling out his hand and waving her to come forward.

Eliza dropped to her knees beside him. Her lips and cheeks were trembling from her unsuccessful effort to not cry. Her arms fell on her skirt, gushing warm air from the many layers of petticoats.

"I thought you knew about the pin," he said as an apology.

"I know nothing!" Eliza shouted, releasing the rest of her storm. "Half the time you are indecipherable! Calling a rope a sheet! Why can you not call it a rope? That is what it is! Port and bow! Why can you not say front and back? Or over there and over here, like people everywhere? And what's that you say for left and right? Starburst and parts? Why not just left and right? You probably have a name for that pin that is not 'pin.' And—" Eliza pointed her finger at his nose— "you did not tell me about the rats. Are you aware your ship has rats?"

She was frightened, Littledove realized, down to her bones. Telling her the ship might sink had not been wise. The pump room with its narrow darkness and foul smells no one liked scared her half to death. And she ran into rats, popular in the lower decks. He had hoped to keep her unaware of them because all cargo ships had rats and mice and other ignominious creatures, a knowledge that did not benefit her.

"Milady. Rest assured you know the important things. You know how to save a man's life. And you have the courage to come out of hiding to do it. You know how to chew out a sea captain proper. And you just figured out on your own how to work the bilge pump. Never met a better seafarer in my life, milady. If you ask me."

He held up his hand to see if she would take it. He was afraid to antagonize her by touching her.

Eliza paused before slipping her hand into his. She eased back into her properness. "I am sorry I spoke so harshly, Captain. You are at a disadvantage and are not at fault because I do not know anything."

"Methinks I deserved most of it. Except for the part of you calling the *Bessie* a leaky tub. That wasn't fair. She's as much a victim as us."

"Yes, she has suffered many indignities."

"She's not the only one. You're too fine a lady to go pumping the bilge. I's real sorry you had to do it, but I's real glad you did it."

"What is— What is the bilge?"

"The lowest part of a ship. It sits under the water. That's why it takes on water. You just pump it now and then, and it doesn't become a problem." Littledove squeezed Eliza's hand. "I count my blessings to have you as my crew, milady, because you know how to overcome your fear. Of everything, seems like."

Eliza was warming herself in the kitchen that Littledove called the galley because every common thing at sea was called a word that did not exist on land. The pirates had not taken the fire in the stove as they had taken almost everything else. She managed to keep it alive by shifting the last of the wood until the fire turned to embers too feeble to use for anything.

She thought of taking the embers to the small stove in Littledove's quarters, but she could not find anything in which to carry them that would not burn, and the pots always got too hot for her to hold, even with padding. Now, the kitchen was cooling. Their source of fire was dying.

Littledove needed warmth brought to him in a vinegar jug. Without that bit of warmth under the blankets, he might very well die because a man in his condition could not battle the temperatures that were causing spilled liquids in the halls to freeze at night. Even she had taken to walking around wearing a blanket under her cloak.

Boiled water, not wine or hot cocoa, became the elixir of life. Boiling water was vital for sterilizing cloth for bandages and for softening peas and salted meat. And to keep drinking water safe. Eliza needed to find fuel, but just as they were surrounded by water they could not drink, they were surrounded by wood they could not burn.

She visited the deck that sometimes felt warmer than the hull because of the direct sunlight. She did her best thinking there. They needed water they could drink, wood they could burn, food they could eat. They needed to survive.

Littledove woke up to the sound of ... of ... Whatever it was, it was coming from the deck. He could not identify the sound, but it had an even, deliberate quality about it. He tried to sit so he could hear better, but the combination of burn and throb flattened him into submission.

Where was his crew? He was never at ease when Eliza was not within sight. By the clarity of sunlight and the gentle bobbing of the ship, he determined she would not be washed off the deck, if that was where she was. He went back to wondering what was happening on deck to cause that sound. Certainly not rigging ...

Too much time later, he awoke to the sound of the door to the hull opening, followed by Eliza's footsteps. By now, he could recognize her footsteps, perhaps even if the *Bessie* were crowded with other people. They'd become like a little melody that always brought him a sense of relief. The door to his quarters swung open, and in came Eliza carrying something that could only be a charred piece of sail filled with ... yellow things with black stripes. He had no idea what they were.

"We can make a fire now," she announced as she dumped what looked like giant splinters beside the stove.

Littledove looked at the wood suspiciously. "Where'd that come from?"

"The masts."

"The masts? The ship's masts?" He tried to sit up and coughed himself flat.

"Captain Littledove, the masts are broken. They are only fit for firewood."

Littledove took a breath with a slight wheeze as he considered. His ears had heard the masts break. His body had felt them fall. His mind understood they were now useless. But his heart never got around to believing his ears and body because he had not yet been on deck to confirm the destruction.

He gave up his indignation. "Let me see. Bring a piece here."

Eliza continued to study him, head tipped to one side.

"What?" he asked.

"I thought I heard you wheezing."

He shrugged, not wanting to admit he might have pneumonia. He'd already heard the wheeze and did not like the sound of it, but he was still holding out fine. Pneumonia in a man already compromised with a stab wound and blood loss was certain death, and a miserable one at that. He put aside his concern. He would deal with pneumonia as he needed to. Today, he had other problems to solve. He waved Eliza over and took a piece of wood from her. Almost immediately, he dropped it and began toiling with the misery of having to give her unfavorable news.

"Milady, we cannot burn this wood."

"Why? Because it used to be a mast? You are nice and warm under those blankets with that jug of water, but we no longer have a way to boil water. Besides, I have not had the privilege of being warm in days."

"No, milady. That's not it. The masts're covered with tar and oils to protect them from sea rot. If we burn this wood in here, we'll choke ourselves for sure."

Eliza looked over her pile of hard labor. "None of it? We cannot burn any of it?"

"None, milady. The oil soaks almost to the core. A single piece'll choke us." He knew how hard she had worked to harvest the meager amount of wood because the masts were rock hard with preservatives.

Eliza dropped to her knees by his side. She said nothing, but by the flicker of her pupils, he knew she was listening to the soft wheeze in his breaths. He attempted to hold his breath but ended up coughing instead.

"Captain Littledove, I am concerned about this new cough of yours. May I ask you to please sit up? It is imperative that your lungs have an opportunity to drain several times a day."

"What's this, you go up a boatswain and come down a ship's doctor?"

"Our doctor always insisted that we sit up whenever we caught colds. Come. Let me help you."

Littledove deplored having to be helped to sit up, of all things, but he allowed her to put her arms around him. Besides, he could not object entirely to her warmth, seeing that he had spent the last half hour shivering. Based on the amount of his weight he had to put on her, he knew he could not sit up by himself. Eliza had taken to placing bits of hardtack soaked in broth into his mouth so he could eat without having to sit.

Together, they slid inch by inch toward the bed until he was able to transfer his weight from Eliza to the corner of the bed and a wall. Eliza pulled a blanket around his shoulders, over his chest, and around his legs.

"I want you to remain sitting while I go and find something else for firewood. Do you hear me? You must stay seated. Please do not lie down. When I come back, I shall make a fire, and the room will get warm, and I shall comb your hair. But you must be sitting when I come back."

Eliza draped another blanket over him and felt his forehead. Littledove leaned into the comfort of her touch, hoping she would not recoil. He forced himself to look at her, despite knowing she was going to fetch wood because he could not.

She rested her hand on his shoulder and squeezed it. "I am glad you are here to show me what to do, Captain Littledove. I would have poisoned us otherwise. Please do not lie down. I shall be back very soon."

"You're real kind, milady." he mumbled.

He could not help wondering how sincere she was or whether she was trying to make him feel better. He forbade himself to even consider lying down as he watched Eliza gather the unusable firewood of her labor and leave.

If she was going to gather wood, he could at least sit up. He listened to her footsteps as she returned to the deck where she probably threw the unusable wood overboard and then came down to grab the ax from the room. Her footsteps continued down the passage. Littledove opened his eyes, wishing he had asked her what she was going to chop down.

With ax in hand, Eliza went to the quarters she had shared with Sarah and Jelly. The room, once neatly crowded with three travel trunks, looked as if the trunks had exploded. The pirates had broken the locks and riffled through them, taking, as far as Eliza could see, all the pantaloons and most of the petticoats.

She rested her ax against a wall, thinking how curious it was that she now thought of the ax as hers, when a day before it had merely been *an* ax. She sat on the bunk she and Jelly shared the last night she saw her sisters and looked at Sarah's bunk. Eliza rubbed her hands. She had failed to touch Sarah before she was taken. She last touched Jelly when she put her hand over her mouth to stop her from screaming. Her memory of Sarah and Jelly carried a fear so fierce it threatened to obliterate all their other expressions from her memory.

The first time she visited the room, she still believed Sarah and Jelly were hiding somewhere on the ship. Even Jelly's screams and Sarah's silence bore promises of their reappearance, and a part of Eliza still expected to run into them when she walked around the ship. Thoughts of them crept up on her even when she was busy and especially when she was not.

Sometimes she thought she heard them as ghosts at sea. She had only recently stopped looking in empty rooms and storage areas, calling "Sarah! Jelly! It's Eliza!" to see if, perhaps, they would show themselves.

Eliza tipped her head back and tried to feel what little of Sarah and Jelly was left in the air. She pressed her face against the mattress for Jelly's scent, but not even that was left of her. There were not enough tears in the world to shed for the sorrow she now felt. She felt more sorrow than there were water drops in the ocean.

The more she grieved, the more furious she became, until everyone was at fault. What entitled the pirates to anything of what they took, most of which was human life they could not use in any way? What made Littledove think that he could hide anything from them behind a closed door? As if closing a door would not cause pirates to wonder about the contents behind it? In a room with a puny lock and three silly trunks as reinforcement? With Dr. Aves to protect them? Twenty Dr. Aveses would not have been effective because he could not bring himself to fire a pistol.

If the hard-muscled sailors could not stop the pirates, how did Littledove expect Dr. Aves to do so? Or Sarah and Jelly to rescue themselves? And she! She was just as guilty, hiding in a closet while everyone was taken or killed. Had she known where Littledove was taking her, she would never have left her sisters to fend for themselves. And why exactly had he chosen her over them? He could have rescued all of them.

Powered by the anger hidden in her grief, Eliza rose and swung the ax into a bunk. She swung and swung until most of the bunk was a pile of boards small enough to fit into Littledove's stove.

Then she brought down the ax on a trunk, feeling violated that the pirates stole their undergarments. To do what, Eliza loathed to imagine. The trunk, reinforced with metal strapping, resisted her strike. She raised the ax again, then lowered it slowly.

She put down the ax as a memory flickered into being and reminded her to flip open a trunk lid. The pirates had hacked out the bottom of the trunks to look for money in hidden compartments that were usually found in false bottoms. But their trunks had been made by an ingenious master cabinetmaker in one town west of Edith's Bay who, having once been in prison, knew about the ways of thieves and placed the false compartment in the lid.

Eliza reached behind the lock on the lid to press a little knob that was no bigger than a pimple. The bottom of the lid released to reveal padded silk pouches with Sarah's jewelry and money. On her own trunk, Eliza pressed another brass pimple and gathered the quilted silk pouches that were strapped inside with her and Jelly's jewelry and more money. Jelly's trunk did not have a brass pimple because Jelly could not be trusted not to brag about having a secret compartment in her trunk, thereby exposing all their hiding places.

Eliza sat on Jelly's trunk and listened to herself gasping, the only human sound in the creaking room. She fingered the quilted pouches in her lap, trying to come to terms that these silk pouches were all that were left of Sarah and Jelly. She was not surprised the remaining essence of her sisters was precious silk and jewels.

With the back of her hand, she brushed her hair back and wiped spittle from the corner of her mouth. She felt hollow and exhausted. That was good. She never wanted to feel again.

Eliza tossed a dress over one shoulder and gathered the wood from the bunks in her arms. She closed the door as she would close the door to a tomb, but she knew she would be back because they would need more wood. The circumstances did not even respect grief.

Eliza walked back to Littledove's quarters and casually placed the apron she tied around the pouches and money on the table before dropping the wood beside the stove. Littledove, still sitting, startled awake.

She announced, "Firewood. From the bunks you built for us. I do not know what kind of wood it is, but it shall have to do for today. It does not look pickled like the masts. Next, I shall start on the bunks in the forecastle."

Littledove frowned. "Fo'c'sle. You say it fo'c'sle, milady."

"Then why is it spelled 'forecastle'?"

"Don't know, milady."

Eliza found the answer unsatisfying and proceeded to stack the boards from the bunks in the stove. Her entire body was sore from chopping so they would fit into the little stove designed to heat the captain's tiny quarters and nothing else.

"What're you doing, milady?" asked Littledove, struggling not to topple over.

"I am making a fire."

"Ah, suggestion, milady?"

Eliza frowned. She couldn't seem to do anything correctly.

"Start with kindling. Get some paper and other little things you can burn out of the wood box, and then put your smallest sticks on them and see if it catches fire. Then you put the bigger sticks on."

Eliza pulled the larger boards out of the stove, grabbed some scrap paper at the bottom of the wood box, and stuffed it into the tiny stove. She forced her thoughts from her sisters to the practical matters on hand.

She was certain she could boil water and make some meals on the stove and keep the heat for themselves. At least the pirates overlooked the tinder box that was full of matches.

She recalled that as children, she and her sister Amelia tried to start a fire by rubbing sticks but were not successful. Sarah had been elsewhere. Jelly had been in diapers. Mary was indoors playing piano.

Littledove shifted. "Milady, don't mind my asking, but you ever made a fire before?"

"Why? Am I still doing it wrong?"

"No. It's catching. Might get bigger flames if you blow on it some. Real soft, so you don't blow it out."

Eliza lowered her head to the opening of the stove and blew a puff into the flames. Soot from the previous fire swirled out into her face.

She glared at Littledove. His eyes grew wide as he held up his hand as if to command the soot to retreat into the stove. Apparently, he had not anticipated that to happen either.

Eliza softened her expression. He had meant none of the wrong she suspected. She wiped her face and threw in another scrap of wood to ensure the health of the new flames. When she felt confident the fire would not go out, she slipped two larger boards into the stove and watched them catch fire with satisfaction. Making a fire was not so difficult.

Self-consciously she said, "The servants tend the fireplaces and stoves at home. Like your cabin boy."

"Come, milady. It'll take a while for the quarters to warm up. Get under a blanket." He lifted the corner of a blanket. "I promise to be a gentleman."

"If I may, I would like to listen to you breathe."

Eliza leaned him forward, surprised that such a stern man could now seem so frail, and pressed her ear against his back. His feverish warmth was delicious in the cold of the room. He was clutching his side, but the wheeze had lessened significantly. She would make certain he sat up several times a day, no matter how much he hurt.

Eliza leaned him back slowly. "I do not think it is pneumonia. I believe it is only because you have not been sitting up. We may have caught it just in time."

She began to shiver, as she did each time she stopped moving. Tired of being worn out from the cold, she slid under the blanket. So, this is where they had come to—sharing warmth from fevers.

She sucked on the base of her thumb to loosen a splinter. Her lips were chapped. Her face was mottled with soot. Her skirt was dusty, stained, and ripped. Her bodice had chips of wood clinging to it. Her hair was loosely braided instead of in the impeccably smooth bun she usually wore. She didn't think she had ever been so dirty in her life. She sniffed, wondering if she smelled. The pirates had taken her perfumes and soaps.

Eliza shifted to her knees and removed the leather strip that gathered Littledove's hair. She brushed out the mats and snarls that developed while he lay on the floor. His head occasionally bobbed as he struggled to stay awake.

"Captain, please stay seated a little longer," said Eliza, concerned the slight wheeze would return if he stretched out.

Littledove opened his eyes wide and nodded, although his head continued to bob. By the time Eliza finished combing his hair and sat beside him again, sleep had overcome him. He slid down with a groan and landed with his head on her lap.

In a brief moment of awareness, Littledove raised his hand apologetically as he coughed. "Give me a moment, milady ..."

Elia could feel the toll Littledove's pain and blood loss were taking on him. The fever wasn't helping. He could still die.

Perhaps the warmth and the comfort of human touch would provide him with some strength. At home, men and women did not touch unless they were dancing, but this was no dance. This was life and death in its rawest form.

Eliza tucked his arm under the blanket and continued to hold his hand. With her other hand, she pulled the blanket up to his chin. She wanted to stroke his forehead, but her fingers were too cold. Moments later, the weight of his head indicated he had fallen asleep.

Eliza leaned against the bed. Kindness was not so difficult.

Chapter Six

FINDING COMMON GROUND

Eliza had gone so long on sponge baths she was having dreams about soaking in a white enamel tub full of scented hot water. Littledove had a small tub, but it was in his quarters, and she could not possibly bathe in it without his having a full view of her. How he fit into it remained a mystery because the tub was quarter-sized, and even a man as lean as Littledove could not fold himself enough to fit into it.

Besides, they could not spare water for a bath. Water was what she preserved most, even if they seemed to have more of it than they had food. She suspected the water barrels had been too cumbersome for the pirates to take at the start of a storm.

The problem was that her hair could not be sponged into cleanliness. Tighter braids with smaller diameters did not disguise that her skull itched. Still, using water to wash hair seemed wasteful. Only after much deliberation did Eliza cut her waist-length hair to her shoulder blades to preserve water when she washed it.

She drew two quarts of water from a barrel and warmed it on Littledove's woodstove before taking the water to the deck to wash, developing goosebumps the size of pineapples from the cold. She cut one quart with sea water to wet and wash her hair and used the remaining water to rinse it.

By the time she got back to Littledove's quarters, her teeth were knocking. She stood by the woodstove and ran her fingers through her hair to encourage it to dry faster. It had begun to billow out of its dampness, but she imagined her hair freezing if it did not dry soon.

"What'd you do?" asked Littledove, who was, after several weeks, now staying awake a bit more each day and asking more questions.

"I washed my hair."

"Nay. Something else."

"I cut it so I would not need so much water to wash it."

"Oh, milady! You didn't."

Touched by his concern, she knelt by him on the floor and brushed his hair off his forehead. "There is no need to be alarmed. No one will know when I put it up. Besides, only on bald men does hair not grow longer. The situation is quite redeemable, Captain."

She tipped her head at a chair by the table and changed the subject because, although she would not admit it to him, she felt self-conscious about having cut her hair so short. "If I bring that chair over here next to the bed, do you think you can sit on it? If you can, I can wash your hair. And then from the chair, you can slip onto the bed. May I ask if you would like to try?"

"Are you going to shave my head before you wash my hair?" asked Littledove with a crooked grin.

Eliza dragged the chair next to the bed. "That, sir, is my second plan."

Littledove took his time sitting up. After several failed attempts, he managed to turn himself onto his knees and rest his elbows on the chair seat, panting from the exertion. A moment later, he slapped his hands on the seat and hauled himself onto it with a groan that was more a shout. By the time he twisted himself and sat, he was sweating profusely and looking as if he might pass out.

By now, his medical needs required her to acquire some comfort when touching him. He, however, had become shyer about being handled, which often amused her. Sometimes circumstances engaged them in a competition over who could more mortified—she for doing the handling; he for needing to be handled.

She waited until Littledove's breaths softened and he nodded against her shoulder to indicate he could continue his efforts. Eliza leaned him back and draped her apron over his lap to keep him modest because he was dressed only in drawers that, in the right light, became translucent.

After reassuring herself that he was not going to pass out, she fetched the pot of warm water from the stove. Eliza gathered Littledove's hair, dipped his ponytail in the pot, and poured some of the water over his head with a mug, collecting as much of it as she could in a pan on the floor. She rolled the bar of soap in her palms until lather formed, then began to work the soap into his hair.

Beginning with slow, firm motions, she allowed herself to explore how he liked to be touched, in what direction to stroke, and the rhythms he enjoyed the most—first slow, then faster, then slow again. Firmly and gently, she ran her hands from the base of his neck to the top of his head.

Littledove closed his eyes and sighed. His chest began to rise and fall with shallow breaths. Eliza began enjoying the new tension in his body that seemed to come not from being in pain but from her touch. When she brushed her fingertip against his neck to remove a bit of lather, he shivered and grabbed the apron on his lap.

All kinds of warmth quivered through her body at that moment. With fingers poised in his hair, she stopped breathing to harvest as much of the sensation as she could. Most of it was concentrated in her abdomen and in places she was discouraged from touching. During the most intense moment, she pressed her fingers against his skull, as if to grab a second course of the sensations. When she emerged from the warm tingles, she studied Littledove's face, wondering if kissing him would cause her body to, as best as she could describe it, unravel into a scream.

Afraid of her newly discovered propensities, she pulled away with a feeling of great wrong. She grabbed the pitcher of warm water and poured it over his head, as if to expunge what was within her.

Littledove jerked out of his reverie. His eyes darted across the room. Eliza dried his hair, too distracted and flustered to notice she was flapping the cloth against his face. She tossed the cloth aside, feeling a prickle of embarrassment crawling over her face as heat. When she tried to step away, Littledove grasped her wrist and held it until she shifted her gaze sideways, unable to look directly at him. The richness of the experience still reverberated within her.

After a moment, Littledove averted his gaze and released her wrist. "Thank you, milady. For washing my hair."

Still looking away, she handed him a brush. "I am going to get the bath water while you comb your hair. Will you be all right seated?"

"I'll stay up," mumbled Littledove.

At least Littledove could finish bathing himself now. She still washed his back and legs up to his knees because he could not yet reach those parts of himself without pain and the risk of pulling on the stab wound. Every bath was cursed with embarrassment but satisfied Eliza's curiosity. Now baths were doing something more for her, although she could not understand exactly how things worked.

She brought the pot of warm bathwater from the stove. The fervor between them intensified beyond any desire she had to subdue it. She did not resist the pleasure of having Littledove rest his cheek against her arm as she prolonged her scrub between his shoulder blades. His pleasure in her touch made her feel she was casting a spell over him. Of her own pleasure ... well, she would think about that later when she wasn't feeling it so directly.

When she knelt to wash his feet, she cast glances at the bulge in his lap, hoping he would not catch her looking. Until now, she suspected Littledove had either been too ill to feel pleasure or had hidden his pleasures behind a deadpan expression. But his clarion was clearly betraying him today. She was unsure what to make of that, but she intuited what it meant.

She was surprised he had that much left in him to react as he had—far from full sails but enough so she noticed. When her married sister, Amelia, first described how that part of men worked, they laughed so hard Eliza doubted she would be able to keep a straight face on her wedding night. Now that she had seen it in action, she had to admit the mechanism had appeals she had not anticipated. Apparently, it did not work alone. It worked with the rest of the man. And perhaps, in this case, because of her.

She ran the washcloth against the inside of one knee and brushed his inner thigh. Littledove startled and pulled the apron on his lap up against his chest.

Eliza turned away to rinse the washcloth but also to hide her enjoyment of his unexpected shyness. Without looking at him, she turned up his hand and placed the washcloth in it.

"Please finish up any little bits I have missed. I shall be back in a moment to help you into the bed."

"The bits ain't so little," blurted Littledove.

Eliza stood still as if suspended between two moments, just as she had done on the deck the time Littledove cursed out some sailors without being aware she was standing behind him. She had let it go too far. Too far. Unable to acknowledge or address the comment, she exited the room as if the moment had never happened.

Littledove went into a panic the moment he proclaimed that his bits were not so little. He had no idea where Eliza went afterward, but he wouldn't be surprised if she jumped ship to get away from him. What had he been thinking? Eliza was no bunter. And after such a display! Although to be fair, he tried very hard to control himself. But lately, his clarion had developed a mind of its own, especially around Eliza.

He was grateful Eliza was not gone for long, although she returned with the precision and crispness of a figure moving in a cuckoo clock. She gave no sign she had heard what he said or seen ... his bits. Littledove played with the idea of apologizing, but that would only bring up the comment again, and no one wanted to forget it more than he.

Eliza positioned herself to slip the nightshirt she was carrying over his head. Angry at himself, he swatted the nightshirt away.

"Not enough you put an apron on me? Now you want to put me in a dress?"

"This is a nightshirt, Captain."

"Looks like a dress to me."

"And what, may I ask, do you usually sleep in?" asked Eliza with a heap of scorn.

She gasped and blushed deeply when she realized what she had asked. He liked seeing her lose her detached calm and took comfort in knowing he was not the only person in the world who bungled.

But her embarrassment invaded him when he began to answer. "I wear—I wear—well, under, ah, things. If someone knocks, I just—put pants on. Then I'm ready. More practical than that thing."

"I think you shall be more comfortable in a nightshirt because it has no ties at the waist."

Eliza slipped the shirt over his head before he could object again. When his head slid out of the neck opening, she glared at him like a schoolmarm until he threaded one arm through a sleeve. In the sleeve on the side of his wound, he got tangled because he had to be careful how he moved. Eliza stepped forward to help him.

"I can dress meself. Don't need a nanny to dress me like a child," snapped Littledove as he flapped the sleeve while trying to thread his arm into it.

Fine situation to find himself in. He, who had been had been in charge of everything on the *Bessie* and, as leader, carried the responsibility of making others transcend their helplessness, now could not even dress himself. All he was fit to do was make lewd comments to an exquisite woman who was trying to help him.

Eliza straightened her back. "Captain Littledove! You are no child! I have seen you in action. You are quite the man. It is just that you are now a bit bruised, and it would benefit you to accept a little help. Graciously, if you please."

Littledove looked away, feeling further reduced for having been rude to her. Without another protest, he let Eliza thread his arm through the sleeve.

"Can you look at the compass and see what direction we're heading?" asked Littledove to shift the conversation to official business he felt comfortable discussing.

"I am afraid the compass is missing."

"Chronometer? Looks like a clock. It's—"

Eliza shook her head. "I have seen no clocks."

"What about the sextants? I's two of them."

"I am sorry. I have not seen either one."

"Filchers didn't leave much behind, did they!"

"Bilge pump," Eliza said before he could draw another breath. "They left the bilge pump in its entirety. No parts are missing. I can vouch for that."

When she smiled, he began to chuckle, holding his side because laughing hurt. Everything hurt, including his pride. A moment later, Eliza's sly smile evolved into a giggle. Somehow, they had struck the elusive jackpot of camaraderie as the shared laughter came upon them like a grace for enduring uncertainties for so long.

After their amusement died down, Eliza nodded soberly toward the bed. Already he knew getting into it would prove to be another humbling experience. He put almost all his weight on Eliza as he shifted from the chair to the mattress. His weight forced her to sit on the bed next to him, but true to her lady-ness, she rose the moment he was securely seated.

Eliza raised his legs so he could lie down, then unexpectedly pulled off his drawers. Littledove yelped and clutched his private bits over the nightshirt. He clenched his eyes to erase himself from the world as Eliza drew blankets over him.

When the flapping of blankets ceased, he opened one eye, afraid to look with two. "What's that mean—that you've seen me in action?"

Eliza almost sniggered at his question, but she responded with utmost seriousness. "I have seen how good you are at managing the ship, how your men respected you. You always care about the right things, however you may express yourself. I have come to appreciate how difficult it is to be the exemplary sea captain you have proven yourself to be. Especially under such circumstances."

Blindsided by the compliment, Littledove opened his mouth. Bewildered, he closed it. He let his head sink into the pillow and took in Eliza as she stood with her hands folded over her waist, exuding a sophisticated, unrufflable calm.

He scrunched his brow. This woman could run circles around him with her sly intelligence, and if he were not careful, he would not know it for days. With an eye twinkle, she could dissolve his cultivated authority and leave him feeling like a naked fool. She was the sort of woman who could pull apart his carefully constructed world into little shreds of chaos. Littledove looked away. Very fine woman.

"Wouldn't'ave offered passage if I'd known this was going to happen," he said to change the subject.

"Do you worry about telling the *Bessie*'s owner about what happened?" asked Eliza.

"Aye, bets are good he knows already."

"Do you think he shall blame you?"

"Blame myself plenty enough, milady."

"You did your best. Surely, he will understand that."

"Milady, I own the *Bessie*. And I don't understand it."

"The *Bessie* is yours? You own her? I thought captains were hired."

"Most are. Stroke of luck blessed me."

"Will you me about that stroke of luck? Come now. Tell me before you fall asleep."

"You drive a hard bargain, milady." Littledove closed his eyes but continued speaking. "I worked for an Admiral Stoop for years and years. Since I's twelve. He left the navy and took up with the merchants. Made a lot of money, he did. Had a fleet of six. He wasn't much of a fool, but he took a liking to me anyway. One day, I come back from being at sea on one of his ships and got told he died. Broke my heart, it did. Mrs. Stoop told me he left the fleet to his sons, except the *Bessie*, his oldest ship. He left her to me. I tell you, I almost had to pick myself off the floor. But I could take her for my own only if I went to the merchant marine academy and got a master's license. You can't sail a ship this size without one—not legally, anyways. Else she'd go to his sons. He arranged it so I went without having to pay too much to go. That was good because I didn't have money then. At least not a lot.

"I knew how to sail the *Bessie*, but I never had to tell anyone how I did it, so I barely passed the entrance exam. But I did, and that was good enough. Didn't realize how much the admiral taught me over the years till I got there. I knew stuff inside out that bamboozled everybody else. Everything went real good until I didn't pass the final test, and they wouldn't let me take the orals. That was because I didn't know what to expect. Not like I didn't know the answers or couldn't sail a ship. I'd just never taken an exam like that. Didn't know you had to answer questions a certain way for them to see it was right.

"I got so mad at myself, I studied until my eyes almost burned out. But then I came in first the second time I took them. Got almost a perfect score. They even suspected me of cheating because no one ever got such a high score before, but that got cleared up quick because you can't cheat on the orals, and I did real good there too. I mean, you either know the stuff or you don't on orals. So, I got my license and claimed the *Bessie* for me own. That's how I got her."

Eliza nodded crisply as if she had expected no less of him. "As you say, the Admiral was no fool. What did you do to impress him? Come, tell me."

Littledove grinned. "Now that's a long story, milady. The short version is I saved the *Bessie* from sinking. We was off the coast of Chile, where we picked up nitrates and some passengers—ah, lady passengers. That kind. Well, the captain got imagination, and before you know it, he got drunk with them. The first and second mates too.

"The third mate probably'd have, too, but he'd the watch on deck. Well, I felt a storm coming. Couldn't get anyone to listen to me because the sky was clear, except the boatswain. He was a rusty bit of ancientness who taught me to read the waves in different winds, real tricky business but reliable like the devil once you catch on.

"When the third mate's watch was over, he went under and sent up the first mate, so drunk he could hardly stand. Was real annoyed, too, that he had to leave the ladies to do his watch. Hadn't even done his fly up proper. Well, the storm came full force, and not a soul was ready. Didn't sober up the first mate none. In fact, he got so seasick with liquor he had to go back under.

"Didn't inspire the captain to come up to deck because he was passed out under. So, the boatswain and me took over with some other men. At least we crew was sober because we didn't have that kind of privileges. He held the helm, and I called the sails until we got through the storm and everybody got sober again. And I got us back on track because I knew how to navigate. Four watches, I did, back to back, before I went below. Think I slept for two days after. Hell of a storm, it was. But not as bad as the one we had here.

"I thought that was the end of it, but the crew got talking about how I saved the ship, and the captain starts to give me squint eye because for every person who said I done something right, he hears them say he done wrong, because he did. A week later, I tied a yard wrong, and he flogged me for endangering others till I couldn't even stand. Tied me to the main mast for two days like an example. If men hadn't passed me food and water, I probably would have died on that mast. Then he put me in the brig for a week. Said my pay'd be docked for the time I wasn't working—like I flogged me own self.

"When we got to shore, I quit the ship without any pay at all, thinking I'd never see the lot of them again. But Admiral Stoop came to see me. Tracked me down somehow. He heard what happened and wanted to ask me questions. So, I told him. Tactful mind you, but you know, tact can't cover for a drunk captain.

"Well, right there Admiral Stoop paid me my whole pay, even for the week in the brig and my cut of the cargo profits, and he even thanked me for saving his ship with extra generosity. Then he went back and fired the captain and the mates in front of the whole crew. He even fired the third mate who wasn't drunk because he let the first mate take over when he was sauced.

"Then he came back and talked me into working for him again. Told me I could apprentice to be third mate on the next voyage, if I said aye. Booted me to second mate some voyages later. That was when we was still going around the Hoorn. Tricky, that was. The Hoorn always is.

"Made me first mate after that. Think he also made me work as a boatswain somewhere in-between. Started saying I was a gifted seaman. I stayed first mate for years under different captains on all his ships. Then I got commissioned as the *Bessie*'s captain when I got my master's license. Still feel sad when I think about him. He was a very decent man. His wife too. Didn't have to do any of that for me. I mean, I's just a sailor."

Littledove looked into the distance, trying to imagine what Admiral Stoop would say if he saw what had happened to the *Bessie*. Then he shifted back to the moment. "Milady, never ask a seafarer to tell you something, or you'll get yourself a long, wild tale of agony and glory."

Eliza drew her arms around herself and rocked herself. "Telling me about your admiral makes me think of Sarah and Jelly. I always imagine I see their bodies floating in the ocean when I am on the deck."

He took her hand, feeling her sorrow more than he had before and wishing he could do something about it. "Milady, the sea's only difficult to us who're alive. To the dead, she's real kind. She cradles bodies in her waves like a mother cradles a baby and rocks it to her bottom. It's like a womb down there, dark and easy. Your sisters'll be fine, but you and me, because we're alive, will be very sad for now. It's the living that carry sorrow for the gone. I'm real sorry about that, milady."

Eliza blinked to clear her tears. Littledove found himself floating into the rich hues of her brown irises.

"Did you ever worry about being attacked by pirates?" she asked.

"Never thought it would happen, to tell the truth. Didn't even really think they were real—the *Black Death* ones, I mean. People was making them sound like some tall tale with red hulls and all. Couldn't believe my eyes when I first saw them. They were down south. The *Andrea* was coming from the south. They stuck to ships with nitrates and lumber from South America. Sometimes a passenger ship but mostly cargo. Never any up here until now. And in the middle of winter, mind you."

"Do you think we shall be all right?"

"I still have hope, milady. But then, the future's always perfect. Always know what to say, where to stand, what to do. Can see exactly how things'll turn out in the future. But I never seen a thing that's perfect in the future survive perfect when it reaches now. Same for the past. Damn past is like the scraps left over from disasters in the now. Everything's messed up in the past. Even what works out fine was messed up before it turned out fine. That's 'cause the past used to be now, you see? But we're doing real good right now, so I wouldn't worry. We're doing good. Real good."

"You provide good solace, Captain Littledove. There is more to you than meets the eye."

"You don't have to call me Captain, milady. Not much left to be captain of."

"May I ask how I may address you, then?"

"Littledove's fine. Everybody calls me Littledove."

"May I ask what your full name is?"

"William Littledove. Nothing in the middle."

"William! A very elegant name. Like William the Conqueror."

"No king here, milady. I's just William the Me. Besides, nobody calls me William."

"So I may assume you prefer Littledove, then?"

He considered. Her question suggested he could change something fundamental about his life. He cleared his throat. "Ah, Will. I always liked being called Will."

"Very well. If you prefer Will, then I shall call you Will."

Littledove clutched his side and almost sat up. "That mean I can call you Eliza? Like your sisters?"

"If you wish."

"Oh, I wish it plenty. Have no doubt, Eliza."

Eliza took her time exploring her fingernails. "I must ask you, Will, why did you hide me and not someone else?"

"I'm real sorry about Miss Jemima and Miss Sarah. None of you deserved what happened. But I had three ladies and only room for one. I figured Miss Jemima might carry on and be found. Miss Sarah was across the room. You were just right there, standing right there, in front of me, there."

He fell silent, then added as if compelled to complete a confession, "Actually, milady, I went to get you on purpose. I couldn't stand the thought of them taking you, if I'd any say about it. Something in me knew the *Bessie* was already done for, and I might as well save what I could. I'd grown fond of you. That's the plain truth. Liked that you asked the cook to make something warm for the men. Didn't think that was in you when we first met. Tell the truth, don't think I saw anyone else in that room when I pulled you out. You probably don't have the same fondness for me, and that's all right. But you asked why I did it, so I'm telling you."

Eliza lowered her voice as she arched toward him. "Will, you have given me many reasons to grow fond of you."

You will do this right, Littledove warned himself before he spoke again. "And you, milady? Why did you come out to get me?"

She leaned forward and kissed him on the forehead, making all possibilities shimmer with viability despite her sly smile. "I could not tolerate the thought of someone making a flyswatter out of your ponytail."

CHAPTER SEVEN

REMAPPING BORDERS

That evening, Eliza gathered blankets from the forecastle and brought them into Littledove's quarters. For some reason, the pirates had not taken any blankets from the *Bessie*, perhaps because the *Bessie*'s blankets were thin and mended, and they had stolen better ones from the *Andrea*. She suspected the *Bessie*'s blankets had never been soft, not even when new. She began folding them into neat rectangles that she piled on the floor.

"What're you doing?" asked Littledove as he looked over from the bed.

"I am preparing a place to sleep."

"No." Littledove brought himself up on one elbow in an effort to get up, then flopped on his back with eyes clenched in pain. "You're not sleeping on the floor while I'm cozy in a bed. Nay. Not right."

Eliza abandoned the blankets and sat beside him, fearing he would roll himself out of bed with indignation. She pressed her hands against his shoulders. "Will—"

"No. Been sleeping on the floor all this time and haven't died yet. Got better things to die of."

"Stop. Stop. Please stop for a moment." Eliza pushed against his shoulders to keep him from getting out of bed. "I can sleep in another room. The fo'c'sle."

"What! And freeze to death? Besides, if pirates come again, I can't go hobbling all over, looking for you. You's got to be here so you can hide real quick."

"Fine. I shall bring a hammock in here."

"No hooks. Haven't got hooks in here."

"Hooks cannot be that difficult to install. Captain Littledove—"

"You said you'd call me Will!"

A silence came over them as Eliza acknowledged they could no longer take refuge in the formalities of being strangers. Still, she was not at ease with what had shifted between them. She clung to the silence, not knowing how to step beyond it, until Littledove spoke again.

"Milady, I know how to solve this problem. But promise me you won't slap me before I finish telling you."

"Your solution already sounds horrid, Will."

"Don't worry. I'm a gentleman. That, I promise you." Littledove pointed to the bed. "You can sleep over here. There's plenty room for two, and I'll be a perfect gentleman. Won't touch you none. It'll be like we're not even in the same room."

Eliza jerked her hands away from his shoulders and stood. Surely, she had not been so forward in her declarations of fondness that he now expected her to spend the night in bed with him. They could not possibly pretend they were not in the same room if they were in the same bed. She recalled his reactions when she washed his hair and became horrified at what he might now expect from her. Or be planning to take from her. She backed away from him.

"Milady, you promised you wouldn't slap me, and I know you want to right now. But I promised I'd be a gentleman, and I'm as good with my promises as you. That includes not saying it to anyone, not even in places where men like to brag. No one'll know by me. No one'll know at all because no one's here but you and me and no one else to judge. Fact is, there's nothing to judge because there's no wrong between us. And I's going to keep it that way. I promise you I'll be a gentleman."

Eliza maintained her silence, not knowing where to take the conversation. Under other circumstances, she would never again speak to a man who made such a suggestion.

Littledove tried again. "Milady, the floor's real hard and cold. And you'll roll all over the place if we get in rough waters. We can put blankets between us. Days're hard here. And also so I don't feel like a worm lying in bed while you sleep on the floor. I's can't let that happen." He paused before adding, "Milady. Give me a chance to be a gentleman so you don't have to suffer."

She was surprised he sounded so hurt at her distrust. Was he really trying to be a gentleman, whatever that meant to him? So far, he had done her no wrong. Not really. He had made some downright horrible *faux pas*, but she sensed he had intended no wrong with his occasional crassness.

She looked at the thin, scratchy blankets on the cold, hard floor. No one could ever fold them enough to turn them into fluffy cushions. The floor was always cold, with drafts skittering over it. Days on a ship were difficult and full of labor, requiring a good night's rest. They could put the vinegar jug of hot water between them.

Without allowing herself another thought, she grabbed a blanket from the floor and leapt over Littledove's legs, landing beside him in bed. She flapped the blanket over herself and, facing up, crossed her arms over her chest like a corpse.

She clamped shut her eyes and muttered through her teeth, "Remember, I am trusting you to be a gentleman. Good night, Captain."

She waited for Littledove to confirm his promise, but he remained perfectly silent and still. She wanted to look at him to affirm he had not died from astonishment but could not bring herself to turn her head. If anything, he would default to behaving like a gentleman because he could not stay awake for long. She hoped.

When she sensed Littledove was asleep, she turned her head a tiny bit to look at him. His nose was like a rudder in the moonlight. The shadows under his eyes were almost blue from loss of blood and fatigue. His hair, thin and bodiless, had a way of spreading with static across his shirts like cobwebs.

He was not handsome. But not ugly either. His handsomeness was in the way he carried himself, exerting a force that made people either step out of his way or follow him, depending on his mood. He respected what was right with deep conviction. He was a considerate soul, even if no one had taught him manners. Sometimes he was difficult to appreciate, but that did not indicate he was not a good person. Perhaps even a gentleman at heart.

Eliza pulled a blanket over him with a tenderness she could not abate. She could no longer deny she was growing fond of Littledove in ways she should not. Perhaps she had presented herself as too forward but could not help wanting Littledove to find a way to kiss her on the lips. Now, as she stretched next to him, she found herself wanting more of the reaction he had when she washed his hair. And more of what she felt at that time.

Her mind positioned him in her world as she once put a paper doll in a cardboard doll house. She envisioned him alarming everyone with his bluntness. His practical nature would not shine well in a parlor of people preoccupied with the subtleties of impressing for social gain. She wondered whether he even knew which wine to serve with what course or in which glass because the only wine served on his ship was red, and it was always served in tumblers that were also used for water.

Visions of Littledove at a dinner party came over her. He was not repulsive when he ate, but he had no real manners. She had never seen him eat with more than a knife, a fork, and sometimes a spoon. Once, whoever was serving mistakenly took his fork, Littledove licked his knife clean of gravy and ate his cake with it. His life reduced everything into simple practicality that somehow did not explain the magnificent, assertive style that flared from him when he was in command or the caring nature he kept hidden beneath his authority.

Eliza put a paper doll of herself on his ship, the only scenario she knew of his life. She was silly to think she could ever belong in such a precarious life, a ninny in the presence of an ever-changing cast of strange, uneducated men who spoke strange languages she had not studied.

Eliza looked at Littledove again. The man came with a life. She came with a life. She was no less bonded to her life than he was to his.

Littledove jerked with a moan, then rearranged himself slowly as he did when pain woke him. The block of warmth to his left reminded him Eliza was beside him. How he could have forgotten, even in his sleep, was beyond him. He was surprised he even fell asleep.

The vulgar comment he made when Eliza bathed him slipped into his mind, and he began berating himself. Even then, full of forgiveness and trust, she was willing to fall asleep beside him. Eliza might be the one woman on earth who could forgive his bungles. Graciously too.

He needed to become a gentleman—a full blown straight and proper gentleman without vulgarities or innuendos. That was what Eliza required if she was to continue being fond of him. At all costs, he would behave like a gentleman. Then maybe she would grow fonder of him.

Or not. Maybe "fond" was too strong a word. She was probably just tolerating him because she needed to. At the first sign of another ship, she would probably jump into a dinghy and start rowing to get away from him.

He still hadn't given her any proof that he could be anything but a barbarian—speaking that way to her! He really wasn't a gentleman, no matter what he claimed or wanted to be. At least not the type she was used to—with distinction, good language, proper manners, and good dress. A real gentleman would have just yielded the bed, even with a stab wound.

Littledove rearranged himself and unintentionally touched the back of Eliza's hand. His body became afflicted with an unnatural, perfect stillness in case she misinterpreted his unintended touch. He waited for her to withdraw, but she didn't. The warmth of the touch caught him in a storm of yearnings he had not seen coming.

You will do this right, Littledove told himself. *You will do this right.*

He pulled his hand away. Eliza rolled over, turning her back to him.

Moods on the ship swung as wildly as a crow's nest in a storm because even on the quietest of days, they were in a storm of anxiety. After several more weeks of drifting at sea, Eliza felt her hopelessness permeating everything as much or more as the cold did.

Littledove was still, for the most part, unable to work. He tired easily and was in constant pain. Even if he were in perfect health, he would not be able to sail the *Bessie*, an enormous ship with two fallen masts and who knew what other damages, without a crew.

Eliza tried not to afflict Littledove with her anxieties and headed to the deck to improve her spirits with fresh air and sunshine. But even there, she felt her hopelessness deepen. She was on a ship that took on water. No matter how often Littledove assured her that all ships took on water in the so-called bilge, she still felt the *Bessie* was singular in that respect and was always on the verge of sinking.

During his best moments, Littledove still looked half dead. The supply of food and drinking water would diminish to nothing because they had no way of increasing it. Eliza tried to fish but never caught anything, not even when she followed Littledove's suggestions about what time of day to fish and from what parts of the ship to throw the line.

"But you won't catch fish when there's no fish," he told her. "Don't matter how good a fisherman you're."

"And what is a better place to find fish than in the ocean?" Eliza retorted, incensed that she was not being successful at what seemed so easy to do.

"At a fishmonger, milady. Costs a little more, but it comes cleaned."

She wanted to be furious at him but could not be. In the end, she laughed with him and felt a little better. Still afraid they would run out of food, she continued dropping a length of twine with a hook at one end into the water as she had once seen some sailors do with great success. The thought of cleaning fish repulsed her but was better than starving.

Then one day, something snapped the line, tightening the twine she had wrapped around her fingers so much and so quickly that her fingers went cold and turned purple. The line jerked her arm with a force that had her stumbling along the deck over fallen yardarms and sails, fearing she'd be pulled into the water. Only when she fell over a mast did the twine unwrap from her fingers. She crawled to the bulwark to see the fins of several sharks swimming by the ship. She gave up fishing that day.

Every time something went wrong, the end of her world seemed to creep forward. The only thing they had in abundance was cold and lack. The world shrank with each passing day as the *Bessie* bobbed on a watery plate suspended in sky. Eliza never thought she would feel claustrophobic in the middle of the open sea, a place where water merged flawlessly with the infinity of sky.

But without land to tell her where they were, the world seemed only as big as what she could see, and it seemed emptier than it was big. She wanted to walk to the edge where the ocean met the sky to shout for help. Why this tiny world was not crowded with people who could help them was beyond her comprehension on some days.

Her imagination took bad turns, led her to dark conclusions, threatened the existence of her hope. She no longer cried, not for herself, Littledove, Sarah, or Jelly. Crying no longer brought her relief or insight. It became just one more thing that tired her.

Before going below deck, she turned into the wind to let its coldness scrape the despair off her face so Littledove would not see it. He had yet to find absolution within himself for having his crew massacred under his watch, and she did not want her despair to add to his harsh sentiments about himself.

Littledove calculated a few weeks had passed since he had been in so much pain he could barely breathe. Eliza had taken out the stitches, and at least he sat through that without carrying on too much. Now that he could sit up without blacking out, he was determined to be useful.

He was tired of drowning in mortification each time Eliza chopped wood or washed clothes. He had always done hard work while in pain. On a ship with a hundred sailors, he could guarantee every single one was in pain from some exertion. He could do things on his ship, even in his condition, that would not be all that taxing and take some of the workload off Eliza.

He sat up, pulled his pants from the hook on the post by the foot of his bed, and began to get into them. The first leg in went well, although the motion made his bad side ache enough to have to sit and catch his breath. The second leg went in better. He bent over to reach for the waistband, and ... a gray blotch swallowed his head.

The worry lines on Eliza's forehead that came into his focus indicated something in his plans had gone wrong. A moment later, he began to feel pains—new ones that concentrated at his hip and elbow. He could not determine where he was or what had happened. Eventually, he realized was sprawled on the floor by the bed, his ankles stuck in pants he had not yet pulled up.

Eliza began swirling around him, causing a commotion around his ankles. Each ankle rose into the air, hovered, and came down to the floor. He heard the clink of a belt buckle, and the chair next to him being up-righted.

"Milady," he mumbled apologetically.

Was there no end to the amount of embarrassment he could suffer around Eliza? Here he was sprawled on the floor in his drawers because she had washed the nightshirt. He had not even tied the waistband because it cut into the stab wound, which was still very tender.

"Let us get you back into bed, Will. When you are ready."

He looked at the chair that now resided permanently beside the bed as if it were the sheer face of a mountain.

"I shall help you as best I can."

"You always do, milady."

Bit by bit, Littledove rolled to his knees and hauled himself upright until his head hung over the chair seat, fully aware that half of his arse was on display. Determined not to groan like an ape, he pulled himself into the chair and twisted to seat himself, fighting the lightheadedness that drenched him in sweat.

Eliza placed her hands on his shoulders to steady him. She tucked a strand of hair behind his ear and rested her hand on the back of his neck as she leaned him against herself. A hug? Was she hugging him? Yes. Her steadying support had slipped into a hug. Littledove considered taking a chance and threading one arm around her waist to snug her against his torso.

You will do this right, he told himself and leaned back before she could think he was taking advantage of her kindness. "Thank you, milady."

What he would give for a book about gentlemanly behavior! Their situation was extenuating, but he was unclear about which lines not to cross. A reassuring hug was acceptable when he sat, but brushing against each other in bed was not, although sometimes during sleep, their limbs crossed their invisible boundaries and they touched. Littledove usually startled awake and withdrew, even though he had no desire to correct the situation.

He sat back and looked at Eliza from the tops of his eyes before he made the final haul of his body onto the mattress. That much he could now do on his own. His head sank into a pillow as Eliza covered him with blankets. She sat by his side while he eased himself into as much comfort as he could muster. Littledove looked at the post by his bed where his pants usually hung.

"Milady, where're my pants?"

"And why, may I ask, do you need your pants today?"

"A captain can't walk around his ship without pants if there's a lady on board. He might run into'er. And then what?"

Eliza laughed. "And may I ask why you need to walk around your ship today?"

"Why, milady? I haven't been on deck in weeks. Don't know how she's doing. For all I know, you painted her purple behind my back with all that time you spend on deck. Besides," he looked down feeling a little sheepish, "I thought I was a little better."

"And you decided to squander your betterment on falling out of bed?"

"Ah, that wasn't in the plan. Neither was having you take my pants away. See? Things like that happen when the future slips into the now."

Laughter overcame Eliza without mercy.

"You're laughing at me again, milady. You're usually sly about laughing at me, but now you do it out open, plain as day. Lost your shame about it, 'ave you, now? No more slyness left in you today?"

Eliza took his hand and pressed it against her cheek. Her amusement drifted out of her, and she became more serious as she rested his hand on his chest, still keeping hers over his.

"Will, you have lost almost all your blood. You shall faint—"

He raised his hand, index finger pointing in protest, without releasing hers. "Black out. Captains don't faint. They black out."

"You shall black out if you are not careful because you are anemic—"

"Not anemic. Ladies get anemic after they have babies. Sailors don't get anemic. Don't have babies either."

"You must not stand up suddenly or do other silly things—"

He wagged his finger, still without releasing her hand. "No. Captains don't do silly things. They—they—miscalculate."

"I think you have used up your quota of miscalculations for the day."

"What about my pants, milady?"

Eliza descended into giggles. "Next time you get up without help, I shall toss them overboard."

She picked the trousers up from the floor and hung them on the post. Littledove closed his eyes when she kissed him on the forehead and turned his head to one side as she kissed his cheek. He turned his head again with an ever so slight pucker of his lips that invited her to kiss him again.

But she did not. Littledove opened his eyes. She was looking away from him. He wondered if she was the sort of woman who needed to be kissed on the lips instead of one who would kiss a man on the lips. Most women were like that. Or maybe men did not have the patience to wait to be kissed and took the matter into their own hands.

It seemed as if her traditions, upbringing, expectations, and propriety made her pull back when he most wanted her to step forward. He couldn't blame her. Under normal conditions, their paths would have never crossed.

"Please do not get out of bed when you are alone, my captain," she said gently.

His throat went dry. "Am I your captain, milady? Am I your captain?"

Eliza averted her gaze, although she smiled. "Yes, you are very much my captain, Will."

"Glad to hear that, milady. I was getting worried you only liked to laugh at me."

Oh no, my captain. I also enjoy hearing *you* laugh at *me*. Now, it is best you get some rest."

Eliza smoothed the blankets over him with a gentleness Littledove wanted to interpret as tenderness but dared not. As he watched her stoke the stove and put more wood into it, he realized he could never kiss Eliza just because he wanted to. He'd have to be chock full of meaning.

Chapter Eight

Waiting for Death

During her next visit to the deck, Eliza noticed the wind was the briskest it had been in days. As Littledove did, without understanding what she was seeing, she checked the waves. They resembled thick chunks of broken glass but did not have whitecaps. No clouds either. Perfect dull blue sky as far as she could see. She abandoned her concerns about impending storms and began a walk around the deck to think.

Lately, Littledove was feeling better and was even walking around his quarters. Sometimes she walked him down the passage to the forecastle and back for exercise. Boredom, the first sign of recovery, was paying him regular visits, although almost any exertion wore him out, and standing quickly without becoming dizzy had yet to come to him.

She contemplated that if he could manage the stairs, he might be able to visit the deck and sit in the sun to get some color on his face. Or he might have a conniption when he saw the deck, just as he had when he saw the forecastle with many of its bunks hacked apart for firewood.

He had been below deck for ... too many weeks to count. Littledove told her he often went from North America to Europe without sighting another ship until they came near a port.

In her desperation, she began using the one hen the pirates left behind as a time piece. She found the broody chicken nesting peacefully on a clutch of eggs and sharing a sack of feed with mice. Completely convinced the tragedy did not apply to it, the hen pecked Eliza's hand when she removed the eggs to mark them. Only eggs laid from that day forward would be unmarked. By that method, Eliza would know which ones they could eat.

Anything other than salted beef and peas was like ambrosia, and on the following day, she carried the first unmarked egg back to Littledove's quarters as if it were a priceless pearl. She boiled it soft and sniffed it before serving it to Littledove, who was in much need of good food so he could heal.

Eliza wished she knew how long it took eggs to hatch. If the other eggs hatched, she dreamed of having something other than salted beef, although that meant she would have to butcher a chicken. Chicken usually arrived to her on a plate, perfectly sliced and barely identifiable as animal under a sauce. All the same, Eliza hoped they would not still be on the ship to see any egg hatch.

Every day she became more conscious of what was left to eat and how much drinking water remained. The drinking water had developed a yellow-green slime when it came out of the spigot, and it stank. Even after she boiled it and skimmed whatever floated to its surface, it never tasted like any water she had ever drunk. But neither of them had dysentery because Littledove mandated that she boil everything. Besides, boiling was the only cooking technique she knew, and she had not found any foods she could cook without boiling water.

They were consuming wood at a good rate between keeping warm and boiling, and Eliza was now considering what else she could hack apart when the forecastle stopped yielding wood like a denuded forest. She was eyeing the furniture without telling Littledove. Her axe was not as sharp as it used to be, and her upper arms chronically ached. They were much harder to the touch and sometimes made her fitted sleeves pinch, although her corset felt looser.

Out of habit, she checked that no one was looking when she hoisted her skirts to her hips and swung a leg over one of the fallen masts. She sidestepped riggings, remembering Littledove had told her in no uncertain terms never to set her foot on a rope because it might pull and hang her upside down, or worse, flip her into the ocean.

Every time she left his side, she received fifteen minutes of warnings about what and what not to do so she would be safe. He always looked greatly relieved when she returned. Eliza supposed she was no different with him, always worrying that he would fall or pass out and hurt himself. The skin over the stab would had mostly healed, but under the skin, the wound was rock hard. She did not know what to make of that.

When she finally subdued a sail that lay flapping on deck to walk around it, she saw the bank of gray clouds bunched tightly against the sky like wool batting ready to unroll. The storm. The storm the wind had been trying to tell her was coming. She should have believed the waves instead of dismissing them.

Littledove would have known immediately. She had seen him sniff the air while on deck to know what the weather was going to be. Eliza abandoned her walk and went below deck. The hatches were still battened from the last time it rained because she had not had the energy to open the heavy contraptions.

Littledove was in a chair, sorting the papers the pirates left behind in an effort to reassemble his life. She suspected organizing his papers was making him realize more undeniably that he had probably lost his ship.

"Where's it coming from?" he asked before she said anything about the storm.

Eliza had no idea. Littledove could look at the sky and tell direction, but she could not.

"I do not know. There are dark clouds beyond the—port? That side." Eliza pointed at a wall.

"That's south. That means we're pointing east."

How easily such calculations came to him. He glanced at the door to his quarters and made a motion to rise from the chair. Eliza stepped between him and the door.

"Milady, you promised me a walk on deck."

"Now is not a good time to be on deck, Will. If the storm breaks and you stumble, I shall need to tell everyone you fainted on the deck."

"You're a hard one, milady." Littledove abandoned his efforts to rise from the chair. "Fancy they'll think real highly of me when you tell them you pumped the bilge in torn dresses while I napped. And then that I fainted at the helm 'cause the waters got a little choppy."

Eliza smiled sympathetically. She knew she could not say anything to make him feel less despair at his inability to pull them out of these circumstances. He was no longer the captain of anything valuable, but he still could not release any of the responsibilities. When he looked away, she squeezed his shoulders in an effort to console him.

Dusk and storm arrived hand in hand, and the ship began to lurch. When Littledove managed the *Bessie* in a storm, he kept it perpendicular to waves, and she moved up and down somewhat predictably. Without his guidance, the *Bessie* rolled in all directions, as if they were in the belly of a child's crazed roly-poly toy.

He could not turn off the thoughts that a ship with such motions was engaged in a slow destruction. Without enough ballast to compensate for the cargo the pirates removed, the *Bessie* rode high above the waterline and could easily tip. Perhaps the only thing that kept her from tipping now was her ungraceful flat bottom. If land or shoals were nearby, she might crash and destroy herself, increasing their chances of getting to land and then dying.

By the time night fell, neither he nor Eliza could stand without being thrown from one side of the cabin to the other. Eliza curled up on the floor, turning paler and paler each time the *Bessie* swooped or randomly rose straight up and dropped just as quickly.

Littledove usually tried to pretend he was asleep because he knew Eliza was reluctant to get into bed if she knew he was awake. But this night, he could not even shut his eyes.

A swell tilted the ship and sent Eliza sliding across the floor. She crashed into a table leg, then slid back to crash against the bed. Littledove lowered his arm and felt Eliza clutch it as she began to slide across the floor again. Despite the pain the odd angle of his arm caused his bad side, he kept it down because he did not want to see Eliza crash into more furniture.

In better days, he would have put his arm around her waist and hoisted her onto the bed, but he could not do that at the moment. He deemed his limitation for the better. A woman like Eliza was not to be handled like a sack of peas with hopes that she would split open and invite him in. She would not tolerate such behavior any more than she tolerated insinuations. She could walk away the first opportunity she had if he offended her, and he would be left to live with her disappointment in him.

"Milady, the best way to weather a storm like this without anyone at the helm is in a place where you won't get flung about." He was careful not to invite her into bed or beside him. He always referred to the bed as if it were a nameless, foreign country in some undiscovered ocean.

She did not respond. The *Bessie* shifted again, and he involuntarily drew a sharp breath and pulled up one leg in pain. By the time he unclenched his eyes, Eliza was climbing into the bed on her own.

She was halfway on it when the ship lurched so harshly she went flying into the wall. In the compensating motion, she rolled back into him, and he threw one of his blankets over her to keep her from realizing he had just gotten a spectacular view of her legs that gave a man, even in his condition, cause for much imagination.

Littledove put his arm around her. Well, around the blanket wrapped around her. When the ship lurched again, she tucked her face into his shoulder. He became racked with imagination but was relieved to know the multiple blankets rendered his reaction undetectable.

What he really wanted to do was make love to Eliza in the storm, even if it killed him, as doing so in his condition most likely would. He berated himself for having become smitten, as if becoming smitten had just happened seconds ago and not when he first set eyes on her, lovely as all hell, waiting by the window of the lounge in the Hansweert harbor office for him to speak.

Only now could he admit the flicker of imagination he felt that moment was so powerful it became the reason he agreed to take them on as passengers. He counted on Eliza being married to guard himself against her and be able to observe her from afar. Now, like a grand lobcock, he was hoping that if he felt enough for her, she would begin to feel for him.

He braced himself for the massive heartbreak he was bound to suffer. She was not just beauty and elegance to please the eye but a complete, complex person of even better quality than he once imagined. She was daring. She was caring. She was a gentle person with the willingness to save a man's life under the worst circumstances.

The the *Bessie*'s stern rose swiftly, lingered midair, and smacked down against ocean. Eliza clenched beside him, digging her fingers into his arm.

Hoping to assuage her fears, he asked, "So, what's the first thing you're going to do when you get home?"

"Home—? First—? Thing—?"

Her reaction made Littledove wonder if he had asked an ungentlemanly question, although he could not figure out how that worked. He'd noticed that except what was ingrained in her manner, Eliza revealed little about herself, becoming a source of mysterious exquisiteness amidst the imperfections of any moment. And she had a way of getting him to talk about himself and say things he normally would not bother to tell others.

Littledove persisted. "Milady, you sound like you're heading to the gallows, not back home."

"Well, I ... We ..." She took a moment to compose herself. "I imagine nothing as exciting as traveling the world on one's own ship. Mostly I sit in a parlor, converse with my sisters, play piano or flute, read, knit, or walk the grounds. Nothing truly exciting. Sometimes I read in French. I know some Latin but not enough to read it comfortably. Oh, yes. I have a meeting of the Ladies' Tea for Charity coming up, if I have not missed it. I am usually involved with that."

"You're a charity lady!" He pulled away and stared at her as if she were a spider on his pillow. "You? A charity lady!"

"I help raise money for charities—"

"You're one of them!"

"One of them? What do you mean 'one of them'?"

Littledove settled back, having heard the indignation in her voice. He pulled Eliza closer after the ship lurched again. Not that he had to do so. Eliza was safe enough from harm where she was. He now felt idiotic about having such a strong reaction to her being a charity lady.

"This's probably before your time, so it wasn't you because I's older than you. Charity ladies—they're these ladies that go around trying to improve poor people's lives. They're all rich, so they don't know a thing about what being poor's. They think they do good, but they just muck around."

"What on earth do you mean, Will?"

He was glad her voice was gentler and expressed more curiosity. "This one time they set up to teach how to cook with cabbage so you can feed a shipload of people for almost nothing. But the people that went couldn't even afford a place to live, never mind a stove to cook on. And where exactly were they going to grow the damn cabbages? In the park? Not like anyone who went was landed gentry. They roast things in open fires on the street. Ever try to roast a cabbage? Those things explode! They just showed up to see if they could get some food. Would have been better off using that cabbage money on giving them hot soup.

"This one time, they decided they're going to improve the lives of poor children. They all get together, raise a heap of money, and start stealing kids from their mums. My mum wasn't perfect, but she was still my mum, and you only get one mum. Not like there's anything better can make do for your mum when you're a kid."

Littledove grabbed the side of the bed and waited for the *Bessie* to ease out of a roll before he continued. "Anyways, they put me in this brick building with hot meals and education and declared me better. Meanwhile, I never saw my mum again. Some charity lady came a few months later and told me she died at the Edith's Bay Sanatorium from something she couldn't say. I suppose she didn't think I'd mind because I had hot food and education.

"Now I'm stuck in this institution. Felt like I killed her, me being away from her. Almost killed me, I tell you. So, I ran away. I walked down to the docks and left on the first ship that said I could come aboard. Swore I'd never set foot anywhere there were charity ladies. I think I stayed on a ship until I got to be of age and couldn't be bossed around."

"May I ask whether your father had any say?"

Littledove hesitated, never having been certain who his father had been. "Ah, he wasn't around."

"I am sorry, Will. I am very sorry."

"Not like it's your fault. I'm sorry I got mad at you. It wasn't you." He clutched her closer, anticipating another heave, and felt her settle into his arm.

"Will, this is as much of a surprise for me as it was for you. I do not think anyone has ever heard about repercussions from charity work or that any of the work was anything but benevolent."

"You think raising charity money makes you not responsible for what happens in some good deed? You ever talk to the people you help? I mean sit down and talk to them over beer? I mean tea." He flapped his hand as if to erase the word. "Whatever ladies drink."

Eliza quivered silently with laughter.

"Ah! You're laughing at me again. I can feel it."

"I'm surprised you can feel anything but this storm. I think you should be a guest speaker at the Ladies' Tea for Charity. I can just imagine it. One outburst of your forthrightness could blast the Ladies' Tea for Charity into extinction. And no, I am not laughing at you. I think what happened to you is horrid, and I am sorry no one was aware of it."

Not pleased with himself at having upset Eliza, he diverted. "You ever think about becoming a nurse? Dr. Aves said you did pretty good when you helped him."

"I suspect when I go home I shall have to sit in a parlor until some fine fellow proposes to me."

"Ah. Engaged?" He kept his tone nonchalant, but his morale sank. Of course she would be engaged. Probably had a mile of men waiting in line for her.

"I have not yet been asked."

"Waiting for the fine fellow to get his courage up, aye?" He made himself sound lighthearted even as hope deserted him. Not that he ever had a chance, really, but he never liked having a fantasy squelched.

"Such fine fellows prefer to marry charity ladies, not nurses."

"Sight of blood doesn't seem to bother you. I mean, someone like a captain wouldn't mind having a nurse on board."

"The thought of you dying terrified me beyond noticing the blood."

"I'm sorry I bled so much, milady."

"And I am still sorry I caused you so much pain."

"Think Dr. Aves said he knew about something better than Whiplash's Tonic. Forgot what he said it was. Anyway, that's the only thing you had."

"I believe Whiplash's Tonic was meant for small cuts. Like shaving nicks." Eliza touched a nick on his jaw.

He sighed. "Wasn't your fault. Dr. Aves said the hardest part about being a doctor is seeing people suffer when you're trying to make them better. I'm better, milady. I'm always better around you."

"Thank you, Will." She stroked his cheek again. "If I may ask, why do you not grow a beard like some captains?"

"Nay, grows in scruffy. Looks like I's got mange or something. Believe me, if I could, I would. It's a trick to shave without slashing your own throat when a ship's rolling."

By now he was certain no one could slip a sheet of paper between them. He took courage and said, "You don't sound happy about going home. Maybe you shouldn't."

Eliza briefly covered her face with her hands and shook her head. "Will, the poor have nothing of what they need. I have everything *except* what I need. I never thought having everything could be so impoverishing. It is too difficult to explain. People think people with means have no needs because they have everything. That does not hold true at all. They have things they can buy, not things of the soul."

He raised the blanket to Eliza's shoulders to protect her from evils and realized he had not been cold since she'd been resting beside him. He could be more of a gentleman, but his arm would not unwrap itself from around her shoulders. She snuggled against his body, revamping his imagination.

"I do not know, Will. In these quarters, I think I have seen more of the world than anywhere else."

Morning might have arrived long before Eliza became aware of it because the dense fog outside the windows made everything outside the *Bessie* disappear. The ship was no longer lurching, but Littledove's arm was still around her, and her head was still on his shoulder. He clasped her hand over his chest the moment he woke.

"Don't go on deck."

"May I ask why? The storm is over."

"Too much fog. I's seen good sailors get lost on a deck in a fog like this. It'll clear up soon enough." Littledove tightened his arm around her when she shifted to sit. "Getting up already, milady? Going shopping today?"

She sank back into the comfort of his arm. "Sooner or later, we shall both have to rise."

"Make it later, then," said Littledove. "Not much to do here today."

They began to drift back to sleep when Eliza heard a distinct clank. She raised her head. Another clank sounded.

"Will! Listen."

Littledove jerked awake. "What?"

"Bells. Are those bells? Listen."

Littledove turned to look out the windows, still obscured with fog. Another clank sounded, not far away. He clutched his side and sat up. "Bells. Aye."

They eased their way out of bed and together tried to look past the fog outside the window. They might as well have been peering through cotton balls.

"Look!" Eliza pointed to a glint. The fog covered it in an instant. "Did you see that?"

More clanks sounded at irregular intervals. Then a few dots of light appeared and disappeared in the fog.

"Fog bells," said Littledove. "To warn other ships she's there. Same for the lanterns. Fog lanterns."

"We can be rescued, Will! We can be rescued!" Her elation almost left her breathless but ended when she saw Littledove's expression.

He pulled her to himself. "Might be pirates."

"But, Will—"

"You don't know, do you? That fog might lift, and we might be sitting right in front of the *Black Death*. We don't know where she is. We don't even know where *we* are."

"But there's nothing of value they haven't taken. They'll see it's the *Bessie* and leave."

"There's one thing they didn't take," said Littledove as he sat on the edge of the bed. "Me. They didn't take me."

"You?"

"They don't know about you, but they know they didn't find me. Maybe they didn't know it at the time, but they know it now. You think they won't remember the captain wasn't found? They tried to set the ship on fire because they couldn't find me. Storm rained it out. If it's them out there, they'll board looking for me."

"Then we'll hide in the compartment. They'll leave again without finding either of us."

Littledove pulled her to himself. "Let me think, Eliza. Let me think a moment."

She fell silent as she leaned against him, playing with the buttons on his nightshirt until he took her hand and kissed it. "I need to get dressed."

Eliza handed him the pants that hung from the post by his bed. She fetched the shirt she had washed the night before from across the room and stoked the fire with her back to him while he struggled to put on the pants without bending over too much. She already knew if she offered to help he would die of embarrassment.

Eliza smoothed her dress because she didn't take it off when she fell asleep next to Littledove. She glanced over her shoulders. His struggles with his pants ended, and he began buttoning his shirt. Already, he looked depleted.

"Comb my hair, Eliza, please. It helps me think."

She fetched the brush from the washstand and knelt on the bed behind him to brush his hair. The perturbation within him emanated, even as he sat without moving, head hanging, hands clasped between his knees.

"Eliza, here's how this works." Littledove finally said when she finished putting his hair in a ponytail. "If we both hide in the compartment, they'll burn or sink the ship, and we'll either drown or burn alive. Either way, we both die. If you hide in the compartment, they'll get what they want with me. They won't burn the ship because they'll want someone to find the captain on the deck. That's what they did with the crew. Left them on the deck for all to see. They've done that before. It's how you know their work. The storm washed them overboard because they didn't see it coming and we were too busy trying to get away to put up the safety nets."

Eliza listened with her eyes and ears and skin until her skull began to prickle. She was trying to understand what Littledove was saying, feeling he was leaving out something vital. She startled when she hit on the missing point.

"Will! They will kill you! The way they did the crew!"

"But you'll be saved, Eliza."

"No, Will, no. That cannot be—"

Littledove grabbed her upper arms. "Eliza, if they get ahold of you, they will make me watch what they do to you before they slice my throat. They will pass you around from man to man, and every damn man on that ship'll have his way with you. Then they'll throw you overboard like an apple core and laugh. Please don't make me watch that. I'll have nightmares in my afterlife. Have mercy on me and stay hid, Eliza. Please."

A stream of light broke through the fog and illuminated the cabin with the force of a clock striking the hour. The *Bessie* was now visible.

Littledove stood with a slight stagger and pulled Eliza against himself. He hesitated, then kissed her with his soul. Eliza closed her eyes and melted into the kiss, feeling every pulse in their bodies reverberate as one—one breath, one heartbeat, one pulse, one desire.

When he pulled away, she tugged him back, wondering how she could ever part her arms and let him go on deck by himself to have his throat cut, or worse. Littledove stroked her cheek.

"Milady, don't let my effort be in vain. Stay hid." He looked at her again, his face holding back all his feelings and added softly before kissing her on the forehead, "Pray for me, milady."

Littledove opened the compartment panel and held it for her more properly and with more dignity than any man who had ever held a door open for her. Eliza slid onto the bench and, through her tears, watched him close the panel. She could smell his fear.

The compartment immediately became a chamber of torments as she imagined Littledove, a man who could barely stand, awaiting death alone on the deck of his ship. Of all the things she had survived, she did not think she could survive this experience. She was certain being on the *Bessie*, a ship so quintessentially Littledove's, without him would cause her to go mad and leap into the ocean.

Sarah and Jelly came into her mind. They had not been shot or thrown overboard, as Eliza imagined, but killed after a lengthy torture that might have lasted days. Littledove had known what would happen to them when he pulled her out of their quarters but never told her.

Overwhelmed by this truth, Eliza began to cry. From the compartment, she would never know if he was being tortured or killed on the deck. She might emerge and find his head stuck on a mast. She began to shake with grief and helplessness at what was happening to Littledove and at her inability to do anything about it.

On this ship, she had cried more than she ever cried anywhere else on earth. On this ship, she learned the meaning and depth of sorrow. She lost Sarah and Jelly, and now she would lose Littledove while she waited submissively in a closet, assigned to be the meaning of his sacrifice.

When the thunder of men's footsteps rumbled down the stairs, Eliza recalled Littledove's description of the ocean rocking a body in her waves to the bottom of her womb and longed for such a sensation to sweep over her. This outcome was not worth surviving if Littledove died.

The rumble on the stairs ended in abrupt silence. Eliza clutched her skirt, waiting for someone to burst through the door. No one came.

Perhaps they had not sent hordes of pirates because the ship looked abandoned. And because they had Littledove in hand. Some of the sounds on the stairs sounded like someone tumbling. Had they thrown Littledove down the stairs? Eliza pressed her ear to the panel, but her heartbeat drowned out the details in the sounds.

She made herself brave and peered through the crack to see a sliver of the empty room. Whatever was happening in the passage was happening almost silently, although she could hear slow shuffling. Was Littledove unconscious? It wouldn't take much. When the latch to the room clicked, she stopped breathing, suspended in cold terror.

A strip of color flashed across the crack so closely and quickly she jumped back and banged her head against a stud. Before the thud from her head bump went silent, the panel snapped open and light blinded her. She screamed and screamed as someone pulled her out. All her life went into her screams, as she shrieked with the same terror she imagined Jelly and Sarah once felt.

No matter how wide her eyes became with fright, she could not see anything before her. An arm wrapped itself around her waist, and a hand went over her mouth. She sank her teeth into the hand, plunged her elbow into some ribs, and hoped she shattered shins when she kicked herself free.

She lunged blindly toward the door and pulled on the door until the latch unfastened, but before she could run out, the man wrapped his arm around her again, dragged her across the room, and landed her on the bed. The arms around her multiplied and became like tentacles as they held her down. She slipped through the hold and began to run again, but she tripped over a chair. The arms wrapped around her again, more firmly than before, and lifted her from the floor as she kicked and screamed.

"Milady! Milady! Look at me. Look at me, milady!" Someone held her face with one hand. "Eliza! Look at me!"

She recognized Littledove's voice before she could focus on him. She stared and stared as if he were an apparition, then gently tapped his cheek with a shaking finger. Littledove! Her Captain Littledove! Alive! A moment later, a blast of gratitude swept through her, and she kissed him on the lips, wanting to stretch the moment into eternity. Littledove kissed her back, breathing hard between kisses, before pressing her against himself and rocking her.

Through his chest, she heard him say, "Milady, Captain Ellsworth of the USS *Vesuvius* is here to rescue us. They're rowing over now."

Chapter Nine

Aspiring to Formality

Captain Ellsworth of the USS *Vesuvius* was a man of decisive action, as Eliza now suspected all sea captains were. Seconds after she and Littledove boarded, he placed Littledove in the care of the ship's doctor and assigned him to sleep in the extra bunk with the mates, just as Dr. Aves had done on the *Bessie*. He sent several boats of men to board the *Bessie* and prepare her to be towed. Then the *Vesuvius* wore around to take the *Bessie* back to Edith's Bay, which was approximately eight to ten days away.

While all this was happening, Captain Ellsworth gave up his private quarters for an hour so Eliza could bathe. Then she was escorted to a room that was evacuated by someone who would now share accommodations with someone else. The room came equipped with a sewing kit so she could mend the rips in her dress. A short while later, a cabin boy delivered a stack of ancient *Godey's Lady's Book* issues.

The notion of reading a lady's magazine at this time struck Eliza as ridiculous. She could not concentrate on anything. Most of the events on the USS *Vesuvius* were happening in a haze she could not clear. After mending her dress, she wiped it down with a washcloth in an attempt to refresh it. Then she slipped it back on and wandered into a passage to learn how the doctor found Littledove. In the passage, she ran into Captain Ellsworth, who was coming to check on her.

"Miss Strauss, Captain Littledove already warned me you were unlikely to stay in your quarters."

"May I ask how Captain Littledove is? How does the doctor find him?"

"The doctor thinks Captain Littledove has no more than a thimble of blood left in him and is lucky to be alive. However, he shall continue to get better. His danger is over. Thanks to you, Miss Strauss, Captain Littledove informs me."

Eliza's knees almost buckled at the news. "May please I see him?"

"Absolutely. Captain Littledove is joining us for dinner. In fact, I was coming to escort you to the officers' mess."

"Oh, I would greatly appreciate dining. I wish to thank you for sending the reading materials," said Eliza, remembering her manners. Her urge to set eyes on Littledove was more compelling than even her hunger.

And there he was as promised, waiting in the officers' mess, hair still damp from a bath, freshly shaved, and wearing what Eliza surmised was a borrowed shirt and tie with trousers of his own. She suspected none of his trousers had been taken because his pants looked as if they had been made for a man on stilts.

"Captain Littledove," said Eliza with a formal curtsy.

"Miss Strauss," said Littledove as he jerked into an exaggerated bow to match her curtsy.

Good. He had taken her cue as to how to address her in public. She hoped formality would prevent misconceptions about familiarity.

The first and third mates arrived not long after with the ship doctor, and dinner was promptly served as a clock struck. Eliza had to stop herself from pouncing on the duck with sides of potatoes and carrots, a glorious reminder that food could consist of more than boiled salted beef and peas. She restrained herself from gulping down the water that was pleasantly laced with lime. The first sip of wine on an empty stomach made her lightheaded, and she abandoned it until the middle of the meal when her hunger began to taper.

As Captain Ellsworth extracted a list from Littledove of damage the *Bessie* suffered, she was relieved to fade into the background. Broken masts, ripped and burned sails, hacked interiors, missing equipment—as the list grew and grew, the corners of Littledove's mouth fell lower and lower until he threw his hands up in the air.

"Maybe we should sink her now rather than tow her back."

"Too early to draw conclusions, Littledove," said Captain Ellsworth. "If the *Bessie* has no canon holes in her hull and survived storms unguided with two broken masts, she's likely to be salvageable, even at her age. Windjammers can take a lot of beatings. I'll send the boatswain with a crew over tomorrow for a detailed inventory of the damages."

Littledove wrinkled his brow and frowned even more, making himself age another decade. Eliza remembered he had already seen the deck with all its devastation while waiting to have his throat slashed.

She forced herself to decline a second serving of fresh pears poached in wine, not wanting to present herself as gluttonous, although her eyes followed the man who removed the last poached pear from the table. She wondered how she could be so full and still feel hungry.

Her haze lifted enough for her to notice First Mate Benka. He had taken to opining sporadically during the meal, then looking at her as if to make sure she remained aware of how significant he was. Halfway through the meal, she was tempted to stand and applaud at the casual statements that he made as if he were a Roman senator.

Aside from being annoyed by his constantly insisting that she remain aware of him, she became wary of Benka because Littledove held his shoulders at a slight angle away from him. Thus far, the two men had not spoken directly to one another, although they were seated side by side. A good bit of enmity was building in the silence between them. She was not surprised. Littledove had little tolerance for self-importance or pretense.

Benka finally spoke to Littledove when the current conversation came to a pause. "Captain Littledove, grace us with a sea story."

"Don't think I know one you haven't heard," said Littledove, appearing so distracted Eliza thought he had not even heard the question.

He stretched his legs under the table and crossed his arms over his chest. His eyes moved quickly as if he were evaluating the *Bessie* in his mind.

"Tell us the story of how you and the lovely Miss Strauss, who pumped your bilge, happened to survive on a ship where everyone else was massacred."

The sounds of tableware ceased. Everyone tensed. Undoubtedly, the question was on everyone's mind, but the topic was a matter of a formal maritime investigation not dinnertime small talk.

Without moving his body, Littledove shifted his eyes toward Benka. Some color rose in his cheeks. His lips began a series of minuscule twitches that Eliza attributed to an inexhaustible stream of silent swear words.

Eliza had no idea what Littledove could say aloud. He could not possibly say he hid with a woman in a closet because a wound rendered him useless, even if that was the truth and he was not at fault.

She spoke up. "I found Captain Littledove when I came out of hiding. I suspect they thought he was not alive because he was lying in a puddle of his own blood."

From his slouch, Littledove looked at her from the tops of his eyes.

"Left for dead?" Benka gave Littledove a once over. "Well, good to see the captain's very much alive for someone who was thought dead."

Captain Ellsworth shifted forward to speak, but Eliza cut him off. "You did not slip on the pool of blood that made them think Captain Littledove had passed away. I assure you it was a horrific moment. I did and was convinced Captain Littledove was not alive until several moments later when he took a breath."

Eliza dabbed her eyes. She hoped the word *horrific* coming from a woman would redirect the conversation because no man wanted to make a woman burst into tears in front of other men.

Benka took the hint. He glanced at Littledove before turning back to Eliza. "And where were you hiding?"

Eliza put on her demure face. "I prefer not to say. I hope never to find myself in a similar predicament, but if I do, I do not want people to come looking for me there first thing. Brilliant ideas have way of being disseminated, I hear."

Littledove's face went slack, except for his eyes that were now the widest she had ever seen. He sat up.

Benka looked Littledove over again. "I am sure Captain Littledove greatly appreciates your brilliance, milad—"

"I prefer being addressed as Miss Strauss, First Mate Benka." She was annoyed to hear Littledove's moniker for her come from Benka's mouth, although she supposed it was a common way for seamen to address women.

Benka backed off as gracefully as a good clod could. "My apologies, Miss Strauss. I did not mean to offend."

"I have taken no offense, thank you. I was merely expressing a preference."

Captain Ellsworth drew a deep breath and nodded with a smirk. "Miss Strauss, I suspect one day you will make an excellent captain."

"Oh dear, I hope it never comes to that. I have learned too much about responsibilities and valor from watching Captain Littledove run his ship, and it is a profession I do not aspire to pursue."

Captain Ellsworth bobbed his head with approval and shifted his attention back to Littledove. "We usually have a quick catch-up after dinner, followed by cards. You're welcome to join, but you look tired, Captain Littledove. I recommend you retire early. Tomorrow, I want to know whereabouts you were attacked. If you have the coordinates, that'd be ideal."

"Haven't got the coordinates precise, but I's a real good idea where it happened because I took readings the night before. You know, they snitched everything—compasses, two sextants, the chronometer, all the charts."

"I, too, should retire early," said Eliza. "The day has been long and difficult, although I am very grateful to be here. Thank you, Captain Ellsworth. I am extremely grateful to you and your crew."

Eliza stood, and in respect, all the men stood and bowed, including Littledove after a slight delay. Growing unexpectedly gray, he swayed and grabbed the back of his chair for support. Captain Ellsworth reached out to steady him.

Littledove held up one hand. "No, no. It's the ups and downs that're bumpy. Everything else goes good."

"I'll walk Miss Strauss to her quarters," announced Benka with grand authority.

Littledove narrowed his eyes, making the shadows under them grow darker. His annoyance with Benka was not entirely undetectable as he pulled a bit of rank.

"Seeing that Miss Strauss has been my crew, I'll see her to her quarters so you can prepare your catch-up report for your good captain, First Mate."

"Thank you, Captain Littledove," Eliza hastened to say to set Benka's expectations and cap the tension between the two men.

By her side, Littledove fumed and muttered to himself all the way down the length of the passage to her quarters. In front of Eliza's cabin door, he glanced over his shoulder, then bent his knees and grasped her by the shoulders.

"Milady, I can't thank you enough for what you just did in there. I'm in your debt forever. With Whiplash, you saved my life—although you nearly killed me. With wits, I think you just saved my career."

"There is no debt between us, Will. You know that."

"Benka's real good at the job, but he gets imagination when there's ladies around. Lob—" Littledove stopped himself. "Aah—fancies himself a lady's man."

Eliza rested her hand on Littledove's arm in an effort to soothe his agitation. He clamped his hand over hers.

"Don't slap me for saying this, milady, but I'm going to miss you tonight. Got spoiled having you to meself all the time." He began to lower his head, but they heard footsteps coming down the passage, and he stepped away from her.

Sensing their moment was over, Eliza said, "Good night, Captain Littledove. Thank you for seeing me to my quarters."

She slipped into her cabin and closed the door behind her. Pressing her cheek against the door, she tried to hear Littledove's footsteps. She very much wanted the door to be Littledove, although the coolness of the wood was a sharp contrast to his bony warmth. She could all too well imagine what being with Littledove on the *Bessie* could be like without the dangers and the wounds and the fears and the expectations they dragged on board from other parts of their lives.

Littledove found the deck speckled with comments about what a fine woman Miss Strauss was (wink, wink). Some even encouraged him with raised eyebrows and grins to engage in braggadocios.

Littledove did not beat around the bush. "Woman like Miss Strauss don't put up with addlepates with imagination."

To Littledove's surprise, he received more respect for that answer than if he had recited a series of adventures through the brothels of the world. Some men accepted his rebuff sheepishly because Eliza's polish was not lost on anyone. Others smiled diplomatically, which he took to mean that the notion of Eliza taking up with him was too improbable to contemplate.

Benka, however, was downright blunt. "So, you're saying she wouldn't have you?"

Littledove leaned in to him and tapped him on the chest with the back of his hand. "Recommend you ask her direct, seeing you did so good at dinner, eh?"

A soft chuckle rose from the sailors who had lingered to listen, making Littledove realize the crew was aware Benka considered himself one of God's gifts to women.

You will do this right, Littledove vowed as he walked away, feeling a little triumphant at not having bungled. He had not been raised to be a gentleman to the degree Eliza had been raised to be a lady. He had barely been raised at all. But he would try his best not to behave like a barbarian.

That said, he often wondered what would have happened if on the night of the storm had he pressed his luck. He liked to flatter himself that he could have seduced her, but in the end, the success would not have been worthwhile if Eliza found any reason to regret it. He did not want to do anything that might make her despise him. The captain of a cargo ship never held much status anywhere, not even with captains in the navy. At best, he was always second class, if even noticed.

The last time he had been around people who were somewhat refined had been at the Edith's Bay Captain's Club that hosted a dinner for the graduates of the Edith's Bay Merchant Marine Academy. Feeling he had reached the pinnacle of his life when he got his master's license, he got drunk, made a fool of himself, and was asked to never again set foot inside the august institution.

Every captain on earth knew about his banishment, and those who did not quickly found out in the small community that extended worldwide. As much as he wanted to dismiss the members of the club as snobs, an inner whisper always held him accountable for that disaster. He had been the one who bungled and deserved ostracism from a place where he might have learned some social graces, furthered his career, and increased his value among mariners. Shamed to the bone, he crawled onto the *Bessie* and fled.

Eliza could accept him, he knew, when they were on an abandoned ship in the middle of an ocean, but in the company of her peers, he would always be the court jester—at best, someone she would always have to explain; at worst, an embarrassing remnant from an unplanned adventure. When Eliza returned home to her world of silk dresses, servants, and foie gras, their paths would never again cross.

A part of him truly feared Eliza would dismiss him as a fool. She had already dismissed Benka as a fool, and Benka had far better polish than he would ever have. A captain always had more standing in the line of command than any mate, but not necessarily in a social situation. Even a naval first mate had more panache than a barbarian captain of a cargo ship.

Littledove sighed. His biggest sorrow was heading toward him as surely as a storm. His dignity was his best weapon against the heartbreak he knew was coming. But he swore that for once, he would do things right, even if he had no chance of winning.

Without doubt, the USS *Vesuvius* towing the *Bessie* into the Edith's Bay harbor was quite the sight. Almost immediately, Littledove got into a heated argument with the tugboat operators that the *Bessie* was not salvage, because they charged more to tow a salvage ship. The truth was, he could not bear the humiliation of having his one ship considered salvage nor the panic of not knowing what he would do next to earn a living. A cargo ship captain without a fully functioning ship was a laughingstock.

Captain Ellsworth pulled some rank and had his boatswain certify the *Bessie* was not salvage, even if she had two broken masts. A deal was struck for regular rates, although Benka chuckled when the tugboat operators began shrugging their shoulders, clearly unable to understand why a military captain would certify a floating pile of wood as a functioning ship.

Captain Ellsworth docked the USS *Vesuvius* long enough to help Littledove arrange for the *Bessie* to be hauled into the shipyard for repairs. Littledove suspected he also took the opportunity to restock the USS *Vesuvius* with fresh fruits and vegetables.

With a bow to Eliza and a firm handshake to Littledove, Captain Ellsworth departed, wishing them the best and inviting them to visit his family in Edith's Bay, together or individually. His voyage was already delayed by many weeks, and he would be returning to sea in search of the *Black Death*.

Without a moment's loss, Littledove began running from one end to the other of the Edith's Bay harbor office, arranging logistics for the *Bessie* and filing reports. Military officials came to interview him, wanting to know where the *Black Death* had struck.

Fortunately, Littledove anticipated being asked this question over and over and requested several copies of his report to Captain Ellsworth that he distributed selectively. Apparently, the *Black Death* had gone after two other ships since attacking the *Bessie* and left a current of blood across the ocean.

Whenever Littledove walked by the waiting lounge, he looked in on Eliza, who waited anonymously by her portmanteau and his sea bag. Most of the time, he found her dissuading some man from conversing with her. She was an incongruous sight, carrying herself with a splendidness not typically found in women who wore mended dresses of extraordinary quality.

When journalists showed up seeking to interview the survivors of a *Black Death* attack, Littledove curtailed all business, grabbed the bags, and slipped with Eliza out a back door. Through backstreets, they picked their way between broken crates that smelled of rotting fish and urine, guarded against snarling dogs and hissing feral cats, and dodged flying sheets of greasy newspapers that always seemed to land on their chests.

Littledove cursed to himself when they turned onto a street lined with brothels and dirty children. He was used to walking down this street alone or with other men and ignoring the sassy invitations. He had never visited houses on this street because he'd always been wary of bunters and the diseases they carried.

Despite having Eliza by his side, he received invitations left and right. Halfway down the street, he put his arm around her, more to protect himself from embarrassment than to shelter her. He swore the hookers were taking extra delight in mortifying him by sashaying across the street in front of them and swishing their skirts in ways that revealed almost everything.

"Ah, don't worry," he explained when he saw Eliza could not stop staring at the women flashing the full length of their legs and with necklines that displayed their breasts like pork loins in a butcher's stall. "Hookers always do this to any man who walks down a brothel street."

Immediately he wanted to kick himself. He wasn't sure whether "hooker" and "brothel" were swearwords, or at least words he shouldn't use in front of a lady. Eliza was too intelligent to not suspect he had once visited places like these. Now that he was older, the charms of brothels rarely hailed him unless he was feeling desperate for human touch. On a ship full of men, he could go for months without more than a slap on the back or a handshake. Oftentimes not even that.

A few blocks from the harbor office, they emerged from the side streets onto the main street again. Exhausted and winded, Littledove dropped the luggage and collapsed onto a bench that over looked the ocean. Whatever rest he had gotten on the *Vesuvius* he'd already spent that day.

"Are you as tired as you look, Will?"

"Enough to fall asleep right now, milady."

His head buzzed with loose ends that needed tying. He could not possibly abandon Eliza at a boardinghouse for women until she could go home. The *Bessie* was at the shipyard being evaluated for repairs, so Eliza could not stay in his quarters (and he at a boardinghouse).

Eliza also sorely needed new dresses because the ones she had were ripped and stained, but Littledove knew she would rather go home in a feed sack than accept a dress from him. Even a barbarian like him knew better than to offer. He struggled to accept he couldn't do anything about her dresses but remained bothered all the same.

Perhaps Captain Abraham Harey and Mrs. Honoré Harey could take her in. They were the closest people he could call family and always imagined if he was not buried at sea, they would attend his funeral on land and even mourn.

By now, the sun was threatening to set, and Littledove knew they could not spend the night sitting on a bench. He put his arm around Eliza and guided her to her feet.

"We're going to the Hareys'. They're real good people, and you can stay with them."

"What about you? Where will you stay, if I may inquire?"

"Depends. If they can put me up for a while, I'll stay with them. If not, I'll take a boardinghouse. Mrs. Beeve runs a nice place." Littledove looked back toward the harbor office. "Them reporters're probably gone by now. Let's get a carriage by the harbor office."

He pulled Eliza's hood over her head, taking a moment to admire the moonlike lines of her face that always beckoned him. "That's just so reporters don't recognize you. Me, they might pick out, seeing that I's taller than some masts. Me mum used to say I looked like a splinter with ribs. If they do, just keep walking like you don't know me, and I'll catch up with you."

Eliza grabbed her portmanteau when Littledove reached for it. "It is not heavy. I can carry it."

He scowled. "Can't let a lady carry something I can carry for her, milady. You might let me be a gentleman once in a while."

"And how shall I claim I do not know you when you are carrying luggage with my initials on it?" Eliza smiled slyly and began walking back to the harbor office.

Littledove followed, making his way through the opulent main street, now avoiding the dirty alleys that ran perpendicular to it. He kept his eyes peeled for anyone approaching Eliza. He had to keep her name out of the newspapers in case word got out that they had been alone on an abandoned ship. Just having that one fact published could ruin Eliza in her circles, if her circles were anything like those of the Captain's Club.

Littledove was about to hail a carriage when a man's voice punched through the din on the street. "Littledove! Good heavens, Littledove!"

Littledove grinned as if a sack of gold and a brand-new ship had landed on him. He dropped his seabag by Eliza and left her standing on the sidewalk while he made his way to the carriage that pulled in front of him.

"Harey! How the hell are you? We were just talking about you!"

"How the devil are *you*?" Captain Harey reached out the carriage window to shake hands. "Look at you! What's happened to you? There're some splendid rumors about you and the *Black Death*. Are they true?"

"Some're. Ah, I need a favor." Littledove lowered his voice. "There's a young lady who needs a place to stay until she can make her way home, if you don't mind. Ah, she's real lovely. That's her there."

Captain Harey followed the quick side motion of Littledove's eyes to look at Eliza. "She's beyond lovely, Littledove. She's spectacular! How did you manage—"

"Didn't manage anything," Littledove said defensively. "She's a lady."

Captain Harey pulled back a little. "You staying with us too?"

"If you got the room, I won't say no." He went to bring Eliza to the carriage. "Miss Strauss, this're's Captain Abraham Harey. I's just telling you about him and his wife. Captain Harey, this'er's Miss Eliza Strauss."

"Miss Strauss, how wonderful to make your acquaintance," said Captain Harey with a bow of his head that he was still sticking out of the carriage window.

"As I am to make yours, Captain Harey." Eliza curtsied.

"Mrs. Harey will be delighted to meet you," said Captain Harey. "Captain Littledove, I'm assuming you and Miss Strauss are also having dinner with us tonight?"

"You know I'm always short a hot meal." Littledove opened the carriage door and helped Eliza get settled and out of sight before passing the portmanteau and seabag to Captain Harey and climbing in himself. Captain Harey knocked on the roof of the carriage with his cane and shouted his address to signal the driver to go.

"Tell me, how is the *Bessie*?" asked Captain Harey as if the *Bessie* were a sick child.

And so began a conversation during which Littledove poured out his worries all the way to the house and into the foyer, where Mrs. Harey was waiting. Mrs. Harey surrounded Littledove in a tender hug and looked him over as she would look over a boy who had been beaten up at school.

"So the rumors are true," she said, "judging by the sight of you."

"Depends on the rumor. The one about me eating pirates, that one's not true by much. Ah, Mrs. Harey, this'er's Miss Eliza Strauss. Mrs. Honoré Harey. Miss Strauss was the other survivor, but we need to keep her name out of the papers."

"I fully understand. That will not be a problem. Good evening, dear. How lovely to make your acquaintance. Please come in and feel very much at home."

"They're staying with us," added Captain Harey.

Mrs. Harey put her arm around Eliza, and they began chatting as if they had known one another for years. How women always seemed to do that was a mystery to Littledove.

Captain Harey pulled him back and asked, "Is she one of the Strauss sisters? From what's-his-name—Strauss Investments?"

"Don't know. Never asked," said Littledove, although with Eliza's polish, she could very well come from that much money. The thought had never occurred to him. If so, she was a member of one of the richest families in Edith's Bay, right up there with the van der Joost ship builders and railroad tycoons who invested their money through such firms.

"Well, we'll pry all the stories out of both of you tonight at dinner. You must both be famished," said Captain Harey.

Littledove remained silent. Now he knew for certain that if he stepped into Eliza's world the best he could ever be was a court jester.

The next day, Mrs. Harey took Eliza shopping for dresses to replace the ones that were in tatters. Eliza had never purchased a dress in a store because seamstresses came to the house to make dresses for her and her sisters, often spending weeks with them.

At the dress shop, she realized that one of her dresses cost many times more than all the dresses most women wore. And none of the dresses was of equivalent quality to the ones that had been ruined on the *Bessie*. Still, a clean dress without rips was better than high couture rags. Determined to not call attention to herself and in an effort to avoid cheap laces and ribbons, she settled for two simple dresses and consoled herself that Mrs. Harey wore dresses of similar quality and managed to look quite fine.

After much debating with herself to whom she should write to inform her family of her safe return, Eliza asked Mrs. Harey for a sheet of stationery and wrote to Mary, one of her two remaining sisters.

My Dearest, Dearest Mary,

Please put your dear heart at ease, for I am well. After too many unplanned adventures, I find myself in Edith's Bay, where I am staying with a lovely family, Captain Harey and his wife, who have promised to bring me home in two weeks' time. I have many stories to tell that will explain my great delay in returning, but please know that I am well, as I wish you and everyone at home are as well.

Eliza paused, uncertain what to say about Sarah and Jelly. Such news should be delivered in person, she knew, but she did not want to leave the question unanswered and for anyone to develop expectations that could no longer be fulfilled.

Sarah and Jelly are safe in God's hands. They shall not be returning with me.

My Utmost Love and Affection, Your Sister, Eliza.

Eliza reread her letter before sealing it in an envelope. She chose two weeks so she would not inconvenience the Hareys by demanding they take her home in a rush that might interfere with their other plans.

At least that's what she wanted to think. Once she went home and Littledove returned to sea, they would never see one another again. The process of losing Littledove to his ship and sea began the moment they were rescued and now seemed unpreventable. In truth, she was not looking forward to returning home at all, Littledove or not. Not in the least.

Chapter Ten

INVESTING IN CHANCES

In the drawing room a few evenings later, Eliza knitted and Mrs. Harey mended socks while the captains got into a discussion about how best to navigate around the Hoorn of Africa, where violent storms wrecked several ships each year. Each man recounted the calculations and passages he thought worked best in more and more insufferable detail until they began sketching maps and drawing strategies. The captains carried on, becoming more and more boisterous until Eliza began to laugh at the glee in their shoptalk.

Mrs. Harey rolled her eyes, apparently having already experienced too many such discussions. She raised her voice just above the animated conversation. "Has Captain Littledove told you about the time he spent in the brig?"

Littledove stopped speaking in mid-sentence and stared at Mrs. Harey, openmouthed and horrified. Captain Harey turned away to chuckle. Mrs. Harey maintained a poker face as she continued to mend a sock toe.

"Now see here, Mrs. Harey," said Littledove, "you make that sound worse than it was. Much worse!"

"Wasn't it for reckless behavior and dishonorable desertion, if I remember correctly?" asked Captain Harey.

"Harey, that makes it sound even worse!"

"Well, if you don't want to talk about it in good company, I certainly understand," said Mrs. Harey. She began to rethread her needle.

"You got me sounding like some degenerate, the both of you!" said Littledove, glaring at both of them in disbeleif.

"Captain Littledove once threatened to put me in the brig if I distracted sailors," Eliza mentioned as innocently as she could. She could not help enjoying watching Littledove squirm.

"I am quite certain you did not deserve it, dear," said Mrs. Harey. "How shameful of you, Captain Littledove."

Littledove rubbed his eyes with two fingers and sank into a chair. Eliza remembered he once warned her that asking a seaman a question often resulted in a tale of agony and glory. She put down her knitting and settled comfortably to listen.

"It's not all bad—despite what these folks here say, mind you." Littledove waved a finger between Captain Harey to Mrs. Harey. "It happened in my first trip. I was a cabin boy. Well, pipsqueak cabin boys aren't allowed on ratl'ns. For good reasons, mind you, but I went anyway. I's angry because I couldn't go on shore because the captain thought I's too young to go by myself and nobody wanted to take me with them. So I thought I'd entertain myself. Waited till almost no one was the ship or under deck and climbed my way up the ratl'ns—and I mean, all the way up—when I didn't think anyone was looking. But wouldn't you know it, the captain come strolling on the pier when I reached the crow's nest, and he caught me. Caught me good too.

"Gave me hell, he did. Lectured me up and down about how a ship wasn't a circus needing monkeys. Probably wanted to call me names but thought I was too young. Made me go under deck for the night. Made me polish every shoe he saw. Made me scrub the fo'c'sle. Made me scrub the galley. Next day, he had me mop the entire deck by myself. Got so everybody was throwing shoes at me and spitting on the place I just mopped. They all had a grand, good laugh, let me tell you."

Eliza tucked her head to stifle a giggle. Littledove shot her a glance.

"Well, I got miserable mad. Took to loathing that captain. Couldn't stand the sight of him. Captain Mighty, he thought himself. Me, I decided to show the Captain Mighty something by abandoning his ship. He could go get himself another cabin boy. He could, for all I cared. So I waited until night to sneak off.

"And, wouldn't you know it, the damn captain catches me again. Personally, I think he was on the watch for me. Marched me right up the boarding plank. Lectured me plenty more. I mean, I thought he got it all out of him the first time, but damnations no! Told me he was going to send me back to my family in disgrace. Told him I didn't have a family and wasn't interested in having none, just in case he was thinking of giving me up to those charity ladies I got sent to once. No, I's just fine on my own, I told him.

"He asked me how old I thought I was that I thought I could just mosey away from the duties I committed to. Now, I forgot I'd told him I's fourteen, like he said I had to be to be a cabin boy on his ship, so I stared him down and told him I's a full twelve. I's almost as tall as him. That's how I got away with that. Well, that was a mistake."

Littledove ignored the outburst of laughter from Eliza and Mrs. Harey and continued.

"He called me a liar as well as other things I can't repeat here because by that time, he worked himself into some good words. Then he called for another sailor and told him to put me in the brig for desertion. Said he would turn me over to the authorities in the morning so I could go to trial, and he would testify against me 'cause it was illegal to desert your duties on a ship.

"Well, that scared me pantless. I'd never been in a brig. I knew people who deserted got hanged. Scared pantless, I was! Now you got the part about me being in the brig, but the story doesn't end there."

Now Captain Harey guffawed, although Eliza wasn't sure whether he was laughing at Littledove being locked up in the brig or being without pants.

Littledove waved away the laughter and continued. "Spent the evening full of nerves. Could hardly eat the food they gave me. But I did because I's twelve and always hungry. Now, the next morning, breakfast didn't come. And you's know, when you're twelve, you set your clocks by meals, especially if you wasn't used to getting regular ones. Lunch didn't come either. Then the ship began to move like it was going out to sea. I knew that feeling, even then. Now I was more scared than ever because I didn't know what was going on. I mean before, I was going to be hanged, but now, who knew? I heard people walked the plank at sea, and I didn't want to be eaten by sharks.

"Finally, a sailor comes and gets me, and he takes me to the captain in the navigation room. I'd never been in the navigation room, and let me tell you, it was grand. Had all kinds of books and maps and things like telescopes, sextants, compasses, protractors, and a fancy parallel rule. Everything was made of brass and mahogany, and the chairs had velvet cushions. I's never touched velvet before."

Eliza recalled the navigation room before the pirates racksacked it. The mahogany shelves were still splendid, although the velvet chairs had gone threadbare.

"But I was still scared. The captain makes me stand there while he tells me he forgot about me in the brig, and he can't turn me in now because they're out to sea. I almost passed out from relief. But then he tells me he's going to turn me into the German officials for desertion because that's where they're heading, to Germany. Well, back to being scared pantless, I was because I knew Germans didn't know English, and how can you explain yourself if people don't understand you? Besides, I already knew I was guilty.

"But then he tells me he'll give me a choice because it costs to keep a useless body in the brig all the way to Germany. He tells me he'll let me work out my commission, but if I go against his orders a single time, I'll be sitting in the brig until we get to Germany, where he'll turn me in because he doesn't have time to be nanny to any fool on board. So I agree. I'll work out my commission. With no disorderly conduct or reckless whatever he charged me with. Anything was better than sitting in a brig, waiting to be hanged in Germany.

"While all this is going on, my stomach's rumbling like thunder because I haven't ate for two meals. So he calls for someone to bring something. Tells me to sit right there and eat it because he has things to do and can't be running around the ship being nanny to a fool. So I sat and ate in the navigation room, looking around all the time. I swear I think I turned into a pair of roving eyes."

"Never seen anything like it. The captain was doing whatever he was doing, and I watched him real close, too. Saw him doing numbers and looking things up in books. Then he pulls out this giant map. By Zeus, I almost flipped over my chair when I saw that map. Never seen anything so big, I hadn't. Couldn't take my eyes off it. And then I look on the shelves and realize he's got plenty more of them rolled up in those shelves. Made me really wonder how big the world was that it needed such big maps.

"Anyway, after a while, the captain says to me, 'Boy, come here and do this.' And I says back, 'What're you doing?' Well, he goes off on me again! Tells me when a captain tells you to do something, the only answer is 'Aye, aye, sir,' not some question about what he's doing. What he's doing none of my business! Then he starts to look at me again like he's going to put me in the brig and leave me in Germany, so I say 'Aye, aye, sir' real quick."

Eliza let out another titter that Littledove ignored after giving her a side eye.

"So he hands me his protractor and parallel ruler and pushes the chart over to me. Let me tell you, I kept fiddling with the protractor and parallel ruler because they were the most fascinating things I ever held. Next to the chart, that is. Then he tells me to do something I never heard of. Well, I thought of pretending I knew how to do it, but I knew he'd know. I mean, even to do something the wrong way, you've got to know something, and I didn't even understand what he wanted. So I raised my nerve and told him I didn't know how to do whatever he wanted me to do.

"By the way he looked at me, I thought I'd just bought myself a one-way fare in the brig and for sure he was going to leave me in Germany because I was so useless. But he tells me to sit down, and he starts teaching me how to do things with the charts and the numbers and the books and the protractor. It took me a while to figure out he was teaching me to chart a course. Next day, he tells me how the compass works and even lets me steer the ship to the compass with the helmsman looking over me shoulder. Next clear night, he wakes me up and shows me how the sextant works. Loved that thing! From then on, he always got me up when he used the sextant. And I got good at it too.

"Well, he didn't leave me in Germany. But I's still nervous when we got back, thinking he'd turn me in to some charity lady, but he tells me I can sail with him again if I wants, and I said 'Aye, aye, sir.' Then he looks at me like he might change his mind and tells me I best come home with him because he still can't trust me not to climb the ratl'ns when his back's turned. So I went home with him for a few weeks and sailed with him the next time. So that's how that turned out. So you see, it wasn't as bad as these two make it sound." Littledove pointed at Captain and Mrs. Harey.

Mrs. Harey tapped her fingers in a silent clap at the tall tale. Captain Harey let out a boom of laughter. "Admiral Stoop was a wily one. You never wanted to find yourself going against his grain. He might do something good for you."

Littledove's crooked smile faded. "A wily fellow, he real was. Turned a pipsqueak cabin boy into a captain."

"Must have got mad at me one day because a few years later he sent you to me," said Captain Harey with a smile.

"Aye, but by that time I wasn't a pain in the aft. I was first mate."

"Littledove, you're always a pain in the aft. That'll never change," said Captain Harey, making Eliza laugh out loud at the salty language.

The following morning before breakfast, Littledove slipped into the kitchen, looking over his shoulder like a spy on a mission. He cracked open the kitchen door after a second thought and looked into the hallway. By now, Mrs. Harey had stopped kneading dough and was waiting for him to speak.

He stuffed his hands into his pockets and leaned against a cabinet, trying not to look concerned. "Ah, Mrs. Harey. You know any gifts a gentleman can give a lady? You know, proper ones."

"The only things a gentleman can give to any lady are candy, flowers, or books," Mrs. Harey recited as if reading from an etiquette book. "I suppose he could also give a lady things like yarn and knitting needles—if she knits—but he'd have to make absolutely certain the combination does not suggest he wants her to make an article of clothing for him."

"Aye. Good. Thanks."

Mrs. Harey seemed to be clairvoyant, because he'd been thinking about Eliza knitting. He felt a kinship with knitting because it looked as if it involved knots like the ones he often tied. When he left the kitchen, he slipped into the parlor to look at Mrs. Harey's basket of yarn. Only then did he realize he had no idea how much yarn it took to make anything or what kind of yarn anything was made of.

After breakfast, he set out to find a yarn shop and get himself educated about proper combinations of needles and yarns that did not make vulgar suggestions. Littledove stood by the window of the first cloth and yarn shop he came across, and the women inside the shop all looked up at the same time. They stretched their necks like ostriches and stared at him, making him feel as unwelcome as a peeping Tom.

He moved on. A yarn shop was definitely a place of women, as much as a tavern was a place of men. He moseyed to a bookshop and bought Eliza a book of sailing terms with illustrations that depicted what things were on a ship and how ships were laid out.

The book included the names of all the decks and masts and sails and pronunciation keys because how a word was spelled usually did not indicate at all how it was pronounced at sea, as in the cases of *forecastle* and *fo'c'sle* or *boatswain* and *bosun* or even *sails and s'ls*. No wonder she couldn't understand him sometimes. He spoke the words as they should be spoken, not as someone decided they would be spelled.

He had the book gift wrapped because he wanted to watch the delicate motions of Eliza's fingers when she took off the wrapping. Mrs. Harey hadn't mentioned gift wrapping, but he felt it was permissible because, after all, it was a gift of the kind he was permitted to give. He also shaved extra close and wore a new shirt because he wanted to look especially presentable when he gave it to her.

"Will!" Eliza breathed out his name when she unwrapped the book with those delicate fingers he enjoyed seeing move and paged through it. "This is exactly what I need! Thank you ever so much, my captain. I so appreciate this. Now I shall not need to go around your ship pointing at things and calling everything 'That Thing.'"

He laughed because that was exactly what she had been doing. "Well, milady. Real glad you can use it."

In her excitement, she ran out of the room to show the book to Mrs. Harey. He leaned back against the sofa, feeling accomplished, although he wished she had kissed him, even if only on the cheek. Or maybe thrown her arms around him. All the same, he was relieved he had not bungled. This time.

After receiving the book from Littledove, Eliza waited until he was with Captain Harey and Mrs. Harey was alone in the parlor, having just left Emma in the kitchen. She slipped in and sat next to Mrs. Harey.

"Mrs. Harey, do you think I would be overstepping propriety if I knitted a cap for Captain Littledove? He is always in need of them and always losing them. Of course, under normal circumstances, I would never consider giving any article of clothing to a man, but with seamen, the rules might be more flexible because sailors need to be warm when they are out at sea, and Captain Littledove is always cold."

Mrs. Harey considered for a bit, frowned, and said, "Such a gift to a man would be considered improper, however unimposing it may be, but it is true that all sailors need to be warm. You could knit a cap but deliver it only as a charitable contribution to someone who knows needy sailors. Surely Captain Littledove knows needy sailors. But you must not indicate it is for him."

That was all Eliza needed. She lost no time going to the cloth and yarn shop Littledove felt he could not enter. She knew exactly what yarn she needed but could not decide the color. After an hour of picking up and putting down various balls of yarn, she bought a teal that reminded her of sea water before storms and a dark blue that reminded her of night skies over a calm sea. She had seen Littledove wearing articles of clothing in both colors and knew he looked handsome in both.

She knitted both caps in one night because the yarns were thick and the pattern was easy. She did not gift wrap them because she did not want anyone to mistake them for presents. Ribbons also implied gifts, so she abandoned that idea.

When she handed the hats to Littledove, she abided by propriety by saying, "I made these for any needy seamen you might know."

"You made these?" Littledove stretched each one with both hands. "For needy sailors?"

"Yes."

Littledove slipped them on his hands like mittens and sniffed them. He rubbed his cheeks with them, then buried his nose in them and took a deep breath.

"Oh, milady! I's a real needy sailor because I's always need things to keep me warm. Thank you very much!"

Eliza had not expected such rapid claim to ownership. She struggled to concoct what she could say in case Mrs. Harey asked.

Littledove looked confused at her reaction. "What? You said they're for needy seamen, and I's one. No one needier for warm caps than me. You know ..." He leaned in closer and whispered, "Especially caps that can keep my head and heart warm." Grinning crookedly, he winked at her.

Eliza burst out laughing, although she had been raised to consider a wink from a man as a sign of disrespect. In Littledove, however, the wink acknowledged fully and with glee what had always been true and could not be denied: She knitted the caps for him, and he was unabashedly delighted to receive them. Neither one of them was fooling anyone, not even themselves with rules that made less and less sense the more they wanted to care for one another.

That evening, Eliza opened the door to her room after a knock. Emma, the maid, stood on the other side, holding an expensive box of chocolates.

"It's from a secret admirer, miss," she whispered, blushing hard.

Eliza looked up and down the hall before whispering, "And may I ask who is the secret admirer?"

Emma turned even redder. "I canna say, miss. It's secret."

"I see …" said Eliza. "Well, let me think. Captain Harey is married, therefore, it cannot be he."

Emma's eyes grew round. "Oh no, miss! It ain't Captain Harey! No!"

"Am I safe in saying it is not Mrs. Harey?"

Emma broke down in giggles at the absurdity of the notion. She shifted her eyes in the direction of Littledove's room and stepped back so Eliza could look down the hallway. A shadow behind the slightly opened door made Eliza almost double with silent laughter. Emma ran downstairs, covering her mouth with her apron to stifle her giggles.

On the following day, Eliza bragged to Littledove that she had a secret admirer and placed a bonbon from the box in his mouth because treats were always better when shared. To Emma, she gave the bon bon that came wrapped in gold foil.

Littledove could not stop festering after Eliza stopped to read a billboard. He waited until she walked beyond it before taking a glance to see what had caught her interest. Music. Symphony. Several of them. On one ticket. Or perhaps one had to choose which one to listen to. He didn't catch all the words because he had to step up to keep up with Eliza, who kept walking down the street, not even aware he was not by her side.

That evening, he asked, "Harey, what's the best way to get symphony tickets?"

"You just buy them like theater tickets. Nothing special." Captain Harey looked over at Littledove. "And if you get matinee tickets, you don't need a chaperone."

"Why the hell would I need a chaperone?"

"Well, I don't know if you're planning to attend by yourself, but a proper young lady would require a chaperone after dark. Not so much during daylight. But if you're going by yourself, that's not an issue."

"Nay. Nothing I need to worry about." He spoke nonchalantly, but when he walked out of the parlor, he thought he heard Captain Harey guffaw.

Littledove did not want a chaperone, so he bought matinee tickets. He waited until Eliza wandered into the parlor before putting down the book he was reading and pulling them out of his pocket.

Although he spent the morning practicing being suave, when the moment came, he blurted. "I got two tickets for tomorrow's symphony. The midday one." He held his breath.

"How very fortunate for you. I am certain you shall greatly enjoy the performance. The Edith's Bay orchestra is magnificent."

He realized he hadn't exactly asked her to go to the concert. And she was not the sort to presume. "Ah, you want to go? I mean, I's got two tickets."

"Will! How wonderful. Thank you ever so much. To think I shall have the honor of listening to music in your esteemed presence. What time shall I be ready?"

Littledove peered at the tickets. "Starts at two. Aye, two o'clock. Ah … We should leave by one?"

"Oh, that is ever so lovely! Thank you, my captain. I shall be ready."

Littledove was shocked she didn't even ask what symphony was playing. For that matter, neither had he. He looked at the tickets but didn't recognize anything that was playing, although the tickets seemed like a good bargain because he'd got more than one symphony per ticket. One usually got only one play per ticket. Besides, his presence had never been called esteemed.

Of Mrs. Harey, he later enquired, "Anything special someone needs to do at a symphony?"

"What did you have in mind?"

"Like, do I tip the person who shows you to the seats?" He had never tipped anyone in playhouses, but symphonies might be different with all the posh people who went to them.

"I believe all you have to do is dress appropriately, sit, and listen."

"So it's just like a playhouse."

"Yes, the opera house is just like a playhouse, except that the music is different. And attire is a bit more formal."

"Aye. Good. Thanks."

He bolted upstairs and checked the tickets to make certain he'd bought tickets to a symphony. He had never thought that a symphony would be played in an opera house, although he would have gladly put up with an opera if Eliza went with him. He had never been to an opera but had been told the women in it sounded like cats whose tails were stepped on, and his instincts told him he would hate a performance of screeching women.

But how would he know? He didn't recognize any of the pieces printed on the ticket. And he sure as hell wasn't going to ask Harey about them.

When the time came, however, he found the symphony quite impressive, especially when someone bashed cymbals followed by rumbling drums. The people who played the violins and flutes were quite scintillating when they swayed back and forth like buoys in rough seas. Littledove concluded he would not mind going to another symphony, especially with Eliza, who never looked more beautiful or delighted, fully in her element.

He welcomed her knowledgeable whispers in his ear about the composer and the music because he liked to feel her breath on his neck. The best part, however, was resting their hands over one another's when the gaslights dimmed. They had to because there was only one arm rest between them.

Mrs. Harey's suggestion that they visit Paome's Chocolatier afterward turned out to be an even finer experience as they flirted and chatted their way through their cups of hot cocoa. Littledove invested in an impressive plate of fruit wedges dipped in chocolate, followed by a second round of hot cocoa.

By the time they left Paome's, they were so giddy from the sugar and chocolate they had to walk twice around the park to calm themselves. The afternoon passed so vigorously and swiftly it threatened to end much too quickly, so they took another walk around the park, leaving trails of wit and conversation.

Littledove would have taken a fourth stroll, but Mrs. Harey drilled into him that respectable young ladies did not walk unchaperoned in the dark with any man, even if she knew him well and trusted him. This seemed a little ludicrous, especially after they had spent over a month alone on the *Bessie*, and she had seen him naked many times. Although the more she saw him naked and cared for his body, the more embarrassed he became. He had not anticipated that.

Being a gentleman was not as difficult an endeavor as it was frustrating because much of the effort involved not doing what he wanted to do. In fact, he now considered it a form of discipline, which helped him deal with its requirements.

He was not sure Eliza knew he was being gentlemanly when he suggested they make their way to the Hareys' house because it was getting dark or whether she simply expected such behavior as people expect rocks to fall when dropped. All the practices that were fresh and prickly to him had been bred deeply into Eliza as expectations, and she seemed to become aware of them only when they were absent.

As they headed to the Hareys' neighborhood, the houses began crowding together until they were cheek by jowl. Every harbor town he'd visited that was highly populated with sailors and sea captains had neighborhoods like the Hareys' because everyone insisted on having views of the water. Wealthier captains built their houses on top of hills so they could see the water all the way to the horizon and so their wives could watch for them.

"It must be lovely to be able to talk to one's neighbors over a fence instead of having to call for a carriage and ride for an hour," said Eliza.

"I can see myself living in one of these some day," said Littledove as casually as he could.

"And what, may I ask, would you do with a house when you are always away at sea?"

"If I'd a wife, I'd need a house. She would want a house. I'd buy her one."

"May I ask why you would marry a woman who stays at home while you are at sea?"

"Ah, well, if there were children, they'd have to stay on land. School and such. You know."

"You could hire a governess and have your wife and children with you while you are at sea," said Eliza.

"You can? That's be good. Would cut down on the missing. If you, ah, married a seaman, would you go to sea with him?"

"What, may I ask, is the purpose of being married if you are not together as husband and wife? If a wife wants to remain on land, then she should marry a farmer."

"Mrs. Harey used to sail with Captain Harey, but she probably didn't see much of him on board because he's always busy because a captain's always got to have an eye on things. Not much can get past him if he expects to keep the respect a captain needs to run a ship and keep things going smooth." Littledove cleared his throat. "You'd probably think Mrs. Harey got lonely. You know—she couldn't have visitors because, well, you're on a ship and when you land, you're in a place where you don't know anyone. But you go back to the same ports over and over and other wives travel with their husbands too, and they meet up at ports. Just like at home."

He looked at her and then away. They continued walking in silence.

Eventually, Eliza said, "I imagine you miss being at sea when you are on land."

"Probably not as much as I'll miss some things I leave on land. Problem is, Eliza, sailing's, ah, well, that's the only thing I know how to do. Not like I can open a shop in town and sell oysters. It brings in good money, though, it does. There's never lack."

"Will, you were born to be a captain. Please do not have any regrets. Or offer apologies."

"You can say that after what happened to my crew? And your sisters? And Dr. Aves?"

"You did everything you could, Will. I hold nothing against you. If you hadn't veered into the storm the way you did, we would all be dead."

"You're real kind, Eliza. Real generous too."

"My poor captain, full of guilt."

Littledove sighed. He tucked his hands into his pockets and looked at the ground as he walked, feeling too tender to pursue the conversation.

Chapter Eleven

TAKING BIG RISKS

The day after the symphony, Eliza awoke still feeling giddy from her outing with Littledove. She suspected the symphony might have been his first because almost everything that happened seemed to surprise him, and he had worn the brown sea boots that he had recently had resoled instead of black evening shoes.

Then her thoughts turned to the conversation they had during their energetic walk around the park. She finally admitted to herself that Littledove was trying to explain why she could not come along with him. He was going to leave, seafarer that he was, and she would be forever marooned in a life without him.

This reality turned into a sense of mourning that would not part. In search of a distraction, she asked Mrs. Harey if she had any interest in seeing the latest exhibits at the Edith's Bay Art Museum.

Littledove was flipping through the newspaper, looking over its edges each time she and Mrs. Harey paused their conversation. Eliza knew he was waiting for one of them to invite him. She wondered how she was going to live without him if she always wanted to be with him, and he could not be with her. Or would not.

In the midst of her mulling, Emma came into the parlor and curtsied. "Mr. Elliot Strauss from Strauss Investments is here to see you, Captain Harey."

Eliza shot to her feet, spilling her knitting on the floor. Then she sat. And gathered her knitting. She stood again, took a step to leave the parlor with her yarns, but backed up until her calves bumped the sofa. And sat.

"Miss Eliza, the visitor does not have to come in here, if you do not wish. Captain Harey can see him in his office," said Mrs. Harey, whom Eliza deemed the most tactful woman on earth.

"He is my father," said Eliza and hunkered down with the anxiety of someone unjustly condemned to be hanged.

Captain and Mrs. Harey exchanged looks before Captain Harey went to greet the visitor who was already demanding loudly to be seen. Eliza took comfort that Littledove repositioned himself by her, although she doubted he would be able to do anything, even if she could predict what would happen.

Her father stormed into the parlor as she remembered him—a red-faced, paunchy bellicosity with little hair. He was dressed, as usual, in a superbly cut wool overcoat diametrically in style to his raucous rudeness. He shook his hat while yelling at Captain Harey about something no one could comprehend. Once in the parlor, he looked around just enough to locate Eliza, who felt so intimidated by his bellowing she could not look up at him.

"Elizabeth! How dare you write to your sister and not to me to inform her of your whereabouts! And to assume you can sport yourself home in two weeks after you have been missing for so long! Get your things! You are leaving this minute!"

Everyone in the parlor remained motionless like the people of Pompeii after the volcano erupted and smothered them in ash. Eliza surprised herself by thinking her father's outburst had all the egocentric rage of someone who had been deposed as the center of the universe by a lowly pigeon.

With a heightened sense of the ridiculous, she went from picking her scarred knuckles to looking directly into her father's eyes. She saw him as if she were wearing clarifying spectacles that brought all objects into a new, fascinating kind of focus.

This time she rose slowly and with poise as she recalled she had once fallen into a slick of human blood because she had stood so long her limbs went numb while supporting a man who might have died in her arms. She pumped a bilge in pure darkness and prevented the *Bessie* was sinking—several times. She killed a rat with a shovel when she found it eating the grain meant for the hen on which they depended for eggs. She cut wood and made stove fires to keep from freezing. She fought for Littledove's and her life and won.

And she had felt ... something she only recently identified as passion, something she had only read about in a cheap penny novel a maid once left at the beach. That experience had been as raw as it had been enticing, leaving behind sparks that had not yet turned to ashes.

Her father could not appear more alien as he now stood in front of her, angrily barking demands. At this moment, she became someone she barely recognized. She faced her father with a rage that vibrated outward, and he fell silent. She could have said anything because she understood the force of her power was entirely in her person, not in her words. And for someone who had been raised to speak hollowly and politely no matter what she felt, this discovery was nothing less than explosive.

"Mrs. Harey and I have an engagement this afternoon. I shall not be leaving until I fulfill that engagement," Eliza said calmly.

Her father pointed to Mrs. Harey as if she were a toad in a garden. "What engagement can you possibly have that you cannot come home this instant!"

"You may return for me tomorrow at eight, or you may wait for me to return home in another few days. My engagement with Mrs. Harey takes priority."

At that moment, the parlor became a chess game of individual moves. Eliza took a step toward the parlor door. Her father took a step forward to grab her by the arm. Littledove stepped toward her father, who then stepped back. Eliza wove behind Littledove's back and left the room.

Her father did not follow her as she expected. Perhaps Littledove was blocking his way. She could not bring herself to look over her shoulder. As she crossed the hallway and began climbing the stairs, she listened to the voices in the parlor as if she were backstage during a play.

As if declaring checkmate, Captain Harey said, "Well, that settles it, then. Miss Strauss wishes to leave tomorrow. Our doors will be open to you at eight o'clock. Please call for her then. I'll see you to the door now."

"Who the hell do you think you are? Keeping my daughter here! And telling me when I can or cannot take her home!"

Littledove stepped forward. "Your daughter keeps herself here, not you, not us."

Eliza imagined him stretching to his full height, which made him far taller than her father would ever be, perhaps even while standing on a stool. She would have laughed at the image, but her father began snarling like a rabid dog.

"Next time, go down with your ship, Captain, like a real man, instead of simpering around my daughter with your thistle in the air."

Eliza stopped with one foot on a step and gasped at the shot her father took at Littledove. She sprang up the remaining steps and slipped into her room, knowing she had to be out of sight when her father left the parlor, or he might say something worse to Littledove.

When Littledove's hands clenched into fists at Strauss's insult, Captain Harey grabbed his sleeve and shook it as if to unclench his fist. Littledove had the wherewithal not to punch someone in Harey's house, but he was still grateful for the reinforcement. Granted, he had not struck a man in years because he had found better ways to cope, but Strauss was just the sort of man who could make him ruin that record.

Strauss turned and stomped out of the house on his own. When the front door slammed, Captain Harey patted Littledove's arm and left the parlor, probably to be sure Strauss had truly left.

Captain Harey returned to the parlor. He made no statement but poured a bit of sherry for Mrs. Harey and two shot glasses of whiskey. He handed one to Littledove. Captain Harey downed his whiskey and poured himself another shot. He held the decanter out to Littledove for a refill, but Littledove shook his head. He had yet to be able to stomach the first shot, which he was certain would not solve his problems by rendering him dead. Not knowing what to say or do, the three nursed themselves in silence.

Littledove caught the Hareys communicating silently with their eyebrows and eye twitches. Eliza and her sisters had also communicated silently at the Hansweert harbor office. He looked out the window, feeling the most alone he had felt in years.

"I am going to check on Miss Eliza," Mrs. Harey said as she left and closed the parlor door behind her.

Littledove downed the whiskey and felt it turn everything in his stomach into muck. He put down the shot glass.

You got yourself imagination and now look what, he yelled in his head. *You think hope wouldn't make this moment come, did you? You lobcock!*

"So what are you going to do, Littledove?" asked Captain Harey.

"Me? Aaah. Do. Ah, I meant to tell you earlier, but all this happened … ah, with the father and all … Anyway, Mrs. Beeve from the boarding house says she's got an opening next week, so I'll be … staying there until I get meself together. The *Bessie* looks like—"

"I mean about Miss Eliza. What are you going to do about Miss Eliza?"

"What do you mean what am I going to do? She's leaving with her father tomorrow morning. Eight o'clock."

"So you are going to let her go home with that beast?"

Littledove felt his head was on the verge of exploding. "What the hell do you want me to do, Harey? Stand in front of her and refuse to let her pass?"

"She is very fond of you, Littledove."

Littledove waved his hand in front of his face. "Stop right there. A woman like that needs lots of luxuries—a big house, nice dresses, maids to look after her, gardens with swings. Gardeners! She needs symphonies. Chocolate shops. She can't be stuck on a ship at sea with nothing but sailors. You didn't see her when she first boarded the *Bessie*. Everything about her was perfect. Hair … little pleats … Then the pirates came and made everything a damn mess. And I tell you, what you see now is not how she really is. Or should be. I can't give her what she needs to should be. Besides, a delicate woman like that needs a man with a lot of polish and lots of money to provide for her. Not like me. Nay. She needs luxuries."

"How delicate is she, Littledove? She just told that frigate of a father in no uncertain terms she was not leaving today just because he said she had to. Told him to come back in the morning if he wanted to take her home or she would make her own arrangements. Didn't even raise her voice. And he yielded! If you ask me, she's plotting a way to get out of going back home with him. I'm tempted to send more bedsheets to her room so she can climb out a window tonight.

"And I heard from you—first hand, no less—that she kicked Death in the bags and hauled you away from it. And did things like an able-bodied seaman. About the only thing she failed at was fishing. Even then, she almost caught a shark. Now, how delicate is a woman who can do all that in a silk dress just because it needs to be done? She could have just fainted and let you die."

"What the hell are you saying, Harey?"

"Littledove, are you dense?" Harey shouted.

"I can't offer her anything she won't get ten times as much of when she goes back."

"Does she look like she wants to go back? Does a girl who really wants to go home write and say she'll be home in two weeks after being stranded on a ship with you and a chicken for over a month? Littledove, do not shortchange yourself! Eliza Strauss is not a flimsy woman. She can have any man she wants, and she's here knitting caps for you. You have until tomorrow morning, and then she'll be gone for good. If she doesn't climb out the window in the middle of the night, that is."

Littledove listened to Captain Harey as a new, intense sense of reality opened before him like an ocean at the mouth of a river. When Captain Harey left the parlor, Littledove hunkered down to process the idea as if about to guide a ship through narrow straits in a violent storm.

Eliza heard the knock on the bedroom door and could not bring herself to answer immediately. She was too distressed.

"Eliza, may I please come in?" asked Mrs. Harey through the door.

"Certainly, Mrs. Harey. Please. Thank you."

Mrs. Harey slipped into the room and quietly shut the door behind her while Eliza tried again to fold a dress so it would fit into her portmanteau. When she failed, Mrs. Harey took it out of her hands and sat her down on the edge of the bed. She folded the dress with an economy of motions that left it in a neat, square form before she slipped it into the bag.

Eliza grabbed a blouse to fold, but when Mrs. Harey sat next to her, she buried her face in the blouse and burst into tears. Mrs. Harey put her arm around her and pulled her to herself.

"Eliza, you do not need to go back with your father. You can stay here for a little longer."

"Were it that easy. He is here to reclaim me and reclaim me, he shall. You have no idea with whom you deal."

"You could get married. I know someone who is very much in love with you."

Eliza stopped trying to fold whatever was rumpled in her lap and focused on Mrs. Harey's face through her tears. Mrs. Harey had a way of bringing all the agonies people thought they could hide into the open and neutralizing them with common sense.

Eliza looked away. "No one has asked me."

"Perhaps Captain Littledove is afraid of you."

Eliza gawked at Mrs. Harey as if the woman had lost her mind. "Afraid? How could he be? What am I compared to the pirates who destroyed his ship and almost killed him?"

"Please allow me to rephrase that. Captain Littledove is afraid he is not good enough for you and will not do you justice. He believes a woman of your upbringing and family line requires a different kind of gentleman. Someone with good suits and the excellent manners he lacks. And more money than he'll ever make."

"Captain Littledove does not need a tuxedo to run a ship. Nor is he an imbecile. He's been learning manners on his own. I've noticed. And he makes a decent living."

"Well then, do not despair. Do you know hope is the very first thing to rise from the ashes of despair?" Mrs. Harey said cryptically.

As if in answer, Emma knocked on the door. "Miss Eliza, Captain Littledove is asking to see you in the parlor, please."

Left speechless, Eliza looked at Mrs. Harey, who smiled back as if she knew something Eliza was only beginning to decipher. When Mrs. Harey nodded, Eliza threw aside the blouse in her lap and ran out of the room, racing down the stairs. She took the last three steps in one leap and barely paused to smooth her dress before she swung open the door to the parlor.

In the parlor, Littledove paced with the same determined, constricted walk he used on the deck when waters were choppy and he needed to keep his balance. He tucked one arm behind his back and swung the other with each step he took. He stopped when Eliza entered and stood before her in a moment of suspended time. Eliza closed the door behind her, giving time permission to continue.

He felt like a blind man in a storm. Not even the perfection of the future could help guide him because he had never imagined this scenario. He had nothing to lose, he reminded himself as he resumed pacing and began to speak, organizing his thoughts as he went along.

"Eliza, I need six months. Six months. To get back on my feet. I got a ship with broken masts that takes on more water than she should. I don't even know how much it'll cost to get her fixed. I owe for the cargo that got stole. I don't even know what that'll come to, if it wasn't insured. I got money stored, so that won't be too much of a problem, I think, but I's ruined because the captain's supposed to go down with his crew, and I didn't. For whatever reason that was. Doesn't matter to people. I don't think I can get two men to sit in a rowboat with me, much less an entire crew I need to run a cargo ship. I need six months. Six months, Eliza! To get back on my feet. Six months. Please."

He was buckling under the weight of all the things that had gone wrong so quickly and that could only be fixed slowly and methodically. He was buckling under the weight of knowing Eliza could say no to him, absurd sea creature that he was, and leave tomorrow after a curtsy.

"What happens at the end of six months?" Eliza asked with the same indomitable calm she used to address her father. Littledove could not read her.

"What happens? I come get you! That's what happens. I'll be on my feet by then. We can marry right away, or we can see each other more if you need to. I'll stay on land until you're sure. Me? I'm sure now. But I need six months to get back on my feet. It's not lack of love, Eliza! It's never been lack of love. I just can't— I can't— We can't— Not right now, the way things are. I need to get back on my feet so I can provide. At least give me that before you decide."

The longer he spoke, the more convinced he became that the only thing keeping Eliza from saying no was the sound of his voice. He might have recovered from the grief had he not asked, but now that he had, he might never recover if she said no.

When Eliza did not answer, he took her hands in his and said, "Eliza, I love you. Please give me six months. To get back on my feet. So we can marry. And be together forever."

When Eliza looked down and withdrew into herself, he panicked that he had made a terrible mistake. She would politely say no and retreat into her room to have a good laugh.

But Eliza raised herself on her toes to wrap her arms around his neck and kissed him on the lips. "Yes, my captain. I shall wait for you so we may marry."

"Yes?" Giddiness came over him. He threw his arms around Eliza and pressed his hand against the small of her back to pull her against himself as he exhaled. "Milady! Eliza!"

Eliza stroked his cheek. "But I believe you shall need more than six months, Will. Six months is very ambitious."

His skin puckered with pleasure when she called him Will. "I can do it in six. I can try, anyway. Six months is a long time to not see you. I'll be at sea for most of that time. I can write to you from ports."

Eliza kissed his forehead. "All the same, Will, you shall need more than six months. You will not be able to sail for another month or two. You are still not as well as you need to be. Remember what you once told me: It is a miserable job, even if you love it."

"I can do it, milady. Trust me that I can do it. I have to. So we can be together."

He took the moment to kiss her after which, she did not seem to want to stop. If he would do it in four months, by dickens, he would.

Chapter Twelve

COPING PATIENTLY

Everything at her father's house was exactly as she had left it. Even the knick-knacks in the parlors were in the same place they had been before she left. The furniture remained carefully positioned as they had always been so the feet aligned with the crushed fibers on the carpets. She would not have been surprised if the sheet music on the piano scroll had not been turned.

Eliza should not have been surprised, but she was. People in her father's house rarely moved anything so as not to annoy him (if you were a guest) or be accused of stealing (if you were a servant) or breaking something (if you were a daughter).

Yet everything felt different. Extremely different.

She stopped exploring the question as she sat by the window where she usually knit. But not even knitting kept her interest. She rested her project on her lap and reclined into the petrified stillness of the parlor. People were holding her recent trauma responsible for the density of her quietness and the peculiarity of knitting constantly. She kept knitting with thinner yarns until she abandoned yarn altogether and was now knitting with silk thread on steel needles no thicker than toothpicks.

The project required enormous amounts of concentration, with almost every row needing to be counted and sometimes taken out and re-knitted. Each stitch felt like a penance. The resulting lace shawl was the likes of which no one had ever seen—as sheer as gauze, as shimmery as light upon the ocean, constructed more of thought than thread. Sometimes when she looked around the parlor, she felt the only moving things were her needles and the stitches that slipped from one to the other.

Beyond the shawl that shrouded the all-consuming thoughts she could not share with anyone, her external life had become a performance. The people around her became the audience of her recital while Littledove remained the audience of her thoughts. Of him, she spoke to no one, not even Mary, who still lived at the house. Eliza glided through the hallways of her father's house as if Littledove did not exist, becoming more and more desperate to end her performance.

Moment by moment, six months was turning into a prison sentence, but Eliza knew Littledove was too responsible to do anything that mattered in a slapdash manner. After six months, she could be with him forever. She could watch him walk the deck with his rolling stride, caring about the things that mattered with an unquestionable respect for what was important in any situation. And she, Elizabeth Anne Strauss, was important to him. Just as he was to her.

She tried to revive her intentions to knit but was unable to concentrate. Instead, she resumed staring at the ocean through the splendid sunlight outside the window. She continued looking out the window even after she became aware of the footman in the doorway. He would not speak until she looked at him, which eventually, reluctantly, she did.

"Miss Strauss, if I may, your father wishes to see you in his office, please."

"Thank you, Burk."

She now regularly thanked the staff and addressed them by name, unlike anyone else in the house. This change was so monumental the servants were still commenting, even now that she had been home for two weeks.

A keen gratitude now also plagued her for the luxury of having people who did things she did not want to do for herself. That she could now do those things herself gave her a deeper, solemn satisfaction. With that in her soul, she stuffed her knitting into a basket and made her way to her father's office.

Her father had barely spoken to her since she came home, not even to ask questions about how she was or whether she had been hurt or how she felt. However unnatural and pending his silence felt, it had given her time to study him with a new perspective she simply could not sidestep. He had not changed, she was certain, although she now could no longer see him in the same way she once had.

When she walked into her father's office, the room struck her as opulent enough to swallow people. Still, she remained unimpressed. Everything in it was coordinated and impersonal, as if he had purchased each wall by the yard.

Her father looked her up and down as she entered his office. "Why are you wearing that dress?"

Out of habit, Eliza averted her eyes, although she was certain he would not be able to describe her dress if she disappeared in a puff of smoke, despite his eye movements over her. A tingle of enlightenment swept through her, as she discerned he simply liked to pick at something—anything, no matter how insignificant—to make the person before him feel uncertain. His week-long silence, which had been a mystery to her, she now understood was part of that.

He took pleasure in such intimidations. The shocking clarity with which Eliza drew these conclusions made her wonder how they had eluded her until now, why she had given him so much significance, allotted him so much of her fear.

"My other dresses were ruined," she eventually said. Any answer would do, she now understood. He would find a way to peck at it.

"All of them? You ruined all of them?"

"They were ruined during the travels," she said, as if floating aimlessly on a wrecked ship with a concerning shortage of food and water and a captain on the verge of death could be considered travel.

"I expect you to change out of that thing the minute you leave this office. Is this another one of those cheap dresses? Like the one you wore when you came home? You looked like a streetwalker. I almost left you on the curb."

"I gave it to a servant," said Eliza, fully aware that the dress she was wearing cost more than what the scullery maid earned in one year.

"Who gave you that vulgar dress?"

"I purchased it."

Eliza did not know whether he was referring to what she was wearing or what she had worn in the carriage on the way home. It didn't matter. She was waiting for the storm she knew was coming. Her unapologetic insouciance was inciting her father, and in that, she took enormous pleasure.

"You purchased it, you say? How could you have done so? You have no money! Any money you have comes from me! You do not even know how to purchase dresses with the money I. Give. To. You. Hand over the rest of it before you squander it!"

"The pirates took the rest," Eliza lied.

She was not giving up the money. Her father gave her almost anything she wanted, except money she could use to implement her decisions. While stranded on the *Bessie*, she discerned that being wealthy without choices was a glorified way of being poor. She knew anyone suffering the hunger she had suffered would scoff at this notion, and rightfully so. But poverty came in many forms, depending on what was severely lacking. She recalled Littledove's stint with hot food, education, and charity ladies. And the misery it caused him.

Her father glared at her. "A cheap and useless purchase! Bring the jewelry."

"The pirates took the jewelry," Eliza lied again.

She had sewn the jewelry next to the money into a petticoat. Not even her father would look at her petticoats as long as she was wearing them.

"It's you the pirates should have taken!"

They took everyone, even those they left behind, Eliza thought, remembering her skirt and petticoats stiff with Littledove's blood, Jelly's screams, Sarah's silent terror. She recalled the bloated men she "buried at sea." Her disgust at their putrefying bodies did not honor their hard lives or the way they died.

Her father knew nothing, understood even less. Of some subjects, she now felt she knew infinitely more than he was capable of learning. She despised him, she realized with a new hardness. She truly despised him.

For years, she believed he was a hapless madman who needed to be endured and valued. She once even wanted to love him. But now, she understood he was made mean by an impulse to control. At that very moment, as a reward for years of unfulfilled tolerance, Eliza ejected her father from her life with a finality that left her feeling strangely detached and clearheaded.

"No jewelry! No money! Fine lot you are!" her father shouted when she did not respond. "They should have taken you, not your sisters! You worthless cow."

Eliza flinched, knowing her father was building up to strike her. She flinched again when he stood from his chair and swallowed with relief when he walked to the window that overlooked the shore and part of the hunting grounds. With his back to her as he looked out the window, he continued his tirade.

"Without my money, you are nothing! Never forget that. When Harold asks for your hand, I expect you to accept. Do you hear me? You are to accept him!"

"I do not love Mr. Bartook."

"Love! A stupid concept invented by useless poets. Only stupid women like you take it seriously. Do you think the paths of women like you are paved with suitors? The only reason Harold will marry you is that my money backs you. Refuse him! What grand duchess do you think you are?"

Fully enraged, he charged right up to her, hand raised to slap her. Eliza ducked under his arm and grabbed the sixteenth-century porcelain figure of Venus off his desk. She froze, holding the brittle figure in both hands as she would a posy, its cold breasts resting on one index finger. She realized her father probably liked the statue, not because it was old or beautiful or made by an artisan, but because it was female and naked.

Eliza waited for her father to strike her so she could drop the statue. It would surely crack, if not turn to powder. The opportunity was perfect. The statue was his favorite, and she hated him.

"Put that down! You are not worthy to touch it!" He lunged forward but lowered his hand.

So, he did have some self-control. She clenched her eyes and continued clutching the statue, feeling her father's spittle in her face as he carried on shouting. His rage carried him like a feather in a whirlwind, more so now that he could not strike her because she might drop his naked Venus.

"You stupid cow! No wonder the pirates left you behind! The second you say no to Harold you'll find yourself on the street in whatever clothes you are wearing. I don't care if you have to work as a whore to keep yourself."

Enraged, Eliza blew a sharp breath into her father's eye. He slapped one hand over his face and turned. Before he could take his hand away, Eliza abandoned the Venus on his desk and bolted out of the office. She ran down the hallway to the sound of her father shouting that she was never again to dress like a whore if she expected to continue living in his house.

The servants, as usual, pretended to be deaf and continued dusting the artwork in the hall. Eliza longed for Littledove, finding his absence from her life unbearable, and not much else mattered.

She made her way to the folly in the woods that was hidden from the house. The folly was, by far, her favorite place in the world, beyond her bedroom, beyond the intimate parlor on the second floor where her sisters usually gathered in the evenings, beyond the library where she spent most of her time during the winter. She always found peace and solace at the folly.

The little building was big enough for five sisters and a governess to have a picnic tea, and it retained a comical whimsy from irregular stone spires. The sisters joked that the folly nibbled dresses because its rough rocks caught fine threads and pulled cloth into tiny puckers. Governesses always made them wear heavy aprons when they visited the folly. Yet, despite the rough stones, Eliza had often fallen asleep in the folly as a child and remembered being carried from it to the house by a footman who had been sent to find her.

When she married Littledove, she would be giving up the folly in the woods. She would have to share a single room on a ship that had no museums or playhouses. Lewd shanties would replace operas. Jigs would replace ballets and waltzes. Cold, basic food would replace the gourmet offerings at her father's table. Tin and crockery would replace hand-cast silverware and porcelain. Walking in circles around a deck would replace lazy meanders through glorious estate grounds. A single cabin boy would replace an army of servants. Her labor would replace the labor of servants.

Was such a life on a ship any less constraining than the one she now had? Was she reacting rationally now that she had glimpsed a new way of living? Instinct clearly instructed her to marry Littledove, but she struggled to understand the why behind such a compelling impulse.

What if her instincts were wrong? What if she was just responding like a ninny willing to take any opportunity that came her way? Was she really in love, or was she desperate to escape?

Mary broke into the clearing of the folly. "Eliza, may I ask if you are all right?"

"Yes. Of course. Thank you." Eliza flipped her hand dismissively.

She had the least affinity for Mary. Mary was a bit of a cold fish and never the sister Eliza sought for solace. But now, only she and Mary remained at the house because Amelia married and moved away. And Sarah and Jelly … well.

In a rare gesture, Mary put her hand on her shoulder. At the touch, Eliza's calm dissolved, and she began to sob. Together, they sank onto one of the stone benches of the folly.

"I hate him," said Eliza, gladly taking the handkerchief Mary slipped into her hand.

"We always hate him after these incidents."

Eliza began releasing enormous tension in tears and trembles, between which she forced out words. "No. I hate him always and—forever. I used—to want to l-l-love him, but he cannot redeem—redeem himself. He has destroyed himself in me. I hate—hated him so much, I picked up that stat-statue on his desk. I was going to d-d-drop it if he struck me."

"You touched it?"

"I did. I took it in my hands. I-I even wished he would strike me so I could drop it. I hate him—him."

"Eliza! He would have killed you!"

Eliza blew her nose, knowing Mary would never again touch a used handkerchief, even after it was washed and pressed. She began to laugh between her sobs, her laughing and crying barely distinguishable, not even to herself.

Over the years, the folly's stones had collected enough tantrums, sobs, anger, and threats of vengeance to power a war. Every sister made wild statements at the folly, beat her chest, declared desires to murder, then went back home, exhausted and diminished. The circle never varied: the house, the folly, the house, the folly, as if they were trapped in an infinite, inescapable loop.

Eliza developed hiccups and began to cough when she realized her victory over her father was miniscule. Showy but miniscule. Nothing had changed for her or Mary. Not really.

The woods rustled, and Eliza stiffened. That their father would show up at the folly always haunted her, even if he never had. The folly was the one place on the estate that did not seem to exist for their father because he considered it a waste of rocks.

She slumped with relief when a footman appeared between two saplings. He pretended not to notice she was wiping her cheeks with her hands and bowed to her and Mary individually.

Then he faced Eliza. "Miss Strauss, your father has expressed strong wishes to see you, please."

Mary rose from the stone bench. When the stones pulled on her dress, she mumbled, "Oh no, I shall have to change now."

Eliza rose from the cold, hard stone and felt a few threads of her dress also catch on the asper surface. The delicate plucks made her recall she had not being able to raise her arms in the dress she wore to board the USS *Vesuvius* because it had a ripped seam in the armpit. The footman stepped to one side in preparation to walk behind the sisters when he escorted them back to the house.

"Please tell Mr. Strauss I cannot return to the house immediately," said Eliza.

Mary stopped fussing with her skirt and gaped at her. "Miss Eliza ..."

"Yes. Please tell Mr. Strauss I am not ready to return," Eliza repeated to the footman.

The footman swallowed hard. The level of confusion in his eyes was outdone only by his sudden gulp. His angst was not lost on Eliza when most of his color drained. If he returned without her, her father could dismiss him and make certain he would never work in any of the great mansions in the area.

Eliza could not allow that to happen. "If it makes you ill at ease to give Mr. Strauss my response, then please take a walk to the stream, which cannot be seen from the house. Going there and back should take you about twenty minutes. By that time, I shall have returned to the house, and he shall not need to ask you where I am. Please let me know which approach you take so we shall not be in conflict."

Mary looked back and forth between her and the footman, eyes flashing with confusion. The footman swayed as he considered.

Then he cleared his throat, and said, "I shall look for you by the stream, Miss Strauss. Thank you, Miss Strauss."

"Eliza, please! You are playing with fire!" Mary whispered after the footman bowed and headed off. "You are going too far. I beg of you. Please!"

To Eliza's surprise, Mary, the sister who seldom touched anyone, kissed her on the cheek. *Poor Mary. She has been coping alone all this time.*

"Mary, go back to the house. I shall return by way of the orchard. By the time I get there, he will have calmed himself with drink. Please, do not worry."

Mary nodded, although her jaw quivered. She walked out of the folly, occasionally looking back at Eliza.

Saying no to him was not so difficult, Eliza decided, although she had yet to suffer the consequences that might follow. A moment later, she headed into the dappled sunlight of the orchard, tapping her fingertips to keep her thoughts in order.

Autonomy. That was the rarity Littledove was offering even if he was not aware he was offering it, because he assumed everyone had it. He certainly had autonomy. Used it every moment of his life on sea and land. The world on a ship was much smaller and more restricted, but the autonomy and unrestricted personal freedoms granted to her on the *Bessie* would move with her over all lands and waters.

Value. Littledove valued her enough to change himself as best he could and to not require her to change. He was changing himself because he found something in her he wanted to emulate, something he felt would improve him. Until Littledove, she had not been sure she had qualities anyone valued.

Respect. Another thing Littledove always showered on her, even when it interfered with what he really wanted. Intuitively, he knew what was important and yielded to it.

And love, the highest form of respect.

Eliza emerged from the orchard to face the splendor of her father's mansion, built from granite with floor-to-ceiling curved, glass windows. The unease of being deprived returned, and she wondered how well she would really cope on Littledove's ship. She weighed the conditions on the *Bessie* against the caveats associated with living in her father's house or being married to Harold Bartook, who would also take her from the house. Eliza stepped forth, appreciating that true wealth was the ability to select one's forms of deprivation.

After his encounter with Eliza's father in the Hareys' parlor, Littledove understood that Strauss most likely would not deliver his letters to Eliza. *We'll see about that, lobcock,* thought Littledove as he gave Mrs. Harey some white envelopes with instructions to address them with Eliza's address in her feminine handwriting. A few days later, Mrs. Harey handed him a box of expensive stationery adorned with little violets on both the sheets and the envelopes she addressed.

"What're these?" asked Littledove as he looked at the plethora of tiny, purple petals.

"These will not raise suspicions," wise Mrs. Harey explained. "No young lady who knows Miss Eliza would correspond with her on plain white paper. Young ladies do not do that."

The explanation made sense, although he cringed when he wrote his first letter to Eliza, feeling silly when he most wanted to present himself in the most masculine way possible.

Milady Eliza,

I hope you're well and in good health like I's now in real good health. Mrs. Harey sends you regards. The Captain too. Methinks Mrs. Harey missed her calling to be a spy when she said I need to use this stationery with flowers to make sure you get my letters. When you write back, address it to Mrs. Harey and put the sign of a wave on the flap so she'll know to save the letter for me.

I's been at Mrs. Beeve's while the Bessie *gets her repairs. Mrs. Beeve runs a nice house. Most of the cargo was insured. The rest I don't have to pay for because it was pirates. With a word from Captain Harey and Captain Ellsworth, someone finally hired me to take cargo to France and several other places. I'll bring you back marzipan from France because they make the best.*

I'll be at sea for about three months and won't be able to send or get letters for the bulk of that. But I'll write you from each port I come to because I's missing you.

Captain Ellsworth's men did a real good job of cleaning up the Bessie *when they came onboard, so the* Bessie *is in good health too.*

My heart misses you all the time.

He hesitated before signing the letter "YCW," code for for "Your Captain Will" in case someone other than Eliza read the letter. He sealed the envelope, fearing he might be misjudged if someone found his handwriting on the frilly stationery. Such a discovery would not bode well for what was left of his reputation.

He did not mention that sighting any ship at sea made him descend into dark moods because he could not block out how the pirates massacred his crew and passengers and almost destroyed his ship. He did not tell her how diminished he felt from the fear that made him feel he no longer belonged on the sea that owned him. He did not tell her he sometimes suffered from fits of consternation that prevented him from thinking clearly. He did not tell her he felt a part of who he was had been stolen from him, just as her sisters had been stolen from her. He did not tell her he had days when he dreaded setting foot on the deck because unspecific anxieties were shredding him. He did not tell her he was always somewhat apprehensive and afraid of things he could not name and of conditions that did not exist.

He wanted to be as brave for her as she had been for him. He wanted her to have faith in him so she could wait comfortably for him.

When he returned from the stint at sea as captain of another man's ship, he wrote to her again:

Milady Eliza,

I gave up my commission on the Jane Seymour *because the* Bessie's *got all her repairs done. I used that cabinetmaker you recommended from West Edith's Bay, and she looks real good. I's heading out in her one more time to Amsterdam with special cargo and will back in a month, give or take. Then sure as ~~the dickens~~ I'll come see you because enough is enough, and I missed you enough for several lifetimes. Please have patience with me. I's probably more desperate to see you than you are to see me. When I see you again, let's talk about what's in the future.*

YCW

Littledove mailed the letter, afraid to tell Eliza the truth about where he was going.

Chapter Thirteen

DEFINING MARRIAGE

Sarah's and Jelly's disappearance was still a little fictitious to everyone except Eliza at their memorial service in the estate graveyard. The denial of the mourners took the benign form of hope that they were misinformed, that the girls would be delivered safely to the house, just as Eliza had been.

The quixotic view repulsed Eliza, who knew the truth was as rough as the stones at the folly. To Eliza, Sarah and Jelly's absence became conclusive and irrevocable when they failed to emerge from the chaos on the ship. Her understanding of what they most likely suffered was an asphyxiating knowledge she did not share with anyone because she could not bring herself to speak about it. While everyone harbored hope of their impossible return, her sisters' absence threatened to overcome their presence in her life because absence was what remained of them.

From the tombstones with their names in the family graveyard, Eliza began to hear Jelly's screams and feel the pressure of Sarah's silence. She felt Littledove's hand on her wrist, pulling her down the passage and shoving her into the secret compartment. She felt his blood soaking through her dress. The entire scene began to recur in the graveyard, surging in Eliza's mind with all its details, some of which she had not remembered until that moment.

She startled when her sister Amelia put her hand on her shoulder and hugged her. "Are you all right, Eliza?"

Eliza nodded, wiped her tears.

"Walk with me back to the house. I have some good news to tell you. It does not compensate for all our losses, but it is good news."

Amelia put her arm around her to prevent anyone from stepping between them. They lowered their heads and spoke quietly, as they often did when they were among others.

"Do not tell anyone, but you are going to be an aunt! I am with child," whispered Amelia.

At bit of light stirred within Eliza. "Amelia! How wonder—"

"Shhhh! Say nothing. Do not let Simon know I told you. He wants to announce it later, but I simply had to tell you. I simply must tell someone, and I know you are good with secrets. You are the only one who knows—aside from us, that is. Let it be our secret for now."

"You have not told Mary?"

Amelia hesitated, her eyes shifting. "Can you please tell her for me after we leave? I do not want to risk being overheard."

Eliza nodded and said nothing more. By now, Simon was walking behind them, almost stepping on their skirt hems, and could easily overhear anything they said. Eliza tried not to be bothered that Simon was denying her sister the joy of announcing she was with child. She suspected that eventually everyone would find out without Amelia having the joy of telling anyone.

Perhaps the secrecy was a symptom of the silly pacts newlyweds made with one another. For a moment, Eliza was tempted to tell Amelia about Littledove, but just as she felt the temptation, she felt the danger of telling anyone unfurl with greater strength, and she remained silent.

She was still not accustomed to Simon's constant presence around Amelia. All Amelia had to do was leave a room, and he followed her. People laughed about how in love he was with Amelia the Beautiful. Amelia was the best representative of the family line, with a long neck that angled gracefully, translucent skin, and hair the color of sunshine with glints of pink.

People joked Simon was concerned a footman would walk off with Amelia. The sisters used to tease him wickedly that, having been around Amelia for such a long time, they were only too happy to be rid of her, and he need not worry that they would want her back.

Amelia was the sister with whom Eliza had the most affinity. She became part mother after their mother died, was always sister, and very often friend. Lately, Eliza felt a little abandoned that Amelia, so involved with her new husband, waited more than two months before coming to see her. Sometimes she wondered with sisterly jealousy whether Amelia would have further delayed her visit had Sarah and Jelly's memorial service been postponed.

Searching for a private moment with Amelia, she invited her to the upstairs parlor to give her the pale lavender silk shawl she had just finished knitting. Within minutes, Simon was in the parlor, making Eliza regret she had not given Amelia the shawl in her bedroom, where she knew Simon could not follow and where they could have settled for a private chat.

Hoping Simon would leave them alone, Eliza pointed out a few mistakes that were so tiny and sporadic Amelia claimed to not be able to see them, even if they were blatant to Eliza. They reminisced about how inept they had been when the governess taught them to knit with thick yarns. They laughed about the glove Mary made that had a thumb almost in the center of the palm; the sweater Sarah made that was large enough to be a bedsheet; the many sweaters Eliza made with crooked necks and one sleeve longer than the other; the sock Jelly made with a toe so wide everyone joked only a mermaid could wear it.

"I believe I still have the mermaid sock," said Amelia, throwing herself back and clapping.

Their laughter slowly died when they once again realized that Jelly would no longer be with them. Eliza suffered a bout of guilt about having tormented her. But they always tormented each other when they were not protecting or comforting one another.

As the conversation progressed, however, Eliza lost her ability to ignore Simon, who remained in the room even if he did not interfere with their conversation. He sat like a customer impatiently standing in line for his turn to buy cheese. Eliza found herself censoring and editing what she was willing to say in front of him and resenting that he was wherever Amelia was. Always.

Annoyed at having to share her sister with him to this degree, Eliza grabbed Amelia's wrist as Littledove had grabbed hers and whisked her to her bedroom under the guise of wanting to show Amelia her latest corset, whose design greatly facilitated good posture. Simon could not possibly follow them into a bedroom where they would be discussing corsets. But moments after Eliza closed the bedroom door, Simon banged his fist against it and called for Amelia to come tend to him, and Amelia ran out as if the room had caught fire.

Stunned at her inability to grab a private moment with Amelia, Eliza slid into a chair and threw the corset across the room. The more she thought about the interactions, the more peculiar she thought Simon's presence was in everything Amelia did. Amelia, in love as she might be with him, did not seem to have the same requirement to be with him at all times.

Unable to come to any sensible conclusion except that Simon suffered from a neurosis, Eliza made her way down the hallway, determined to find another opportunity. Perhaps she and Amelia could escape to the folly without Simon.

"I shall wear it tomorrow, Simon. It does not match my dress."

The panic that tightened Amelia's voice made Eliza stop at the bedroom door, unable to prevent herself from eavesdropping.

"You shall wear it now! She just gave it to you! Or do you plan to be rude to her for the rest of your life?"

"Simon, it does not match my dress—"

"Who the hell cares about your dress!"

Eliza swung the door open without knocking to find Amelia flattened against a wall while Simon held the lavender shawl as if he were going to strangle her with it. Again, for Eliza, time splintered into still frames as it had done when she first crawled out of Littledove's compartment to help him.

"Are you not in the habit of knocking?" shouted Simon.

Eliza marched to the settee and picked up the blue shawl that matched Amelia's dress. She threw the shawl around Amelia's shoulders and escorted her across the room with her arms around her.

To Simon she said, "I am afraid to say your sense of fashion is inadequate. The shawl I gave to my sister does not match her dress. Besides, this is the one she wants to wear."

Eliza did not need to look behind herself to know Simon was stumbling with rage as he followed them down the hallway, down the stairs, through the great hall, and into one of the smaller parlors on the first floor, where, with a single glare, he made Amelia move from the chair Eliza had sat her in to a settee where he sat down beside her. Eliza could feel his rage focus on her as she puttered around the parlor with hopes that he would leave. Eventually, she caved in to the pressure and stepped out of the parlor, leaving Amelia and Simon alone in it.

One parlor over, Eliza pulled Mary aside. "Forgive me if I exaggerate, but am I the only one who notices Amelia cannot take breaths without Simon being present?"

Mary shrugged. "I dare say you are not exaggerating. We all thought he would calm down after marrying ... Not even working for Father has calmed him about Amelia."

"Simon works for Father?"

"Oh. Well. I imagine there is no reason for you to know if no one has told you. Simon sold his company to Father and now works for him."

"He did? May I ask what he does at Father's company?"

"I am not certain. But Father is mentoring him for some great position. Perhaps to head the company."

Eliza nodded as if she comprehended but felt even more perplexed. What could her father offer a man used to successfully running his own company? Almost every man she knew, great and small, dreamt of managing his destiny by having his own company. Simon had already accomplished that.

Littledove was no different. Captain Harey often teased him about his maternal instincts toward the *Bessie*, but Eliza understood the *Bessie* was not merely a ship. She was Littledove's life, his company, his home, his wealth.

The next time Eliza had a chance, she cornered Amelia at the buffet in the dining room. The room was crowded—not exactly suited for a private conversation—but she pressed on.

"Amelia, if I may ask, are you happy in your marriage?"

Amelia answered as she placed petit fours a dessert plate. "Marriage is for financial security, not for love, because love is bound to fade."

What Eliza heard was that Amelia did not answer her question. Amelia recited what her father told all of them, and her answer did not resemble anything Eliza would be tempted to say about marrying Littledove. *Was she wrong?*

Her doubts revisited her. Perhaps she was being naive. With Littledove, she would certainly not go hungry, but his resources were considerably more limited than her father's or Harold's. And she would be away from her sisters for long periods of time.

The conversation frittered as Eliza became aware that Amelia had put enough petit fours on her plate for two people. Eliza looked around. Simon, standing across the room, still had not taken his eyes off Amelia. He was now glowering at Eliza because she was distracting Amelia from him. Amelia reached to add another petit four to the plate, and in the blast of summer light from the window, Eliza saw pale smudges above her collar bones.

Their mother often had marks like those—little gray smudges the size of fingertips. Soot marks, she called them. As a child, Eliza never understood why her mother had soot marks on her face and neck when only the servants dealt with fires. Neither did she question why her mother was always walking into doors, although Eliza had never seen her do so in person. Eliza had once deliberately walked into a door and walked away with a sore nose but not a black eye.

Then her father backhanded her. She developed a green and gray blotch on her cheek that eventually faded to gray, just like the dots on her mother's cheeks, but bigger. He forbade her to come downstairs for dinner because she looked so horrible, and her sisters had to ask maids to take dinner to her.

Old facts about her life came together in new configurations Eliza did not like. She marveled at what she could now see so clearly, at the absurdities she always thought were normal and that her sisters still thought were normal—or at least not worth questioning. For all she knew, they might be afraid to even question the issues for themselves, so deeply convinced were they that nothing could be changed.

She recalled people's comment that the Strauss governesses worked very hard because five girls were a handful, but now, Eliza saw clearly that their governesses worked very hard because their mother would not let them stop teaching. The main job of the governesses, the music teachers, the art teachers, the archery and tennis instructors, and the math tutors was to keep the sisters out of their father's way. If they got in his way, he often accused their mother of being incompetent to raise children, or worse, added smudges to her face.

All that academic protection of governesses ceased after their mother died. Overnight, their father dismissed the governesses, including Jelly's. She and her sisters stepped in to instruct Jelly with various degrees of success and watched her slowly turn feral. Their father's new mission became to get his daughters married.

Eliza shifted her eyes to Simon. What grandness was their father training Simon to perform that inspired him to sell his company and marry Amelia? The two events seemed related. The question made Eliza look across the room at Harold Bartook, the man her father was determined she should marry. She had spent the day avoiding Harold, plunging into other people's conversations whenever he came near her, keeping herself across the room from wherever he was.

Harold was nothing like Simon. Not much was wrong with Harold, she had to admit. He was a sound man, steady in his habits. He was as reliable as a good clock when wound properly. Harold was the youngest of three sons who ran Bartook Investments, a firm smaller than Strauss Investments Incorporated by many degrees. He was not unintelligent, but he lacked guile.

Eliza could not imagine Bartook Investments enhancing her father's firm in any way, or her father convincing three brothers to sell their company to him. Perhaps Harold was truly in love with her? But she could not reciprocate, not even before Littledove came into her life. Now she received Harold's attentions in limited amounts to not arouse suspicions about Littledove.

July. That was when Littledove would return. July was six months from when they last saw each other at the Hareys'. Two months of the original six remained. Give or take a month, Littledove said, he would return by July. Despite understanding that Littledove most likely would take longer than six months to get on his feet, Eliza's life still began and ended with the promises of July.

Eliza tingled when she recalled that in Littledove's most recent letter, he explained he had to go to sea one more time for a short trip. Afterward, he would take no other commission and come to see her without fail. It was now early June. She smiled as she imagined seeing him by the end of July.

July came and went without incident. By August, Littledove's letters stopped arriving, but he did not appear. He was at sea, and the sea had many ways of delaying a person's return, Eliza knew firsthand. But no sooner did Eliza console herself with that thought than she became burdened with the knowledge that the sea had pirates from whom he escaped one time.

The chances of Littledove surviving another attack were nil. They would burn the *Bessie* in the middle of the ocean if they did not find him on it. He could disappear without a trace, and no one would ever find the *Bessie*'s ashes or his bones at the bottom of the ocean.

Eliza wrote to Mrs. Harey to inquire whether she had heard from Littledove. By leaving off the little wave on the envelope flap and underlining "Mrs. Harey" on the address, Eliza hoped Mrs. Harey would have the sense to open the envelope.

A week later, she received a response:

My Darling, Sweet Miss Eliza,

I hope you are better than you sounded in your letter, although I cannot blame you for being so worried. I wish could put you at ease as much as I would like by saying that Captain Littledove is fine and sitting in our parlor. Unfortunately, Captain Littledove is at sea, probably between ports where he has no means by which to send letters.

Coping with the prolonged absences of seamen and not knowing where they are is always harrowing. Many times I have lost sleep over Captain Harey's whereabouts. I recommend checking the Ship Observation Report in the newspaper where ship sightings are reported, although I dare say you probably do so already. Perhaps the Bessie *will appear in the list and by that you may deduce Captain Littledove is well. It is a game of patience, and the one who waits always wins because she has no choice but to wait and win.*

Sincerely and always with Affection,

Mrs. Abraham Harey

Having no choice, Eliza took Mrs. Harey's advice. She read the Ships Observation Report with religious fervor and waited. She feared the price for waiting with such patience would be news that Littledove could not return. Such news would certainly end her waiting, and she would win the game with a prize she would not be able to bear.

In early September, many things were happening, none of which distracted Eliza from her despair at not having heard from Littledove. She contracted into a pillar of strength, becoming quieter, knitting more elaborately with even finer threads. At this rate, she would soon be knitting with filaments of yearnings.

Mary had gotten engaged to Richard, a fellow who met their father's approval, and they were planning to marry in a month because they were too in love to wait longer. That they were in love seemed undeniable when every evening they walked the shore together, arm in arm, circling the folly nestled in the patch of woods, and returning enchanted as could be. They were always nestled in a corner of a parlor, flirting and tending to one another to the extreme of ridiculousness. The sight was refreshing to Eliza, who had never seen Mary so open to expressions of affection, and for a while, Eliza was glad Richard was in Mary's life.

Of all the suitors their father allowed any of her sisters to consider, Richard was the most insouciant, as if he were incapable of suffering. Richard was not extremely handsome, but he had a charming way about him. So charming in fact, that the maids would not stop smiling at him until the housekeeper lined them up and forbade them from even looking at him, lest Miss Strauss, of the variant Mary, fire all of them.

Eliza was not surprised that even Eunice, an older, second cousin, giggled like a girl when she met him, so overtaken was she with his charm. Cousin Eunice, who never missed a wedding, arrived with her young daughter and son as soon as she received the invitation to help with the preparations. The son was having his fifth birthday the second week of September, and Mary was keen to plan a party for him while she also planned her wedding.

With the flurry of activity and planning and an endless list of errands that needed to be run for the birthday party and the wedding, Eliza began to welcome the daily tea at three when the activity in the house came to a pause and the women sat in quiet respite. Usually, the tea lasted an hour, but nowadays it lasted only until someone leapt up after remembering she had left something undone.

"Master Andrew, please say thank you to Aunt Mary for taking time out of planning her wedding to help plan your birthday party," prompted Eunice.

"Is it going to have balloons?" asked Andrew as he practiced balancing himself with one leg in the air.

"If you are good," answered Mary, who could not stop admiring her engagement ring, a thing that reminded Eliza of a garlic bulb because of its enormous diamonds.

"I've been good all week," bragged Andrew, making a face at his sister, who shot him a side-eyed look to express a contrary opinion.

"How good have you been if you have not yet thanked Aunt Mary?" his mother prompted again.

"Thank you, Aunt Mary," Andrew recited. "Can you cut glass with your ring? Papa says you can cut a mirror with a diamond." He did not wait for an answer because his sister stuck her tongue out at him, and he chased her out of the parlor.

Mary turned wistful. "I hope to be as wonderful a mother as Richard shall be a father."

Eunice laughed. "You shall have many doubts at first, but eventually you will catch on. The best thing you can do is to hire an experienced nanny. They can make all the difference."

"I suspect I shall need much help when the time comes."

"The time shall come soon enough. Have you decided where you will honeymoon?" asked Eunice.

Eliza declined another cup of tea from the maid, much amused by Mary's declarations to become a mother. Mary was so meticulous she often changed her dress if it became wrinkled. She was in for a surprise if she thought she could dress immaculately when she had a child.

Eliza almost laughed when she imagined the diaper on Mary's adorable baby leaking over one of her dresses. Certainly, Mary thought a child would sit perfectly still like a houseplant until she needed it to become adorable so people could admire it.

"Oh, Cousin Eunice, I have been so preoccupied with the wedding and the birthday party, I have not considered a birthday present for Master Andrew," Mary was saying.

"Your attention to his party should be enough, but I suspect he shall not fully appreciate that."

Eunice began to rattle off a list of toys her son enjoyed, including commentaries about what he already had and what he lacked. Slight impatience flickered through Mary's eyes before she hunkered down to appear interested in what Eunice was saying.

Eunice could drone on forever, and Eliza's thoughts drifted to a time their mother gave each sister a moniker that reflected what she thought was her most prominent trait. Jemima the Impetuous. Sarah the Pious. Eliza the Unrepentant. Mary the Impeccable. And Amelia the Beautiful.

One time, behind their mother's back, Eliza referred to Mary as "Mary the Immaculate," and they all giggled nervously at the sacrilegious pun, except for Mary the Impeccable, who became furious, and Sarah the Pious, who stormed out of the room to pray for their souls.

As if insisting under dark clouds that no rain would fall because she was on a picnic, Mary said, "I believe Richard shall be an excellent father."

An inner prompting made Eliza bypass Mary's words and focus on the depth of Mary's sourness. Eliza shot to her feet under the force of revelation, bearing Eunice's gripping stare. Mary did not look up as she smoothed the napkin on her lap before taking a sip of tea as if to hide behind the teacup.

Oh, the secrets the folly keeps so diligently! Eliza realized. *Mary is with child!*

That was why the wedding was happening so soon. Eliza now saw the components of the deception. Mary was helping with Andrew's party to reverse the suspicion that she did not like children, whom everyone knew she found annoying.

In that same moment, Cousin Eunice might have turned into a cobweb, leaving only Eliza and Mary in one another's presence. Eliza crossed the room and rested her hand on Mary's shoulder, feeling Mary twitch at the touch. She would not look up at Eliza as she blinked furiously to keep her tears from spilling. The spell broke when a footman came into the parlor to announce the mail had arrived.

At a loss for what else to do, Eliza left the parlor and headed to her father's office. They lived in a house of secrets. She could not tell Mary about Littledove. Mary could not tell her she was with child. Amelia could not tell anyone she was expecting. Eliza was so distressed that her ability to take her letters from her father's hand while feigning lack of desperation ran thin.

Strauss slammed a letter with Amelia's handwriting on the envelope in front of Eliza. He sorted through the letters in his hand and was going to slam another one on the desk but pulled it back as he squinted at the writing on the envelope. He shook the envelope next to his ear, as if expecting to hear something in it rattle.

"Who is this Havey"—he squinted at the feminine scrolls—"Harey person?"

Eliza filled her cheeks with false enthusiasm and beamed a smile. She began to mimic how Sarah spoke when she finally unloaded the anxieties she usually experienced in her silence.

"Oh, Mrs. Harey is an avid knitter who knows everything! We exchange knitting patterns and advice because she knows, oh so many, many things. She specializes in lace knitting but only recently taught me a new way of shaping sock heels. But I do wonder if it is as durable. Those techniques can be used as well to shape clothing, especially bodices, and ..."

Eliza spoke, watching her father's eyes glaze over until he slammed Mrs. Harey's letter on his desk to indicate Eliza was to become silent. He continued to his next thought, as if reciting a list of tasks the other person had failed to complete.

"Your sister is marrying Richard at the end of next month. Now, Harold—"

"Please excuse me, Father. I feel unwell."

With one hand over her mouth, Eliza bolted into the hallway. Her father would not stop her because he did not want anyone getting sick in his office.

Eliza ran out of the house, opening doors for herself instead of waiting for footmen to do so for her. She ran until she reached the rocky shore and came to a halt because she was out of breath. Facing the ocean, she hoped the sight of the water would ease her anxieties, but it increased them.

Where was Littledove? Was he all right? Was he well? Was he alive? Did he still have plans to return to her? He promised that he would, he did. Surely, he was not abandoning her.

She pulled out Mrs. Harey's letter from her pocket. No wave on the flap. Eliza considered it might contain information about Littledove, but she would not dare read it except in her room behind a locked door, and she could not go back into the house without feeling she would suffocate. Even outside, she felt constrained, as if her corset had shrunk with her still in it. She stuffed Mrs. Harey's letter deep into her corset, then rested her hand over a lump of jewelry in her underskirt.

Eliza sat on a boulder to read Amelia's letter. Amelia apologized again for not visiting, but Simon would not let her travel because she was advanced with child. Simon was of the opinion that women prominent with child should not be in public. And it was best not to visit her for the same reason. He might make an exception for Mary's wedding, seeing as it was a significant event, but they might have to leave after the ceremony and not be able to stay for the reception.

Eliza slapped the letter on her thigh. Did Simon expect Amelia to spend her time with child unseen? Her entire life unseen? Amelia wrote as if she lived hundreds of miles away and not a short distance by carriage. Eliza was tempted to ask for a carriage and visit her but was not sure whether Simon would allow her into the house or whether Amelia would suffer afterward for her visit.

Beneath the letter on her thigh, Eliza fingered another bulge next to the jewelry and money—Littledove's letters. If her father put her on the street, at least she would have these things. At times, she felt she could barely move from the many weights she carried, most of which were not made of gold, precious stones, or paper.

The last time she had not had random feelings of confinement was when she stayed at the Hareys' house, where she could walk around freely with or without anyone, where her life was not being constantly manipulated and controlled. Where she was heard when she spoke. She and Littledove could converse for hours, during which she discovered the true polish of the man was in his integrity and intelligence and not on his weathered surface.

Littledove! How she ached for him. She closed her eyes and imagined his scent coming from the sea. Eliza began to take deep breaths when a shadow darkened her lids.

She opened her eyes with a start when she felt a motion by her side to find Harold about to sit beside her on the rock. Panic swept over her and made her bolt upright. If she did not marry Harold, her father would put her on the street. Amelia would take her in, if Simon permitted, but who could say Simon would permit it if it went against her father's wishes or if it pleased Amelia? Or that living with Simon would be any better than living at her father's house?

Perhaps Cousin Eunice would take her in. But Eliza did not know how Eunice was beholden to her father. After all, Eunice's husband worked for her father, and her father had a knack of making sure everyone was beholden to him because the penalties for defying him were always catastrophic. One had to go before him naked and leave naked if one expected to survive because he took everything when defied.

Eliza tried not to look at Harold as she wondered what exactly motivated him to pursue her when she never sought him. She was not so beautiful or charming that a man in whom she showed no interest would continue courting relentlessly. Harold was not brilliant, but he was not obtuse.

He would make a wonderful husband for someone other than herself. Eliza wished Amelia had married him instead of Simon, but Amelia was available for marriage when her father developed an interest in Simon's company.

Eliza was now willing to accept that marrying Amelia had been part of some greater business contract for Simon, although she was still not sure how all the parts fit together. She wondered again what Simon got from being an employee of Strauss Investments that he had lacked when running his own company.

Bartook Investments had nothing Strauss Investments did not already have ... although some benefit might come to Bartook Investments in a merger with a larger company like her father's. Perhaps Harold was courting her to facilitate a merger, but did Harold even think that way? Harold had ... a fundamental nature.

Her thoughts raced on. Mary often joked she would have more diamonds than she could wear because Richard's company had a finger in African diamond mines that were worth a small fortune. Perhaps that was the distinction Richard's company offered. The diamond business had to be what her father wanted, or he would not have even allowed Richard into the house, much less to court Mary.

Eliza remembered Richard's one flirtation with her around the time Mary began to be interested in him. He made her feel she was the center of his universe, but she curtailed the next flirtation in no uncertain terms because of her loyalty to Mary. Eliza was always loyal to her sisters, although for several months afterwards, she resented Mary, coveted Richard, and questioned her judgment.

Mary did not know about her encounter with Richard, but she knew about the housekeeper lining up the maids and threatening to fire them if they flirted with Richard or allowed Richard to flirt with them. Not that Mary had a choice now. She tied her future to a motherhood Eliza knew Mary would not cherish. Perhaps their father had offered Richard a harem on the side. Eliza released her helplessness in a sharp, scornful exhale.

Harold took her hand. The gesture was very kind, and she, having little strength against kindness, squeezed his hand before withdrawing hers. They had not touched in months, not even casually. Even now, his touch felt misplaced against her skin.

Harold was not a bad person. She tried to smile but could not, so she looked to the ocean whose waters could express as many moods as a person could feel. She thought of the last time Littledove held her in her arms and kissed her. Littledove was somewhere on the ocean or perhaps under it, and that was why she had not heard from him.

"Elizabeth, my darling. Please give me a chance to make you happy," said Harold.

Eliza thought her heart would blow a valve. The first detail that struck her about what was sounding like a proposal was Harold calling her Elizabeth, a name only her father used. As Eliza's insides expanded with despair, she felt the invisible walls around her shove against her chest. She jumped up to run into the ocean and swim away from everything but caught her toe on a clump of seaweed and fell hard against a rock. The last thing she remembered doing as she fell was pushing down her skirt because her petticoats were full of secrets.

Chapter Fourteen

PREPARING THE RETRIBUTION

Littledove contemplated rounding the bay by coach to the other side where the grand estates were to visit Eliza, but a strong caution was making him wait to see her until he was ready to walk away with her. If she could not receive his letters, she could be in other dangers. That caution insisted with a strength that made him concede to remaining on his freshly repaired *Bessie* on the pier.

To compensate for his longings, he went about his chores with great determination and posted several notices at the harbor office, soliciting sailors with military experience. Within the week, he began hearing rumors that his cargo was valuable and had to be protected. An equally strong rumor went around that he, who had not gone down with his crew, was terrified of being attacked by pirates again and wanted to be protected. He made the best of the situations in public while seething in private.

On the first sunny day after he got back the *Bessie*, he set up a Windsor chair and a table on her deck as he always did to interview men who came to apply for work. Only two men showed up. He hired the first one, a young, quiet fellow named Alton Neve, fresh out of the navy. He had no battle experience, but he had military training, and that was enough for Littledove.

The second man seemed promising until he began to ask advice with a sneer about the best ways to avoid going down with a crew that was being slaughtered. Littledove rose so quickly from his chair that the man ran down the boarding ramp until he tripped and rolled the rest of the way to the pier. When he got to his feet and saw Littledove was not coming after him, he smirked and swanked away. For the rest of that day, no one came to apply for jobs on the *Bessie*. Rumors went around that the pirates had made Littledove volatile, and he had punched a man who applied for a job hard enough to make the man roll down a boarding ramp.

With a crew of one that night, Littledove went into his quarters, the most desolate place in the world now that Eliza was not there. There he braced himself, knowing he had an important mission to fulfill before he could see her.

He began to despair, fearing he might not be able to find crew to sail with him. People were doubting an angel of mercy emerged from the woodwork of the hull at the eleventh hour to resuscitate him from death, which was how the story was being relayed with chuckles and eye rolls.

He always responded indirectly, if at all, when asked how he survived, not wanting to insist on the veracity of the story because he wanted to shield Eliza. A woman alone with a man on a ship for over a month always gave people imagination, no matter what the circumstances. He had done things right for once with a woman he loved—and who seemed to love him back—and was not about to have everything ruined by bungling. He was doing this right.

That night in taverns, Littledove became the subject of many discussions. Sailors could not deny he ran a tight ship with military-style discipline that made every man confident of his place and job at any given moment.

And he taught. If someone was interested in learning something, most likely Littledove would teach it or assign him to learn it so every man felt an opportunity to become more than just a sack of labor. And his voyages usually resulted in a profit for all, unlike with other captains who essentially offered little more than room and board on a ship for long hours of work.

Then someone reminded everyone that he had not gone down with his crew. Among the scowls and mutters, someone else mentioned that he didn't flog, and the conversation diverted: He fed them plenty, and the food was edible.

His hardtack was rarely infested with beetles because he made sure it was fresh and well stored. He had a peculiarity about boiling all water, and any sailor who overlooked that mandate usually got dysentery and a good cursing from Littledove, who always found out everything that happened on his ship. His tongue-lashing could impale a man, but those who had worked for him for years knew that he cursed generously but had to be pushed hard to lose his temper.

When the topic that he had not gone down with his crew resurfaced, some speculated that after so many years of running a good ship, Littledove might have been granted an angel. Many went home from the taverns that night shaking their heads at the fall of a good captain, only to stand in line the following morning to apply for the jobs Littledove posted.

The pay was too good for a common voyage to Amsterdam, and some mentioned there had to be a catch somewhere. But the pay was so good that men stopped fortifying their apprehensions. Perhaps the catch was sailing with a captain who did not go down with his crew, but how often did pirates attack the same ship twice?

The night he finished filling all the positions, Littledove fell asleep peacefully, only to wake from a nightmare in which Eliza disintegrated into dust when another man kissed her. Captain Harey was right in saying Eliza could have her pick of men, and the men at her house spoke as properly and dressed as royally as she did. Formal manners flowed in their blood.

He could become obscure or worse, ridiculous, the moment she crossed the threshold of her father's house. That she had chosen him could change after so many months among her stock, when the intensity of their experience waned and she came to her senses to realize he was only the captain of a cargo ship. A ridiculous sea creature, at best.

Littledove tried to assuage his insecurities by rereading Eliza's letters that Mrs. Harey saved for him. They were discreet about her feelings, as a woman who knew she could be uncovered and compromised was bound to be. Eliza bubbled with enthusiasm about all his missions, rejoiced in his milestones, comforted when he expressed concern. She always found a way to say she was waiting for him to visit as soon as he could. She mentioned no other men except for one that her father expressed wishes for her to marry—someone named Harold. In this sentence, she underlined "Father" as if to suggest she was of a different opinion.

All the same, said fellow made Littledove nervous. He knew he was no competition for any man in Eliza's world who at a moment's notice could snap his fingers, shower her with anything she wanted, and equip her with a mansion full of servants. He could barely offer her a small room in a ship's hull in a society of uncouth sailors who bathed infrequently and mistook piss for beer when drunk. And he had not yet found a way to rid the lower decks of rats.

Still. Each letter seemed encouraging. She tossed in a word or two about the solace of feeling safe in bed while storms raged outside. She spoke of nursing the fevers of her restless soul, a phrase that gave Littledove more imagination than any man should have to suffer.

Everything she wanted to say was said between the lines of her tightly managed words, except for her enthusiastic opening, which was always "My Dearest, Dearest Captain Littledove" and her sign off, which was without fail, "Your lady always, Miss Eliza Strauss."

On this necessary coldness, Littledove subsisted, after having become accustomed to the intensity of her tenderness and care. Before he left for Amsterdam, he wrote a letter on the last sheet he had of Mrs. Harey's purple-petaled stationery. He told her he had one more voyage before he would come to see her without delay, and perhaps they could go for a walk and have a chat about what the future held.

From the men Littledove hired as crew, some stood out more than others. Among those was a retired soldier named Cosmos Pias, who had three fingers on one hand, two on the other, and walked sideways like a crab. He was tattooed across his chest and back and arms with images of all the places he had visited while sailing. Cosmos applied for the position of cook.

"A bastard cannon got loose an' made me unworthy for battle," he explained.

"That teach you anything?" asked Littledove, skeptical the man was suitable for this voyage.

"Dun stand in back o' dem damned things. Jus' as stupid as standin' in front o' one!" Cosmos boomed with laughter as if he had merely tripped over a shoelace and bruised his knee.

Littledove hired him because he thought the ability to learn harsh life lessons without becoming bitter was a highly valuable trait. He needed a man with Cosmos's spirit.

For the ship's carpenter, Littledove hired a Midwesterner nicknamed Bolt who spent a few years as a cattle rancher after leaving the army. He packed a lasso on his belt for sentimental reasons but had sailed long enough to know he did not get seasick. On Littledove's invitation, he displayed an amazing ability to throw a lasso over almost anything and to do fancy footwork around the whirling loop.

"Prairie ain't no different from this he-ah ocean. Jus' miles and miles o' the same thing trying to make you think there ain't nothing beyond it," Bolt said. "Only way to travel through them places is in the company of Hope and Faith."

Littledove hired him because he needed someone who was level and did not have dark feelings about himself. And who could remind him about hope and faith during this particular voyage.

The secret cargo that required military protection began arriving, and Littledove personally supervised its loading on the *Bessie*. The single crate contained an enormous pig—a white showy thing with brown and black patches. He'd be damned if anyone skimmed this cargo. Littledove gritted his teeth when people on the pier began laughing at him in front of his crew even as the pig was being lowered under deck.

"Flying pigs and holy cows! Tha's the secret cargo!"

"And angels to shoo pirates away!"

People snickered when he walked through the harbor office. From them, he learned he was so terrified of pirates that he hired an army to protect his precious pig. Littledove scowled, conducted his business in the harbor office at breakneck speed, and left as quickly as he could. The derision served his purpose for the moment, but he still resented it. He worried he would never get his reputation back. He considered leaving early before his current crew thought to abandon him.

The next day, the rest of his cargo arrived, neatly packaged in crates that were low to the ground, no longer than a donkey, and heavy as sin. As the stevedores loaded the crates on the *Bessie*, the dock crowded with people trying to guess what the secret cargo was and what its relationship was to the giant pig that was always grunting and screeching loudly. The crates were deemed too small for holy cows, too big for flying pigs. And angels, everyone agreed, could not be contained in crates.

For the first time in weeks, Littledove smiled when he heard the rumor that his cargo had to be something very valuable if it came in only ten relatively small but heavy crates and he was unwilling to mix it with other cargo. Except the pig. The most common speculation was munitions. For the sailors with military experience to protect the pig. Followed by laughter.

On each crate, Littledove had someone stencil: SLECHTS WORDEN GEOPE BIJ HET MINISTERIE VAN EDELE METALEN—not an easy bunch of letters to memorize from a distance, especially while the crates were swaying from a hoist when they were being lowered into the *Bessie*.

It had taken Littledove forever to find someone who knew someone who could translate TO BE OPENED ONLY BY THE DUTCH MINISTRY OF PRECIOUS METALS into Dutch. He counted that by the time someone on the pier found someone who knew someone who knew Dutch, the *Bessie* would be out of the harbor and in the open sea.

Littledove knew when the stenciled letters had been translated into English because people stopped laughing when they looked at him. As the translation spread through the public, a different set of rumors began circulating.

Ten small crates heavy with precious metals was an unspeakably valuable cargo that would be delivered point to point without any other stops. No wonder sailors with military experience were necessary to protect the cargo. Littledove finally grinned when he heard that he might not go down with his crew, but he was a hell of a merchant marine because the profits from such a cargo would be stupendous.

Littledove sailed for twelve days at top speed with his best sails. Even on clear days, he did not bother to use his older, thinner sails. If a sail so much as puckered from lack of wind, he snapped at the mate in charge to pay attention. Then he brought the *Bessie* to a stop in the center of the ocean with not a scrap of land in sight.

Aware of the puzzlement of every man on deck, he called the ship carpenter to the lower deck to help uncrate the cargo. As he went into the hull, Littledove could hear the buzz of sailors asking why they were uncrating cargo when no land was in sight.

Littledove pried off the first lid with a crowbar and let Bolt look inside the crate. Bolt did not speak for seconds. His eyes flickered from the cargo in the crate to Littledove's face.

When enough silence passed, Littledove ordered, "Make bases for them."

"You mean cannon stands?"

"Cook'll help you."

"Cook? What does he know about cannons? With all respect, Cap'n, he only got five fingers between two hands. I don't think he can hold a hammer."

"Ask him how he lost his fingers. Then make the stands. One in front of each port."

"Ports?" Bolt looked over the walls in the hull.

Littledove went to a wall and pulled a discreet handle that opened a row of portholes. Eliza had recommended a top-notch cabinetmaker in West Edith's Bay to build the portholes and their covers so they were barely detectable. The carpenter's price was astronomical until Littledove explained his purpose. Then he lowered his price to something Littledove could well afford. A decent fellow, the carpenter was. His reputation was well earned.

Bolt stuck his head out of a porthole to look at the ports from the outside. He pulled his head back in and said, "These are real good! You can't even tell from the outside." He inspected the porthole again and pulled away, slightly less impressed. "You plan on havin' real good weather? I don't think they'll keep out storm waters."

"I's got reinforcements made for storms." Littledove already knew the port covers were too flimsy, that they would not last, that they would leak. He needed them to last for only one day, albeit a special day that was guaranteed not to have a storm.

"Aye, aye, sir," said Bolt, rolling his tongue in his cheek. "You want all six stands on this side?"

"Make six stands on each side. Put three cannons on each side. Every other one. For now."

Bolt shook his head. "Aye, Cap'n. But you telling us what all this be about, ain't you?"

"In good time," said Littledove and abandoned Bolt to visit the galley. "Pias!"

"Aye, sir, Cap'n," said Cosmos in the middle of emptying a bag of peas into a pot.

"You're promoted to Cannon Master."

"Beg pardon, Cap'n?"

"You hard of hearing? Cannon Master. That's you now." He turned to the sailor who stopped slicing salted pork fat to listen to the conversation. "Neve, that your name?"

"Aye, sir?"

"Stand up when I talk to you! You're now Acting Head Cook. Pias, come with me. You're going to work with the ship's carpenter."

From his peripheral vision, Littledove caught Cosmos shaking his head to indicate to Neve that he should remain silent. He followed Littledove to the lower deck. There, Cosmos stepped up to a crate and peered into it with Bolt by his side. They exchanged looks, remained silent, and looked at Littledove for further instructions.

"Make cannon stands. Six on each side to line with the ports. Bolt'll show you the ports. Grab more men if you need 'em." And with that, Littledove left the two men.

Word swept through the crew: Six cannons. Twelve bases. Six openings on each side of the *Bessie*, a ship that in no way could withstand a battle of any kind. A child's toy arrow might sink her if it struck her right. And of course, the mystery of why they needed six cannons to deliver a pig to Amsterdam. Never mind volatile—Littledove might be a little touched.

By overhearing whispers, Littledove became aware the crew figured out they detoured south after heading north, a circuitous way of getting to Amsterdam from Edith's Bay. They were consumed with suspicions that the trip to Amsterdam was a ruse. According to rumors, he was now planning to engage them in a South American war. Cosmos assured them such could not happen because he had taken inventory and knew they did not have enough stocked food to get to South America.

All the same, Cosmos instilled the fear of God in the crew by telling the men about impenetrable iron clad frigates and galleons packed with cannons and munitions. If they needed to abandon ship and swim to shore, savage men in loincloths who ate human flesh awaited them. By this time, Littledove was sure some of the men would have gladly jumped into the water and swum ashore had he not stopped the *Bessie* where no shore could be seen, days away from any land and where the ocean was too deep to anchor.

After hearing the rumors being disseminated, Littledove called the men together under deck. He strode with his best unapologetic roll, and without fanfare stood in front of one of the empty crates and looked over the men. Their mutters slowly ceased until the only sounds were the creaking and groaning of the hull.

"For those of you who haven't figured it out yet, we're going after pirates," Littledove announced. "*Black Death* pirates."

"Ee be touched in ee head!" someone whispered, but not so quietly that everyone in the hall did not clearly hear.

"Not one bit touched. Quite clear-headed," Littledove said. "But I respect you thinking that. Hear me out. I've selected you because you're all experienced military men with good reputations. Some of you more experienced than me."

The men perked up at the suggestion that he had military experience. He hoped running his ship with military precision and practices as Admiral Stoop had done would stop the crew from questioning his sanity.

"How you 'spect to catch the *Black Death* in this 'ere ship?" someone asked. "She's a galleon. Real quick. In both directions—away from us and to us when we's got to get away."

"We stand still," said Littledove. "She comes to us. Besides, she's no galleon. She's a brigantine. I's seen her."

A ruffle of murmurs went up, and someone else said, "Yay? We sit still an' then do wha'? You plannin' to bring her down with six bitty cannons? She got more cannons than us! She got more men than us! She got more everythin' than us!"

"We don't show her what we have until she's next to us," said Littledove.

"Next to us! What yee sayin'?"

The men began to grumble, but he held his ground. "We trick her."

"Exactly how you plannin' to outsmart the *Black Death*?" asked Cosmos, crossing his arms over his chest.

"Do we look dangerous?" Littledove shot back. "Would you think the *Black Death* would ever think the *Bessie's* armed? Would any other ship? Anyone here? Already on board?"

"You dun even know where the *Black Death* is!"

Littledove pointed to a crate that held cannonballs. "She'll find us because it's known we got small boxes of cargo that can only be opened at the Dutch ministry of precious metals. That's what those words on the crates say in Dutch, and by now, those words are known around the world."

"We got gold?" someone squeaked.

"They'll just sink us and take it!" called another sailor.

"And how'll they get the gold from the bottom of the ocean?" asked Littledove. "They can't sink us if they want the cargo. We got to be above water for them to take it. And they got to come close to get it. Close enough to board the *Bessie* because gold doesn't float. That makes the opportunity we need to sink her."

An astonished silence fell over the men as they stared at the words on the crate and pieced together the plan. Littledove could feel the cogs in their heads begin to turn.

"We dun got enough cannons," said Cosmos. By now everyone knew about his encounter with cannons.

"We got six, "said Littledove. "We put three on each side until we figure which side she comin' from. Then we move the other three to the side she's on. Not that hard. They're on wheels."

"Six won't sink her none!" said Cosmo.

"Six'll sink her at point-blank range if we use exploding cannonballs. We go at her munitions deck first and disarm her, and then at her lower decks and sink her. If we're good, one'll hit her magazine because you know they've a magazine. If we're not so good, fire'll spread there 'cause that's what fire does."

"What if we catch on fire? We got powder too, if we got cannons."

"Our sails'll be doused. They'll be rigged to release easy from deck. Less chance of catching fire that way."

"What if they fire on us?"

"They won't have time. We're taking them by surprise. They'll think we're just the cargo ship they see. By the time they figure otherwise, her hull'll be gone."

The men fell silent, and he let them consider the plan for a moment without distracting them. Cosmos wrinkled his nose and scratched his temple as he frowned and arched his eyebrows, all at once.

"Don't give up this opportunity," Littledove said when he next spoke. "If we don't get the *Black Death* now, she'll surely get some of us some day, if not most of us eventually. The only certain way to avoid the *Black Death* is to never go to sea. How many of you are willing to do that? To have your choices cut by fear?"

No one answered, but Littledove knew that one attraction of sailing was a savage sense of freedom and promises of seeing things men had never before seen. Sailors were a community of antsy, curious sorts with itchy feet who had to leave and return, leave and return to find their peace.

"I've seen firsthand what the *Black Death* can do," he continued, "and it's real bad. Won't deny that. I've got scars enough to prove it. And memories worse than any scar. But I know something about the men she's got. They're common thieves! They think they can rob their way to wealth and murder their way to glory. How committed to anything is a man who steals? Is that kind of man superior to you? Smarter than you? More important, I've seen how she works, how she comes about. I know the assumptions her captain makes, and by that, I know how she can be deceived. Men, we have the upper hand in our humility. You can go down in history as thems who took the *Black Death* down."

He paused to take in the new sparkle of potential glory in some of the men's eyes. He then applied an important lesson he learned from Kraken, the slimy harbormaster in Port Hansweert. "Plus, there'll be a handsome cut of the reward money for each of you."

Those who could do math began to mumble and keep track of the amounts on their fingers. Littledove knew all the men had seen the reward amounts because he always posted his fliers by the reward fliers.

Finally, someone asked a question that indicated they were buying into the plan. "What about ee pig? Where's tha' come in?"

"Ah, the pig." Littledove grinned. "He's real important. You'll see. Tomorrow, we start training, and I'll explain the pig. Everything'll fall into place, and you'll all understand. Remember: You are the men chosen to take down the *Black Death*! Keep that in your souls. Get back to your duties."

Littledove stepped back as the men, overwhelmed with awe, stood with respect. Some saluted him military style, and he saluted back, silently thanking Admiral Stoop for having taught him how to salute.

He went back to his quarters without speaking to anyone because he did not want to reveal information in a haphazard way by answering questions on the decks and in the passages. Everyone would have the same information at the same time as he metered it out. Tomorrow, he would begin to train the men to execute The Plan.

That night when he crawled into bed, he gathered a pillow under his arm, but it was no substitute for Eliza. Simultaneously he wished she was with him and was glad she was away during this ordeal.

In truth, ridding the world of *Black Death* pirates was less altruistic than people imagined. His motives were self-inclined. He could not take Eliza to sea if they had a good chance of running into the *Black Death* again, and he wanted to rid himself of the pernicious apprehension that made him feel chronically uncertain. He knew the pirates would come again, not only for precious metals but for him. And not least, he wanted to honor the crew and passengers who died under his watch. They deserved the honor.

As the night wore on, Littledove became more and more conscious of how carefully he had to lead the men who, stuck in the middle of the ocean, had no choice but to follow him. And he had misrepresented himself as a military man. The last time he led men on the *Bessie*, he failed them. That the odds had not been even and he had done everything possible would never compensate for the fact that they all died. At least not for him.

From the night table, he pulled a flier and unfolded it to bolster his optimism. A consortium of American nautical industry leaders, as well as the English, German, Dutch, Spanish, French, and United States governments, were all offering rewards for the destruction of the *Black Death* and the capture or death of its leader, Benedict Pascal, a man with a long history of ill doings. If all went well, he planned to use the money to buy a new ship. If things did not go well, he was certain he would not need any ship. But he had to take that chance.

He closed his eyes and recalled the brilliant yellow silk brocade vest on a man who stood on the deck of the *Black Death* waiting for his minions to storm the *Bessie* and kill everyone on board. Littledove was certain none of that blood ever stained that vest directly, and the men who did the killing were too blinded with greed and grandeur to be aware of how ignominiously they were being used or to care about what they were doing. When a strong man leads, weaker men will go anywhere he steps, even if straight into hell. And most men were not that strong.

He was keenly aware that any man who gave such sadistic orders was not to be underestimated. Most pirates allowed crew and passengers to live if they were not fussy, and even the captain, if he was not arrogant. Most were honorable to women on board.

But this *Black Death* captain belonged in another realm, too disconnected from the essence of compassion to live among humans. The absence of compassion, more so than the presence of any brilliant criminal quality, was what made such a being dangerous.

Littledove wondered about the men who joined forces with such a leader. Surely wealth could not compensate for marring one's soul with such destruction. He hoped that such men were less aware than they were brash and their blindness would panic them as easily when they were taken by surprise. Hope and Faith.

Chapter Fifteen

FACING THE NEMESIS

Littledove trained and trained and trained the crew. He trained them every day, sun or rain, calm seas or not. He even trained them at night, just in case, because nothing could be predicted. He trained them for when they thought they would be prepared and for when they thought they might be taken by surprise. He trained until the men spoke of nothing else and could recite what they were supposed to do, whenever he asked them.

He made certain they knew the key points of what would make the plan work and that they were prepared to improvise to preserve those points if things went wrong. And then he trained them some more. He had chosen well. The men's military training rose out of their shadows and took them over.

When he felt the men were ready, Littledove reversed direction and headed north again, deviating slightly to pass two ports so his direction would be noticed. He wanted the *Bessie* and her direction mentioned in the Ship Observation Report. He stopped the *Bessie* at the Gullen Straits, a place where several ships had been wrecked in storms. In the straits, he angled her so she looked as if she had drifted from the open sea.

He commanded Cosmos to slaughter and cook the pig and gave another sailor the honor of spiking the pig's head, with the skin still attached, on the main mast. Then they waited, hiding in the hull, except for the men who had the watch on deck, and eating cold meals to not create smoke. Training continued every night so they would not be seen by day.

Eleven days passed with the stink of the rotting pig on the mast spreading over miles. The skin of the body was threatening to separate from the head when the poor sailor stationed in the crow's nest below it pulled a cord that released a red flag at the base of the mast, because voices carried over water. Another sailor snatched the red flag and ran into the hull.

Upon seeing the flag, Littledove gave the signal, and every man on the *Bessie* slunk into position with the instinct that comes from thorough training. Some men ducked into crates that appeared to be haphazardly abandoned on the deck but that Littledove arranged to allow his whispered commands to be communicated around the deck and into the hull without needing to raise his voice and risk being heard across the water. Each crate hid one or two men.

One crate obscured the helm so the helmsman could not be easily seen, even if he was camouflaged in burlap. His job was to keep the *Bessie* pointed at the same angle. Littledove assigned another man to replace him in case something went wrong.

If all went well … If every man did what he was supposed to do … If no man panicked … If no man made a serious mistake … If the plan was well conceived, the action would be quick, decisive, and glorious.

If.

Everything was still in the future state of "If." Now had not yet arrived with its infestation of imperfections.

Seemingly abandoned but adorned with a rotting pig on the mast, with sails neatly dowsed, and with randomly strewn crates marked for the Dutch Ministry of Precious Metals on the deck, Littledove hoped the *Bessie* had the aura of a true mystery. He wanted to entice with a riddle that invited exploration.

Inside one of the crates with his spyglass, Littledove found himself wanting to be everywhere on the ship he was not. He wanted to be on the foredeck so he could have a better view, but he did not want to raise suspicions by placing a crate in an obvious place. He also wanted to be under deck where the cannons were so he could supervise those preparations, but he had to be on deck in a crate to call the shots.

His breath grew shallow as he became hyper-vigilant and silently recited a variety of phrases to keep himself calm: *Be patient. Trust your men. Be patient. Let the moment come to you. Be patient.*

The *Black Death* stopped a fair distance away. By the angle of her bow and how the men were aiming the deck munitions, Littledove determined the *Black Death* would enter the strait from a specific point. He sent the helmsman a correction that would bring the *Bessie* parallel with the *Black Death*'s broadside when the *Black Death* slipped into place. At least that part would go well.

The man nearest him relayed his command to another who then relayed it to another until the command went around the deck and made its way into the hull. Littledove drilled the sailors for hours to relay tongue twisters around the ship so words would travel accurately and undistorted through all the accents. Eliza would have termed the practice as elocution for sailors and perhaps even have been proud of him.

The *Bessie* tilted a bit at the redistribution of the cannons' weight. He had trained the men to move the cannons with excruciating slowness, so the shift appeared like a ship's natural movement on water.

The *Black Death* held her position to the *Bessie* outside the strait for such a long time that Littledove began to question the logic of his plan, so carefully thought out and rehearsed in his head for months and so carefully distilled into his men for weeks. He hoped his men trusted their best weapon was patience, although his was already fraying.

After much too much time, the *Black Death* moved into the strait. Her sailors began loading the small deck cannons. Her cannon ports opened.

The sight was intimidating enough to make Littledove feel he might need to piss. Knowing the *Black Death* would not fire if they wanted the cargo was not as comforting now that he faced the open ports. His assertive hope now felt like a mere assumption.

"All men. Hold!" commanded Littledove in a loud whisper. His word whipped around the deck and under. The men held. To himself, he chanted, *Be patient. Trust your men. Let the moment come to you. Be patient, patient.*

He comforted himself knowing Bolt reinforced each crate, so if something heavy landed on it, anyone inside had a good chance of surviving. Bolt built the walls thick with wood and iron plates so bullets would not penetrate. A bonus was that if a bullet struck the iron plate, it might ring against the metal, presumably a precious one.

Littledove explained over and over that pirates would not sink a ship before they boarded it to see if she had cargo. All he needed was for each man to have faith in that and not panic. He drilled into them that they would be safe in the crates on deck because the pirates did not want to damage the precious cargo. The first shots were always meant to intimidate the crew and to stop the ship. For their convenience, the *Bessie* was already stopped, and no crew appeared to be on board.

"All men. Hold," he commanded again in a hoarse whisper.

And just in time because the *Black Death* fired four of her deck cannons. Small cannon balls crashed onto the *Bessie*'s deck and rolled into crates that did not move because Bolt screwed them into the deck to behave as if they contained metals too heavy for a small cannonball to shift.

A chain struck a yardarm that cracked and fell across the deck, unraveling a sail that obscured Littledove's line of sight when the wind flapped it. Another chain struck his crate. He startled at the sound of cracking wood and banged his head against the top of the crate. Other projectiles skittered over the deck, banging against the bulwark.

The future had slipped into the now, and imperfections were manifesting rapidly. Fortunately, Bolt had drilled several peepholes in each crate, and Littledove moved to another one. From the trajectory of the missiles, Littledove knew the *Black Death* had intentionally tried not to hit the crates head on.

"Cannons starboard and ready," someone reported in a whisper.

Littledove whispered back, "Aye. All men. Hold."

He was surprised he could speak because his mouth was so dry. He continued migrating among four peepholes, depending on how the fallen sail flapped, feeling each peephole was shrinking in size the more he needed to see.

With no evidence of men on the *Bessie*'s deck, the *Black Death* inched closer. A man on the *Black Death* fired with a rifle into some of the crates. Instinctively, Littledove pulled away from a peephole. He strained to hear if anyone in another crate was struck. It had not occurred to him to leave tourniquets and bandages in each crate in case someone was injured. Imperfections, imperfections everywhere. He released the thought when no one complained and continued to bob between peepholes to get the best view possible.

The *Black Death* bobbled in as close as she could come, then reoriented her sails to keep the wind from filling them and making her move away. The *Bessie* was now within boarding distance.

Through his spyglass, Littledove kept track of a group of men conferring on the deck of the *Black Death*. They were passing around a spyglass and gesturing to the pig with its crown of flies and seagulls. They studied the crates strewn on the *Bessie*'s deck, frequently pointing at one, then another, and another.

They were dying of curiosity. Only now was Littledove certain they would board and The Plan might actually work.

He spotted a bright green striped vest with the shimmer of silk. Only a man who could wear a vest as yellow as the one Littledove saw before would also wear a vest as green as this one. He was looking at the same man, the captain of the *Black Death*, rumored to be the infamous Benedict Pascal.

"Pias. Prepare," whispered Littledove with a burst of gusto.

His command was whisked around the deck and into the hull where Cosmos waited with the cannons and the men he had trained to fire them. Littledove kept his eyes on the *Black Death*'s deck with his spyglass. Someone began preparing to again shoot the deck cannons at the *Bessie*, but the green-vested captain turned and gave an order that made the same men turn their attention to lowering lifeboats into the water. Other men positioned themselves on the deck with rifles to shoot at anything that might move on the *Bessie*.

Littledove waited. A minuscule bit of time would pass between when the pirates left their ship and when they could board the *Bessie*. He could not see when the men in the lifeboats reached the water, but he knew how long it typically took sailors to lower a lifeboat.

Now. All the future had turned into Now.

Littledove whispered, "Pias. Fire!"

He felt, more than heard, his command tumble down the stairs as it was relayed one man at a time to Cosmos in the hull. Littledove had timed this delay over and over until any variation fell within seconds, but he always underestimated how difficult it was to wait until the command was executed. He barely breathed as he waited for his words to make their way down the stairs, into the *Bessie*'s newly minted cannon deck; for the exploding cannonballs to be lit; for the ignited balls to be rolled into the cannons; for the cannons' fuses to be ignited; for the ports to be flung open; for the cannons to shoot.

The new design of the port shutters allowed them to be opened in an instant so as not to give the *Black Death* any more warning than necessary. But for that to happen, the timing of all the other actions had to be impeccable because any cannonball that exploded before it was shot out of a port would destroy the *Bessie*'s hull.

He was almost in hives from nerves, imagining the hundreds of mistakes that could be made, but he did not take his eyes off the green-vested captain. He knew the moment the ports opened, not because he heard them but because he saw the captain's jaw drop as he leaned over the bulwark to get a closer look at what he probably did not think was possible.

"Lobcock," hissed Littledove, and the *Bessie*'s cannons fired.

Six cannonballs shot across the water toward the *Black* Death, which Cosmos would later claim he could almost touch, she was so close. One took out the rudder before it exploded over the water. The other five ripped into the *Black Death*'s hull before exploding. Seconds later, the deck boards went flying into the air when a flame spread to the magazine.

"Bolt. Fire!" Littledove shouted, knowing he could no longer be heard through the commotion of explosions and panicking men on the *Black Death*.

Bolt, an army-trained marksman, shot into a target disguised as a pile of seaweed on the shore. The shots triggered a mechanism that made the pile of straw under the seaweed catch fire, subsequently igniting a fuse that sent white, blinding fireballs toward the *Black Death*. The explosion was a harmless distraction to confuse while Cosmos again prepared the cannons to shoot a second round. The men on the *Black Death* had no idea no one was on the shore. For all they knew, they were surrounded.

The next set of cannonballs crashed into the part of the hull closest to the water, as Littledove instructed in The Plan. Those cannonballs exploded, blowing out the outer boards of the hull and making the *Black Death*'s cannons fall into her lower deck. Water flooded into the *Black Death*'s hull at such speed that she immediately tilted, sending all men stumbling to one side of the deck. Several bodies flew out of the hull like birds from a tree. Pirates began lowering lifeboats in whatever order was possible, every man for himself.

With an enormous sense of satisfaction, Littledove watched the *Black Death* spurt geysers of water while going down in flames. The *Bessie*'s cannons fired again, this time directly into the angled deck.

"Clear the rigging!" shouted Littledove as he jumped out of his crate, a signal that the other men should also spring into action.

Some men began to untangle the rigging from the fallen yardarm so the *Bessie* could depart. Other men began to put out fires from *Black Death* boards that had landed on the *Bessie* during explosions.

"Captain, she's gonna fall on us," reported Neve, his voice quivering.

"Aware of that," said Littledove. "Clear the rigging."

The *Black Death* tipped dangerously close to the *Bessie* with a mast that was turning into a pole of rolling flames. If the mast fell on the *Bessie*, her rigging would surely catch on fire.

Littledove ran under deck, shouting "Pias! Pias! Hold! Hold!"

He flailed to a stop in front of Cosmos. "These three. Fire these three. No! No! Regular balls. Not exploding ones. Regular ones. These three."

Cosmos began loading the three cannons. He pulled Littledove out of the way just before the cannons blasted. The *Black Death* released more boards into the water and jerked to one side. Then she continued tilting toward the *Bessie*.

"The last two! Fire the last two. Fast!" shouted Littledove, hoping to push the *Black Death* away from the *Bessie* with the force of cannonballs. He thought of one hundred other things he could have done on deck to prevent fire from spreading if the *Bessie* caught on fire, but having the mast miss the *Bessie* was the only action that would now prevent the disaster.

"Stay out of the goddamned way!" Cosmos shouted at him as the men loaded the last two cannons on one end.

Littledove shifted his attention between the mast of flames and the *Bessie*'s hull. The mast was destined to fall on the *Bessie*. Nothing was going to stop it. The *Black Death* was tipping faster than the cannon fuses were burning. The *Black Death* groaned mightily as she continued to lower her flaming mast over the *Bessie*.

Littledove shoved Cosmos aside and threw himself over the last cannon to tip it down to the *Black Death*'s deck. The last thing Littledove heard before the cannon went off under his belly was Cosmos shouting curses. Littledove's next sensation was being drenched with a bucket of water that Cosmos threw on him because his shirt was on fire.

Still sprawled on the floor, Littledove looked through a port in time to see a cannon-ball shatter the *Black Death*'s deck at the base of the mast, causing the burning mast to collapse into a shower of less deadly sparks over the *Bessie*. With a series of deafening groans, the *Black Death* finished tipping without her mast.

Littledove almost passed out from relief. He checked his side to find it red and weeping from a burn. The pain had not yet registered. He took Cosmos' three-fingered hand to rise from the floor.

"Good work," Littledove muttered and bolted up to the deck.

From there, he could feel the heat of the fire on the *Black Death*. He sent Neve to evaluate the chances of the *Bessie* catching fire.

"Water's full of burning things, Cap'n, but there's little fires on deck now almost out," Neve reported when he returned.

Littledove looked around. The rigging was still tangled from the fallen yardarm. The boatswain was directing every available person to work on untangling the ropes. Anyone not working on the rigging was pulling up buckets of water and dumping them on small deck fires. Everyone was working fast, but not fast enough to quell Littledove's anxieties.

"Make another round. Tell me if the ship catches fire anywhere. If it does, take as many men as you need to put it out and reinforce from the inside."

Neve was about to take off when he stopped short and squinted over the water. "That the cap'n, sir?"

Littledove swung around. "Where?"

"Over there, sir?"

He saw the spot of bright green bobbing in a lifeboat with four other men. The four men toiled hard at rowing the boat because as the *Black Death* sank, she was creating a suction that was pulling everything around her toward herself, including the *Bessie*, which might then still catch on fire.

"Bolt!" shouted Littledove.

"Fifteen minutes. We'll be loose then," called Bolt. He returned his attention to the rigging.

Littledove pointed toward the water. "Take him down."

Bolt scanned the water with wild eyes before he grinned. He picked a path through the deck toward Littledove and said with a deadpan humor, "Aye, aye, Cap'n. But he's got a nice vest, and dead men don't tell who their tailor is."

"Do it in ten minutes. Then go back to the rigging."

Bolt raised his rifle and shot each man in the boat, taking care to miss the green-vested captain. Then he shot several holes in the rowboat. Little springs of water began to sprout between the dead men's bodies. Captain Green Vest, as Bolt took to calling him, began to frantically look around while trying to form a plan to stay alive. He put his hand over the little springs of water in an effort to stop the boat from filling. Bolt continued to methodically shoot holes in the boat.

He reloaded the rifle and handed it to Littledove. "Can you shoot? Keep his arms up. Shoot anything he tries to touch, all right? Just keep his hands in the air."

Littledove knew he was no Bolt when it came to hitting targets from a distance, but he was accurate enough to hit a rowboat. He released a shot each time Captain Green Vest tried to touch anything. He shot at the sides of the boat, a dead man (again), a sprit of water, the one oar that had not yet fallen off the boat. He shot at the water filling the rowboat.

Captain Green Vest sat crotch deep in water with his arms raised, too afraid to lower them in case he lost a hand. Littledove could see by his rapid glances that he was measuring whether he could hold up against the suction of the sinking *Black Death*, which he most likely could not.

Bolt began swinging his lasso. He swung it until he got into a rhythm, then gently sent it gliding across the water. The loop landed around one of the captain's wrists. The captain's instinct to preserve his life prevailed, and he grabbed the rope as the rowboat began to slip under water. With a tug, Bolt tightened the noose around the captain's wrist.

Bolt and Neve pulled the rope hand over hand, as if hauling a giant mackerel on board. They rolled the green-vested captain over the bulwark and landed him on deck, a wet mess of a man. Together, they manhandled him to his feet.

Littledove stood back and waited, feet apart, hands loosely resting on his belt. "Captain Pascal?"

Pascal nodded as he blinked through the saltwater running into his eyes.

"Welcome aboard, sir." Littledove pulled the pistol from his holster and shot Pascal in the knee.

Pascal screamed and tumbled forward. He would have fallen on his face had Bolt and Neve not held him up.

Littledove replaced his pistol in his holster. If Pascal could not feel the heartache he caused, he could suffer from the same physical pain he inflicted on others.

To Bolt and Neve, he said, "Put 'im in the brig."

"He'd be easier to handle dead," said Bolt. "And you can just take the vest, Cap'n."

"Nay, he'll stink up the ship. Like the pig. Take him down. If he gives you trouble, take out his other knee."

"Aye, aye, Captain," Bolt and Neve said in unison, as if shooting people in the knee was common practice on the *Bessie*.

As they dragged Pascal away, a sailor came running from the hull. "Cap'n! Cook says the *Black Death* ain't gettin' up no more. Ee says we got extra balls. You want 'im to use 'em up?"

"We sure got balls to spare," said Littledove with great satisfaction now that Eliza was not around to hear him. "Tell him to stop. We're moving out."

He checked to be certain the *Bessie* could still exit with all the debris on the water and a missing sail. The first mate and the boatswain were now instructing men to clear a path around the deck so the sailors could shift the sails. Bolt and some other men were unscrewing the crates from the deck so others could move them to one side.

"Five minutes, Cap'n!" shouted the boatswain.

Littledove held up his hand to indicate he'd heard. The *Black Death* was almost completely under water, and he wanted to fix landmarks in his mind so as not to run the *Bessie* into her if she disappeared entirely.

He took in the commotion of the pirates in rowboats who were trying to row away from the sinking ship. Already some had gotten pulled under by the suction. Those who did not drown would die, marooned on the straits without food or drinkable water. Some might turn to cannibalism in their desperation to live another day.

Littledove hardened his heart to all of them, refusing to even consider that some of them might have redeemable qualities despite what they were doing. The success of ridding the sea of these pirates was tarnished by knowing it could not bring back to life his old crew, Dr. Aves, or Eliza's sisters. At the moment, being a creature without a conscience became something Littledove could envy.

"All clear, Cap'n!" shouted the first mate, recalling him to the moment.

"Loose all s'ls!" he shouted.

The men on the deck pulled on ropes to make the sails magically unfurl without having to release them from the foot lines. Afraid to set men in boats to tow the *Bessie* into the open ocean, Littledove guided her out of the strait one inch at a time at the speed of a snail, with a quick string of precise commands.

Once out of the strait, he took another look at the smolder that was the *Black Death* and shouted, "Set course!"

The sailors cheered triumphantly.

"Wha' about ee pig?" someone asked.

Littledove looked up. Everyone, including men with strong stomachs, who thought they had gotten used to the stench of the rotting pig, coughed with nausea when the wind created a downdraft to the deck. He instructed the mate to bring the pig carcass down when they were under a steady wind and to throw it overboard. It could sink like the *Black Death*.

To reverse direction, Littledove tacked the *Bessie*. When she was well on her way, he left the first mate in charge and went to his quarters where Eliza had once been, where he had hidden her and where she had come out of hiding to care for him, and where they once comforted one another during weeks of misery. The day, despite all its success, was miserably incomplete without being able to tell her what he had done.

He heard the carcass of the pig land on the deck with a squelch amidst cheers and disgusted groans. A little later, sailors cheered when someone threw it overboard with a pitchfork. Littledove now noticed his side stung from the burn.

He took off his shirt and began to dab his chest with an ointment, wishing Eliza were there to tend to him. He stopped dabbing when he caught sight of a pen by the ship's journal and felt the urge to write a letter to her to tell her he had done it as much for her as for himself, to say that even if the world that did not know his true motives, it would benefit from what he had done. He reached for the pen before remembering he had already used the last of the stationery with the little violets. Besides, the nearest post office was in Edith's Bay.

Eliza flickered between grayness and light as consciousness entered her head in flashes. She opened her eyes to accept the sunlight and bolted upright with such force she almost fell out of the bed.

Mary caught her just in time. She pushed Mary away, first mistaking her for Harold, then slapped her hands all over her skirt to feel if anyone had undressed her and uncovered the secrets in her petticoat. Parts of her skirt were still wet from her fall, but she was still fully dressed. Eliza fell back onto her pillow. Her head hurt so much she felt sick. She let her head sink fully into the pillow.

"Mr. Bartook informs us you took quite a fall," Dr. Haskell said.

Mr. Bartook informed? Had Harold proposed? She could not remember. Dr. Haskell held her eyelids up while he looked into each eye, making her head hurt even more.

"Miss Strauss," he said to Mary, "please do not allow Mr. Bartook to visit for the following week on the chance that he might incite another incident of hysteria in your dear sister. Keep away anything that might incite her. As you well know, Miss Strauss, women are delicate. And please make sure she stays awake for the next four hours. She has a serious head injury."

Mary nodded demurely. She folded a wet cloth and draped it over Eliza's forehead.

Women are only delicate in the minds of feeble men, Eliza thought as she filled with indignation that made her head hurt even more. Angry at everything and everyone, she wanted to shove Dr. Haskell out of the room, but he began gathering his medical implements with one hand, making clickety, metallic sounds that annoyed her to no end. Eventually he left, escorted down the hall by a footman.

"Come," said Mary. "Let me undress you and get you into a nightgown."

"No!" Eliza sat up and slapped her hands over her skirt. She clutched the edge of the bed as the room swerved around her. "What I mean is— I shall be less tempted to fall asleep if I am fully dressed."

"But your skirt is wet. I can get you another dress."

"No. It is not too wet. I do not feel I want to change. Thank you."

"Then so be it. Will you drink the chocolate I asked for you? Chocolate helps with headaches."

"Yes. Thank you." The last thing she wanted was chocolate, but she would drink it to appease Mary.

"Shall I read to you?"

"No! No. Thank you. My head will hurt more. Read for yourself."

Eliza took two sips of the hot chocolate when it arrived and abandoned the cup. She waited for Mary to leave, but Mary stayed forever, occasionally offering her something to eat or to amuse her.

Eliza refused everything. She could not understand why anyone could expect her to fall asleep with the headache she had. Or would want to play a board game. Or eat anything. When Mary finally left after the prescribed four-hour eternity, Eliza crawled out of bed and fumbled into her nightgown. She put her petticoat where she could grab it easily if she needed to do so. It was still damp with saltwater and smelled like seaweed.

Eliza began milking her recuperation beyond Dr. Haskell's recommended week by mumbling incoherently to people who came to visit her and pretending to get easily confused. When asked, she acted surprised that Harold had been with her and allowed her to fall.

If she did not remember, then Harold would have to propose again, if he *had* proposed. What if he told people he proposed and she had said yes? She could not imagine Harold being sufficiently guileful to do that, but she still worried about the possibility.

When not being observed, Eliza read avidly with a clear mind, stitched together another petticoat of coarser linen with deeper pockets, and thought of Littledove. She all but memorized the book of nautical terms he gave her because every word in the book seemed to spell his name. She waited for letters from any Harey. None arrived. She worried her father had caught on and was withholding them. She worried Littledove could no longer write letters.

At long last, her pretense became too difficult for her to sustain. Feeling defeated, she dressed and went down to the breakfast room in search of a newspaper in which she could check the Ship Observation Report for sightings of the *Bessie*. Dr. Haskell had forbidden her to read newspapers in case the news upset her, and Mary had followed his orders to the letter.

The breakfast room, set up as a buffet, was not crawling with footmen and maids. Eliza served herself toast, coffee, and a small scoop of fruit salad. Littledove loved fruit, craved it when he was at sea, could not eat enough of it when he was on shore. She ate it on his behalf, imagining the gesture might call him forth from the salty, desiccating waters of the ocean. She sat at the table with Mary and her father, avoiding eye contact with both of them.

"How do you expect to recover if you do not eat?" Strauss demanded when she ignored the scrambled eggs, bacon, and potatoes on the sideboard.

"I shall start with this," said Eliza, hoping no one else would tell her to eat something else.

Strauss folded the newspaper in half and slapped it on the table before leaving the room in a steamy silence. Mary leaned back in her chair to make sure he was down the hall before picking up the newspaper.

"How are you feeling?" Mary whispered from behind the newspaper.

"Better, thank you. And you?" Eliza whispered back. She had been ordering tea and crackers and passing them to Mary to help her with the morning sickness.

Mary nodded. "Harold is coming to dinner tonight. Perhaps you shall be well enough to join us."

Eliza nodded, knowing Mary was warning her. Eliza imagined herself reenacting the scene at the beach. Instead of falling, she would push Harold into a rock. Or throw a rock at him. One could not marry a dead man—a notion that brought her thoughts to Littledove. Eliza lost her taste for fresh fruit and put down her spoon.

"Eliza!" said Mary, unable to part her eyes from the newspaper. "What was the name of that captain on that ship?"

Eliza, who was about to take a sip of coffee, let her eyes look over the rim of the cup at her sister. With her lips still on the rim, she asked, "Ship?"

"It says here a captain sank a ship that attacked his ship, the *Black Death*. No, the *Bessie*. That is the name of his ship. The *Black Death* is the name of the ship that attacked. What a horrible name. I cannot imagine what they were thinking. Oh! No wonder. It was full of pirates. It says he captured the other captain ... Benedict Pascal. That sounds French, does it not? And has been awarded ... Oh! That is quite a large sum. William Littledove—that is the name of the captain who sank the pirate ship. Was that the ship you said attacked you? The *Black Death*, I mean? Were you on the *Bessie*? Oh no! I think there is a reference to you here. However, most fortunately, not by name."

Eliza grabbed the newspaper, tipping over Mary's coffee cup in the process. A corner of the paper caught on Mary's plate and dragged bits of scrambled egg across the tablecloth. Toast bounced and fell on the carpet.

"Eliza, sincerely! Have you no manners left in you?" said Mary as she wiped her dress and patted the tablecloth with her napkin. Coffee stains and egg crumbs were everywhere. "Now I have to change. And I was so looking forward to wearing this dress today."

Unable to contain herself, Eliza moved her lips as if tasting the words on the paper as she read:

The pirate ship known as the *Black Death* was sunk at the Gullen Straits by Captain William Littledove of the *Bessie*, a cargo Windjammer. The notorious pirate Benedict Pascal has been turned in to the custody of Edith Bay officials, where he will face trial for his crimes at sea after his leg is amputated due to an injury during his capture. No other men were turned in to custody.

Captain Littledove declined to be interviewed, but Cosmos Pias, a retired army lieutenant and the Cannon Master during the battle, said the *Bessie* was armed with six cannons that were fired with exploding cannonballs to sink the *Black Death*.

The *Black Death* sported black sails when attacking ships but wore typical white sails when docked, thus evading officials who sought her. She was also rumored to be a Galleon that was painted red when she was, in fact, a Brigantine painted gray. The name on the ship was not *Black Death*, but *Emmaline*, a ship stolen in the Pacific Ocean under the name of Petite Dragon.

The *Bessie* was the ninth ship, first above the Meridian, to be attacked by the *Black Death*. The pirates previously operated in the south, where they pillaged eight ships and took countless lives. Only two persons survived the attack on the *Bessie*, one of which was Captain Littledove. The other passenger remains unidentified.

Navy ships were sent to the Gullen Straits, where the battle took place, to search for survivors, although it is thought that none shall be alive by the time the rescue ships arrive. None of the crew on the *Bessie* was killed or seriously injured during the attack.

Captain Littledove shall be receiving significant fiduciary rewards from the United States government, as well as the French, English, German, Spanish, and Dutch governments, the United States Association of Shipping Industrialists, the United States Navy, the Edith's Bay Captain's Club, and the Van der Joost Foundation. Additional bonuses will be paid by the United States government for the capture of Captain Benedict Pascal and his return to stand trial in Edith's (continued on page 5)

Eliza stopped reading and crushed the newspaper into her lap. She was so relieved that she could not hold up her arms to turn the page. With her forehead in one palm, she tried to not giggle as a zephyr of lightheadedness whisked through her.

When she looked up, Mary was staring at her, brows arched, eyes wide, lips slightly parted. Eliza imagined she must have looked the same in the parlor when Mary was declaring her desire to become a mother.

"Yes," said Eliza to set the tone of how much she was willing to discuss. She straightened her back. "I believe the captain mentioned in the paper is the same Captain Littledove of the *Bessie*."

Eliza eyed Mary as Mary continued to study her until they both smiled and, on the verge of laughter, looked away. They were close, despite lacking affinity for one another. They could not keep secrets from each other, not even secrets that had never been articulated.

Mary looked at the mess of stains and bits of food around her place setting and after a moment asked, "Is that all you are going to eat?"

"Perhaps I shall have some eggs," said Eliza, feeling her soul unclench.

Chapter Sixteen

PINNING TAILS

When Littledove announced his plans to visit Eliza, Captain and Mrs. Harey exchanged looks and twitched their eyebrows. He immediately became suspicious.

With oodles of enthusiasm, Mrs. Harey then said, "Perhaps you should pick up a few of the traditions people like them follow."

"What's that mean—traditions?" asked Littledove.

"They tend to have some peculiarities when they dine. It would do you well to make them feel comfortable by doing things the way they do them."

Littledove was not exactly sure what Mrs. Harey was suggesting, but her polite subtlety made him think she had been waiting, perhaps for years, for the opportunity to make this suggestion. He glanced at Captain Harey to see if he knew what was going on, but Captain Harey poured himself another cup of coffee without revealing anything.

Eating traditions? The only thing he could think of was table manners. Mrs. Stoop once taught him table manners when he was young enough to stay with Captain Stoop at his house, but he usually forgot them during voyages because no one else practiced them, and everyone made fun of him when he did.

Littledove recalled Eliza always put a napkin over her lap when she ate, even when they were eating salted beef and peas and no one was watching. Eliza always sliced the beef with precise, delicate gestures that made him feel as if he had giant, floppy duck feet for hands.

At the Hareys' house, she ate everything using a variety of utensils that to him always looked like a collection of knives and forks and spoons without much to distinguish one from another of its kind. He usually ate what was on his plate with whatever utensil his hand touched first.

Far more intimidating than a ship full of pirates was the number of plates Mrs. Harey placed on the table and the rows of silverware she laid out the day lessons in eating traditions began. She began by showing him how to remove a napkin without sending the artillery of silverware on it clattering to the floor. She stressed keeping the utensils in order so he would know which ones to use as the meal progressed.

To his surprise, Mrs. Harey laughed when he proudly put the napkin on his lap (at least, he thought he knew that much) and informed him that only women placed their napkins on their laps. Men tucked it into their collars and spread it across the front of the shirt to prevent their shirts from getting stains.

"What about women? Don't they spill on themselves?" he asked.

"Ladies do not spill," said Mrs. Harey.

Littledove complied. He remembered the men on the *Benjamin Stuart* tucking their napkins into their collars, and he could not imagine Eliza spilling anything on herself.

Mrs. Harey held up cards with the names of foods, and he was to engage in a pantomime of properly picking up the correct utensils and eating the food from the correct plate. Steak, bread, butter, fish, salad, artichoke, bacon, asparagus, peas, potato, custard, cake, coffee—each had its own set of utensils and ritual of how to be consumed. He did well until she held up a card with the word "Escargot."

"Snails?" Littledove clenched his eyes and stuck out his tongue. "Ah, don't need a fork for something I'd never eat. Even a marooned man can find something better to eat on shore than snails."

To his further apprehension, Mrs. Harey mentioned that some foods came with additional silverware, as in the case of escargot that were presented with tongs with which to hold the shells and a tiny pitch fork with which to extract the snail. She didn't show him examples of the implements but said he would be sure to recognize them because they came on the plate with the snails.

Then she consoled Littledove by telling him that if he simply could not eat what was served, he could push the repulsive food around the plate and cut it into smaller and smaller pieces while conversing with charm until a servant removed the plate. The lesson did not comfort him because she also told him never to cut escargot. It was to go into his mouth whole—a thought that almost made him gag.

Captain Harey, although he did not associate with the like of the Strausses, was familiar with people like them because he was a member of the Edith's Bay Captain's Club, and those people often attended fundraisers for the club. Captain Harey took him to a tailor to be fitted for day and evening attire, and they packed the clothes with precise notes about when to wear what tie and vest with what suit. Littledove was astonished that he would have to change for each meal that was served under the same roof only hours apart.

Then Captain Harey passed him back to Mrs. Harey, who taught him how and when to bow and what to say when greeting people. She handed him a list of subjects never to discuss and a list of topics with which he could start a conversation with anyone. She warned him that if he swore at Eliza's house, the butler would be instructed to remove his tongue with pliers.

She filled him in about what to expect in general, including the hierarchy of butlers, footmen, groundskeepers, kitchen workers, cleaners, valets, and lady's maids. She taught him where he would be most likely to run into them and how to address them—the only part at which he felt he might do well because he was used to addressing sailors.

Mrs. Harey gave him a book of etiquette that he read cover to cover in one night while trying to memorize everything in it. By the wee hours of morning, he realized manners had to be why women always had headaches. He left the Hareys' house convinced he had visited many foreign countries whose people had fewer questionable customs.

Fully armed with etiquette, Littledove approached the enormous, multi-turreted mansion where Eliza lived. It made his *Bessie* look like a dinghy. He sat in the carriage, studying the mansion and suffering doubts about whether he could pull off this deception about having manners.

After all, he had only had manners for a week while everyone else in the house with Eliza had been raised with them until they were second nature. He still wasn't even clear about the purpose of having half a dozen different forks for one meal when one would do just as well if he licked it clean between savory and sweet servings.

Using European castles for guidance, Littledove aimed the carriage toward what he thought was the front entrance. Two men in matching uniforms came out of two little doors that flanked the massive front door. One opened the carriage door for him to disembark and escorted him to the front door. The other bowed to him and drove the carriage to the carriage house.

They seemed dressed better than he was, and Littledove felt his ability to command servants as he did sailors waver. He had to remind himself not to bow to them because they were servants, so said Mrs. Harey. Inside the entrance, he came across a man dressed like a giant penguin.

"Good afternoon, sir. Who may I say is calling, sir?" asked the butler as he took Littledove's brand new hat and overcoat.

"Captain William Littledove, sir."

The butler's eyelids twitched when Littledove addressed him as sir. "Please come this way, sir."

Littledove almost lost his balance twisting around behind the butler to look at the enormous height of the great hall whose walls were covered with paintings of every conceivable item on earth. He was shocked to see, tucked among the paintings, statues of naked women, some without arms or legs but still retaining the bits that distinguished them as women.

The only other place Littledove had seen statues of naked women so prominently displayed had been in a high-class brothel in Japan where, early in his sailing days, he had spent nearly a month's salary on steam baths and pleasures. Fortunately, after that indulgence, he got wise about money.

With a deep sense of relief, he turned his attention from the statues to children who were giggling and cheering and some adults who were laughing. At least he understood those sounds. Already he was feeling like a barbarian, and he had not yet seen Eliza.

The butler led him through the etched double-glass doors into a parlor where children dressed in party clothes were engaged in a happy raucous. He immediately saw Eliza, who was in the center of a commotion, blindfolded and holding a paper donkey tail.

Children were turning her around. They stepped back, giggling with mischief. Eliza took a step forward, her back to the paper donkey that was pinned to the wall.

"You terrible children!" another woman scolded playfully as she stepped forward to turn Eliza around so she would at least be facing the donkey on the wall. "Please carry on now, Miss Strauss."

Eliza tottered toward the wall, holding the paper tail in her outstretched hand. The butler took a deep breath, but before he could announce Captain William Littledove's arrival, Littledove placed his hand on the butler's shoulder and raised a finger to his own lips. The butler's polite smile wavered at the irregularity, but he abided.

By now, everyone in the parlor was becoming progressively quieter. Only a few children playing a board game remained oblivious to Littledove.

"Am I that far off?" asked Eliza as the chatter diminished. "Oh, do tell me I have not wandered off into another room."

Littledove stepped in front of her. He slipped his hand over her hand holding the paper tail. Eliza stopped at his touch. Her soft fingers stroked his calloused palm. He folded his hand around hers and, with his other hand, pulled the paper tail from Eliza's fingers and blindly slapped it over the ribs of the paper donkey.

"Milady," he said softly.

In one motion, Eliza pulled off the blindfold and threw her arms around him. She buried her face in his neck.

"Oh, milady. Milady," Littledove mumbled.

The contours of her body become his new firmament. He lifted Eliza and twirled her around while taking deep breaths of her and feeling the gentle slopes of her waist. They released one another into the astonished silence of the room. Even the children fell quiet.

Littledove swung out his arm and slapped the butler on the shoulder. "You can go ahead now."

"Captain William Littledove," announced the butler and neatly stepped out of the parlor.

With that formality over, Littledove seated Eliza and knelt by her side to stroke her tears off her cheeks with his thumb. "Milady, I didn't come this far to make you cry."

Eliza was mouthing *Will, Will, Will,* apparently unable to speak out loud. He wiped away more tears with his thumbs and took in the sheer loveliness of her face, even with tears and puffy eyes that welcomed him so openly.

"Who the devil are you?" shouted Strauss as he came charging through the guests.

Littledove rose to his full height in front of Strauss, knowing well that good height could make even a spindly figure like him look intimidating. He had not forgotten what Strauss had said to him at the Hareys'.

Eliza rose and slipped between them. "Father, may I please introduce Captain William Littledove from Edith's Bay. Captain Littledove and I are good friends. No disrespect was meant or taken."

"Ah, none," affirmed Littledove, looking at Eliza with a happiness he could not constrain. He scanned the parlor, wondering who on earth all these people were and why they had to be here now.

A woman with some of Eliza's facial features quietly stepped toward him, discreetly looking him over. "May I ask if you are the Captain Littledove of the *Bessie*?"

"Yes ma'am. I am. Well, was. Sold her." He now remembered to bow.

She curtsied back slowly, still looking him over. "And the un-doer of the *Black Death*, if I may ask?"

"Nay, not by meself. I's got lots 'n' lots of help with that, I did."

"Miss Strauss, may I present to you Captain William Littledove," said Eliza. "Captain Littledove, my sister, Miss Mary Strauss."

"Did you see real pirates?" asked a little boy, wide-eyed with fascination. "Aunt Eliza was attacked by pirates. But she says she didn't see much because she was hid."

"Hidden," someone corrected gently.

Littledove crouched to be eye level with the boy, a gesture that drew the other children toward him. "I saw lots of pirates. Lots of them! And I made them all afraid!"

He let out a loud, maniacal laugh that made the children back away, but when he winked and smiled, they all swarmed toward him again, laughing and clamoring with questions about the pirates and what happened and how he did it. Even the adults began to laugh as he gave huge, playfully exaggerated answers to the children's little questions.

A man stepped in next to Eliza and glared at him as if he were an ashy chimney sweep who showed up on the wrong day. "Perhaps Captain Littledove has so impressed the children he would now like a try at pin-the-tail."

Missing the undertone of insult, the children cheered at the suggestion as Littledove crouched on the floor with them. Triumphantly, the man held out the blindfold and a paper tail.

"Captain William Littledove, Mr. Harold Bartook," Eliza said almost in a whisper.

Littledove took in Harold's proximity to Eliza and narrowed his eyes. Harold had all the makings of a first-class twit, including thick glasses, oily hair, and a chin pointier than a leprechaun's. He could not believe Eliza's father wanted her to marry this man.

He stood from his crouch and glanced at the paper donkey on the wall. "What's the prize?"

Now, everyone laughed at the notion that a grown sea captain would even play, much less care about the prize.

"You get to pick!" said a little girl. She held out a basket full of cast-iron animals. "There's a white pony, a brown pony, a cow, a pig, and a sheep left."

"Now, how can anyone resist that?" Littledove said to the girl.

He snapped the blindfold out of Harold's hand and handed it to Eliza, sending Harold and Eliza's father into a smolder that was not lost on anyone.

Littledove bowed his head while Eliza set to task. He wrangled with the impulse to kiss her while she blindfolded him and afterwards as well. She turned him a few times, as he noted the difference between a turn and a hug was negligible, but any sign of affection would be caught by everyone, and he still wasn't sure what Eliza had told anyone.

"Am I at least facing the ass?" asked Littledove as Eliza held his hand longer than she needed to slip the paper tail into it and patted him on the back.

"Yes, Captain. I have made certain of that."

"Good, because I seen what they did with you."

He tucked the tail into his vest pocket and moved forward with a strong but cautious stride, one arm extended. He stopped when he touched the rectangle on which the donkey was printed.

With both hands, he stroked the paper until he located the edge and felt his way toward the tail end of the donkey. He ran his fingers to the corners and back to the center. With one finger pressed to mark the center, he pulled the tail from his pocket with his other hand and pinned it about two knuckles in from the edge of the sheet.

The astonished oohs and aahs in the room confirmed he was right on target. He pulled off the blindfold. The tail was perfectly placed, closer to the correct spot than any other tail.

"That was very impressive, Captain Littledove," said a grandfatherly gentleman. "I must say, I have never seen it played with strategy."

"Helps to have a plan. Can't just flail around like a fool." Littledove held out the blindfold to Harold. "Your turn."

"I should say not," said Harold.

"Perhaps Captain Littledove would like a glass of wine instead of a toy as his prize?" Eliza asked to diffuse the tension.

Littledove looked around. No one else held a wine glass. "Nay, thanks." He turned to the little girl holding up the basket of iron farm animals to him. "I don't know. What do you think I should pick?"

The little girl shrugged. "I like the white pony."

"Me too. That's what I'll pick." Littledove reached into the basket and pulled out the white pony. "Tell you what. Why don't you keep it safe for me?"

The girl giggled, immediately becoming the envy of the rest of the children. After all, no one else had a toy pony from someone who'd defeated pirates.

Littledove gave Harold a jaundiced eye, regretting having wasted concern about him. Eliza's father concerned him more because Littledove was certain her father already suspected what Eliza might not yet have told him. The man was a brute, but he did not lack intelligence.

A new, more serious game had begun. Harold was not yet aware he had been eliminated. The real game was now between Littledove and Strauss. Eliza was still the prize.

During dinner, Strauss studied Littledove's mechanical caution when he ate, first checking what utensil everyone else was picking up before picking up his own, as if he had just read a lady's magazine article about table manners before sitting at a table for the first time. Strauss festered as he listened through the din of voices and table clatter to the conversation Littledove was having.

"If I am not being too impertinent, Captain, may I ask if you shall be retiring now that you have sold your ship?" asked Mrs. Bodun on his right.

"Retire? Nay, nay. I still got some life in me. I's got a new one on order. She's being put together now in Edith's Bay. A van der Joost ship, she is. Always wanted one of them. I'll still miss the *Bessie*, though. She was my first."

"May I presume you have made the acquaintance of Mr. van der Joost?"

"Me? No. Don't know him personal, but I's real familiar with his ships."

"Was the *Bessie* badly damaged during the attack?"

"Not so much. She just got old and needed more new parts than she'd good ones left. I's going to scrap her, but the Edith's Bay Historical Society offered a good penny for her, so I sold her to them. That covered most of what I put into her. At least I can go see her if I get homesick. Ah, the *Bessie*! She was a good little ship. Plenty proud of her. Admiral Stoop was always fond of her."

"Admiral Stoop? May I ask how you were acquainted with the admiral?"

"He trained me, ma'am, aye."

"Well, that certainly explains why you were so successful at defeating those pirates. My father was a contemporary of Admiral Stoop ..."

As the conversation tolled on, Strauss tallied the sums of reward monies (or the sums he imagined because he had not yet had a chance to look them up). In newspapers, he read the prize for destroying the pirate ship was substantial enough for Littledove to buy one of van der Joost's ships and have loose change. He knew several European countries offered substantial rewards that Littledove would certainly claim. Perhaps delivering Benedict Pascal alive gave him another coin or two. And Littledove managed to sell an insignificant, half-rotted ship that should have been scrapped to a museum where it would gather the dusts of posterity and bring him honor.

This Littledove could, indeed, be more formidable than his crassness suggested. A man whose astuteness was greater than his education or financial resources could become dangerous. He didn't seem to be the kind who could be easily bamboozled.

And he had come to claim Eliza, who had never mentioned him or received a letter from him. Now, Strauss clearly saw Eliza had been waiting for Littledove with the patience of a stone on a shore waiting for the tide to arrive. Strauss looked Eliza over. The stupid girl had made a fool out of him. He began to fume.

The difficult child. Had been since the moment she was born, purple and screeching. Had not changed since. Would not be molded into being submissive in any way. Thought too much. Did not have the grace of her sisters, who were tall and willowy with the coloring of pastel watercolors. Eliza was short with curves a hooker would envy. She was ... impasto oils senselessly smeared on a canvas with a knife.

Her embrace of Littledove revealed everything, as did the tenderness with which he wiped away her tears. Her awareness of Littledove predominated her attitude and infused her with a levity she had not had until he stepped into the house. She looked even happier whenever Littledove's voice drifted across the table.

Too furious to even look at Littledove, Strauss turned his attention to Harold the Fool. By now, Eliza had all but finished abandoning Harold, if it was possible to imagine she could become more negligent toward him, always going out of her way to avoid him and to be absent when he came to visit. Perhaps Strauss overcompensated with Harold's mildness when Eliza reacted so violently against the notion of Simon courting her.

He should have kept Simon for Eliza. Eliza required a man who could control a woman firmly. But within a week, Simon requested permission to court Sarah. Strauss gave him Amelia instead. She was older and needed to be married before she aged into worthlessness. He was not going to support a single spinster when their marriages could benefit his company.

Even if Eliza never took to Harold, she thought well enough of him to make a marriage possible—had this Littledove brute not shown up, that is. Strauss would have to determine how Eliza managed to pull this egregiousness over on him.

Perhaps Mary helped her. He turned his attention to Mary, smiling brilliantly at Richard, who, between smiling back at her, took furtive glances at the breasts of Mrs. Devens, who sat across from him. Mrs. Devens, a woman well past her prime, occasionally pressed her upper arms against her breasts to increase her cleavage because she knew it was being admired—by a young man, no less.

As far as Strauss was concerned, European royalty had been marrying off daughters to maintain peace and foster prosperity among countries for centuries. He was merely adapting the practice to merge corporations. If he could not have a son to lead his company, he would use his collection of worthless daughters to benefit it.

A fleabag sea captain who crawled out of a cargo ship brought him nothing. Harold—the weakest third of Bartook Investments that had a quiet but powerful real estate division specializing in industrial properties worth a fortune—was far more useful. That real estate division could some day make Bartook Investments more powerful than Strauss Investments.

Harold's two brothers ran the real estate part of the business, leaving Harold to handle established accounts. Even they realized he was a fool.

Strauss smirked. Harold had been easy. He'd been so flattered to be given a prominent office next to Strauss' and slathered with praise and promises while instilling him with unbending loyalty. Within the year, Strauss manipulated Harold into exercising his singular talent for making any accounting ledger tell any story it needed to tell.

By the time Harold caught on to the implications of breaching legal business practices for reasons of loyalty, Strauss had taken possession of the ledgers with the creative accounting. He began to terrorize Harold by implying bad outcomes until Harold became afraid and too ashamed to seek help from his brothers. Racked with fear he could end up in prison or bring down the family company by writing lies in ledgers, Harold was too much of an idiot to realize such a ledger could also bring down Strauss Investments.

Strauss waited until Harold could barely function and suggested that marrying well might protect him from bad consequences. Harold, who lacked imagination, except with ledgers, persisted in the courtship, thinking his problems would be quelled if he married Eliza. Besides, the fool sincerely liked Eliza.

Strauss frowned because controlling Harold would not necessarily bring down Bartook Investments. The plan had to be bigger because the remaining two brothers had strong characters. However, one brother was rumored to have a preference for men, and a scandal would bring him down for good, perhaps even land him in prison. Even if he truly preferred women, enough people would be willing to believe he preferred men to make a scandal effective.

That left the third brother. He could never bear the weight of such damage alone. The third brother would then be vulnerable to a merger, and Harold would support a merger if he were married to Eliza. The plan would take time, but Strauss was certain it would work if he worked it slowly. Yes, it would work perfectly.

Strauss nodded to himself, having replaced his anxiety with a sense of being in control. Eliza would marry Harold, the high-ranking magic accountant. Littledove would never have her because Strauss knew that Littledove, like all men, had a price. Even Eliza had a price, and Strauss knew exactly what it was.

After dinner, Eliza perched herself delicately on a parlor sofa across the room from Littledove and concentrated on not looking at him. The majority of guests had already left in an exodus, and the handful of adults who remained collapsed onto sofas, waiting for the servants to serve evening tea.

She kept her head down and listened to the conversation around her as she wondered how Littledove's reserve of patience was faring. Hers was certainly waning. They had exchanged words no more than a half dozen times since he arrived.

Eliza took the opportunity to relinquish her seat to Mary when Mary returned from changing her dress because a child had run into her skirt with a powdered sugar confection. Eliza took several deep breaths to settle her nerves before approaching Littledove.

"Captain Littledove, I recall that you enjoy coffee. May I ask if you would prefer it to tea?"

Littledove jerked into standing when she did not sit next to him. Eliza looked down and smiled, suspecting Mrs. Harey had instructed him to stand whenever he spoke to a woman, even if empty chairs surrounded both of them. He then bowed. Eliza stifled another smile and curtsied back. He was trying so very hard.

"If it's no bother, aye. I'll've coffee. Please."

"It is no bother at all, Captain Littledove." Eliza lowered her voice, and Littledove lowered his head toward her. "My father has a visitor. When he leaves to see him, shall I take you for a tour of the beach?"

"Aye, aye, mila—

"Miss Strauss," whispered Eliza.

"—Miss Strauss. I's real clear that'd be nice."

With enormous restraint, she turned away from Littledove and asked a maid to make coffee for the captain, then sat down across the room next to Mary. Every one of her gestures was choreographed. She was exhausted from pretending.

Her waiting would soon be over, however. Whoever was scribbled in her father's calendar—a man named Bins or Bims or Rems—would soon arrive. Even if her father had forgotten about the appointment, he would have to see the person in his office. Were Littledove not present, her father, who had no real interest in people, much less children, would have already retreated into his office.

Shortly before the hour at which the visitor was scheduled to arrive, Eliza stood up. Littledove's instant sobriety in the form of an eye shift confirmed he understood the moment had arrived. She began an outstanding commotion of promising the ladies around her to be back with the new silk thread of some fabulous, variegated colors and the pattern for the shawl she intended to make with it.

Eliza left the parlor and tucked herself in the opening of the servants' hallway that permitted the servants to move around the house without getting in the way of the house's inhabitants. Her timing was perfect. She sidestepped the butler, who was making his way into the parlor to announce the arrival of the visitor. She watched her father leave the parlor and usher the visitor into his office. The moment the door to the office shut, Eliza sent a footman to fetch Littledove.

The footman fetched Littledove and returned to his post without indicating he saw Eliza pull a houseguest into the servants' hallway. Eliza tugged Littledove through the hidden corridors until they were in a stretch that had no doors to rooms in the main house. Only then did they indulge in the embrace and kiss that had taken godlike restraint to not have happened earlier.

She took the moment to reaffirm Littledove's realness to herself and to release the feelings she had barely been controlling. She might have stayed in his arms forever had she not felt an urgency to continue pulling him by the hand until they emerged through the servants' entrance to the beach at the back of the house, which faced the shore.

Once on the shore in the autumn coolness, she took a deep breath and exhaled forcefully to empty herself of the oppression from the house.

Littledove put his arms around her and pressed her to himself as he stroked her cheek. "Eliza, are you all right? Tell me. Are you all right?"

"I was so worried about you, Will. I thought the sea had taken you. You cannot imagine."

"Almost died from missing you, milady. That's the truth, all right. Didn't mean to leave you hanging, but, you know, I couldn't explain what I was doing and make more worry for you."

"Yes, I read the newspapers. I am so proud of you."

They walked a little farther, holding hands, until Littledove coughed to clear his throat. "You, ah, thought about what I asked you? I mean, I'm on my feet now. The rewards from the *Black Death*'re good enough to buy me a new ship and maybe a house on shore for you a little later. Nothing big like this one here because this one's bigger than the new ship, and a captain can't have a house bigger than his ship, if you get my drift. More like the one Captain Harey's got, with all them neighbors you want. Got to be honest about that.

"But I can hire you a maid for the house and a proper cabin boy to keep the ship quarters tidy when you're on board. Someone older with experience, not some young pipsqueak like I was who needs to be taught everything and still does everything wrong. But a professional cabin boy so you won't have to clean and wash and do things like that. And we can get a steward who knows how to cook real good, someone besides the crew's cook. And I asked for three rooms in the captain's quarters instead of just one, so there'll be room—in case, you know, there might be little ones. Do you think you can be happy with just that, Eliza?"

Eliza frowned superbly. "What about the captain? After all, what good is having a ship, a house, a professional cabin boy, a maid, and a steward if there is no captain in the offerings?" She released her best sly smile.

Littledove threw up his hands. "Milady, why do you laugh at me when I's most defenseless? The captain's what you've most of. You've all of me. All my love. All my soul. All of me is yours forever."

"You are aware that if you marry me, you shall be stuck on a ship with a woman who laughs at you?"

"That mean yes? You're saying yes to me? You haven't changed your mind?"

"Of course, I shall marry you, my captain! I love you."

"Milady!"

Littledove leaned forward to kiss her, but Eliza grabbed him by the arm and pulled him in the opposite direction. "They might see us if we go past this point."

Littledove frowned at the house and settled back to business, albeit with less enthusiasm. "Then all's that left is me asking your father, according to the rules and all that."

"Oh, please do not, Will. Please. He shall say no."

"What? You want to elope?"

Eliza stopped walking, knowing her father would never fund her wedding to someone he did not approve of. "I think a better approach would be not to ask but to inform him. We shall tell him together and see how he responds. But I shall warn you: Father does not like to be defied. Let us go back now. Let us try to get back before he leaves his office."

She looked over the ocean. She hoped Littledove's proposal would have filled her with the happiness her answer had made him feel, but at best, it cast more worry over her. Littledove did not comprehend the dangers that were overwhelming her. She understood confronting her father probably seemed docile after blowing up a ship full of pirates. But she knew better.

"Eliza, are you unhappy with this? Why do you prefer to marry me over any other man in that house?"

"What a silly question, Will. I prefer to marry you over any man on earth because I love you. And because you love me."

Littledove gathered her in an embrace and kissed her. For the moment, Eliza felt her worries replaced by a glimmer that things would work out. She pressed her breasts against Littledove, and from the second kiss, she knew she was making him suffer a bolt of shameless imagination—much like the one she was feeling.

Etty, the kitchen maid, heard one of the footmen say he had seen Miss Eliza and Captain Littledove entering the servants' hallway that emptied on the shore. Thus, when Mrs. Simmons, the head cook, sent Etty into the pantry to get coffee because some guest requested it, she was delighted.

The pantry was always dark because the window had a copper awning to keep the sunlight from ruining stocks like the expensive spices. The awning also had an unintended effect, which was that a person on the shore could not see into the pantry, although a person in the pantry could clearly see everything happening on a stretch of the shore.

Etty lost track of time as she watched Eliza and Littledove strolling down the beach in the dusk, holding hands, heads tipped toward one another in conversation. Then Mrs. Simmons came in, wound up with impatience for the coffee beans.

Catching Etty's fascination with whatever was happening on the shore, Mrs. Simmons stepped beside her to have a look, just in time to see Littledove tip Eliza until her body was almost horizontal to the ground, and with great agility, throw one leg over her and kiss her in a way that would become legendary among the kitchen staff for years. The kiss was a wild, raging, uncontrolled phenomenon that left Etty gasping and Mrs. Simmons with eyes that bulged almost as far as the awning protruded.

"Did yee see tha', missus?" breathed Etty, who could not progress beyond what she had just witnessed.

"Mine yee business, Etty. Take tha' coffee inta ee kitchen. They's waiting," snapped Mrs. Simmons, although she was thinking, *Mr. Bartook, ee really dun stand a chance now.*

Etty scrambled out of the pantry after the rebuke. Mrs. Simmons stayed behind to watch a little longer as Miss Eliza and Captain Littledove disentangled themselves and settled into a whispered conversation punctuated with sly smiles and crooked grins. They approached the house by an angle that indicated they would be entering through the servants' entrance. Mrs. Simmons was surprised any of the Strauss girls knew where the servants' entrance was.

Once in the house, Littledove slipped into the parlor as if he were returning from the lavatory while Eliza remained in the servants' hall so she could enter separately. Before Littledove could even sit down, a maid offered him coffee, which he was more than happy to accept because he felt he needed his wits sharpened for what was coming.

He sat as casually as he could next to a Mrs. Oyl, who was discussing how the French were never to be trusted, based on the horror from Benedict Pascal. He joined the conversation by defending the French on account of his experience with French sailors and food, but Strauss' ceaseless glaring from the corner of the parlor deflated the elation he was feeling after his conversation with Eliza.

Until Eliza entered so many minutes later, he had to force himself not to stare at the doorway to monitor when she arrived. He took in the language of Eliza's body when she skirted her father slightly cringed, eyes averted.

Eliza was afraid of him, and she had already proved she could put her fear aside—with wild pirates and men with knives sticking out of them. Her sister also skirted the father with caution, as if he were a napping, fire-breathing dragon who could wake up and incinerate them in an instant.

Eliza sat down with a dramatic flap of her hands and told the woman beside her, "I am afraid I could not find it, try as I did. It must be with the pattern because I could not find that either. I am so sorry. I am sure it will turn up, but I did not want to spend more time looking for it when I could be spending time with you."

Without missing a beat, Eliza turned to a maid who offered her tea. "Yes, please. Thank you."

She's magnificent, Littledove thought as he grinned to himself. He could not wait to leave the house and begin his life with Eliza.

Chapter Seventeen

RACING THROUGH MOONLIGHT

Littledove braced himself to speak with Strauss. He never imagined he would feel so concerned about asking for Eliza's hand in marriage, but apparently, this was no ordinary father. He composed himself and approached with authority as if to reprimand an unruly sailor.

"Sir, need a word in private."

"About what?"

"Aye, that's the private part," he said firmly. The bastard already knew what this meeting was about.

Without another word, Strauss stood and headed to his office. Littledove followed, feeling his gait constrict as it usually did when he approached dangerous waters. Eliza slipped behind him and walked on tiptoe to be silent and go unnoticed until Strauss opened his office door and saw her. He allowed Littledove to pass through the door but stood in the doorway when Eliza approached.

"This doesn't concern you," he said.

"Actually, it does, sir. Pardon." Littledove reached over Strauss and pulled Eliza into the office by her wrist.

"What waste of my time is this?" Strauss demanded. "Why are you still here? What the hell do you want?"

Littledove evened his weight over both his legs and got to the point. "Your daughter and I're getting married. Suggest you feel the honor of being the first to know."

Strauss's brown eyes turned yellow with a simmering rage as he looked over Eliza. Littledove stepped forward and put one foot between them. He stood still as Strauss eyed him as if inspecting a cow patty in a pasture.

To Eliza, Strauss said, "This? This is what you want to marry? Look at him, Elizabeth! He has a donkey tail and dresses like a shyster. He could not even go down honorably with his ship when his crew was killed! What was he doing? Hiding like a coward? And you want to marry him? This primitive ... orangutan?"

"Captain Littledove and I are to be married. You may approve or not, but we shall be married," Eliza said with utmost calm.

Littledove almost smiled. Eliza's calm never flared into a storm. It *was* the storm.

"How often did you please him when you were with him? Is that why you need to marry him?"

Littledove stepped forward, but Eliza stretched her arm in front of him. "Goodnight, Father. Captain, please come with me."

"Are you aware that I shall disinherit her if she marries you?" Strauss said triumphantly. "Or did you imagine you'll be getting rich by marrying her? Not one penny shall see the inside of your worn pockets. She goes to you in what she wears."

"I came for Eliza, and I'll have her as she is," Littledove said with contempt.

Strauss turned to Eliza. "Well, you think about what this will means for you. Not only will I disown you if you leave here with him, I shall forbid you from ever setting foot in this house again. And from consorting with your sisters. You shall be no one to them! You shall be like the dead, as you so deserve to be instead of your other sisters! You couldn't even give your life for them."

Tears welled in Eliza's eyes, but she spoke clearly with a mournful sense of destiny. "I shall always be someone, Father, even to those who think me dead. Goodbye."

Strauss brown eyes turned leopard yellow. "Leave this house. Right now! Go into the night like the whore that you are with your cock bawd! Go live in Hell, where whores are welcomed! You'll never see your sisters again! No wonder he wants to marry you! You think people do not know about your sordidness on his ship? Why, it's already all over town. Why else would he want to marry you? Go into the night like the whore you are! I forbid you to corrupt your sisters with your putrid wretchedness!"

Littledove felt Eliza's hand on his lapel as she pulled him out of the office and shut the door behind her to block her father's voice.

"Get the carriage, Will. We must depart immediately. I shall meet you in front. Hurry."

As Eliza ran down the hall, past the guests who were gawking, the office door swung open and Strauss stepped out, shouting for the world to hear, "You goddamned whore! Go into the night with your cock bawd!"

Littledove's patience disintegrated. Before his brain could catch up to what he was doing, he smashed his fist into Strauss's face so hard Strauss tumbled backward into his office. He flipped over his enormous desk, sending inkwells and assorted statues skittering off his desk to shatter on the floor.

With every one of his gestures unwinding as if in slow motion, Littledove pivoted and pointed to the footman by the front door. "My carriage."

The footman stood petrified. Littledove narrowed his eyes and took a step toward him. The footman bolted, abandoning his composure and shrieking, "Captain's carriage! Captain's carriage! Get the captain his carriage!"

In the dark of the night, Littledove paced while waiting for his carriage to arrive. He would have rather gotten the carriage himself so he would not have to wait with an idleness that was driving him mad. He began considering going back into the house to retrieve Eliza because she had yet to come out.

A scruffy barn hand, not a footman, appeared with the carriage but did not evacuate the driver's seat. "Get in, Cap'n! Miss Strauss be down back. I'll take yee there quick now."

Littledove jumped in. The barn worker snapped the reins to the horse's back and took off. Littledove spun into a panic. Where exactly was Eliza? Why were they moving away from the house without her? He looked over his shoulder at the shrinking mansion door. If he did not leave with Eliza now, he would leave her in danger. He drew a deep breath and raised his foot to knock the driver off the seat so he could take control of the carriage.

He almost fell out of the carriage when the driver took a sharp turn onto a narrow dirt road and headed to the back of the house. The driver shouted to be heard over the horse's gallop and the rattles of the carriage, "She said to git her in ee back!"

Littledove lowered his foot and looked up. He could now see Eliza in her cloak as a dark triangle surrounded by servants in white aprons. She stood beside a portmanteau, her hands clasped with so much tension they looked as if they had been welded together.

The moment the carriage stopped, two kitchen maids hauled the portmanteau into the carriage while an older woman who seemed in charge walked Eliza to her seat. The driver stuffed the reins into Littledove's hands and assisted Eliza into the carriage. A moment later, they took off, leaving behind a swirl of grit.

Eliza's sister came running out of the servants' entrance and dashed toward the carriage. In a last-ditch effort to say goodbye, the sisters waved at one another, a tiny gesture that could not possibly overcome the heartbreak Littledove felt pulsing between them. He wanted to stop so the sisters could say goodbye, but he was sincerely afraid Strauss would come out with a shotgun and shoot everyone.

Littledove continued to drive the horse hard until they were on the main road and the mansion was out of sight. Then he allowed the horse to slow to a comfortable pace. Eliza sat beside him, looking as if her soul had fallen out of her.

He was coming aware he could not spend the night with Eliza without being married. Not on land. Not in a parish where everyone knew her. She would be ruined.

He had wanted to do things right, to take Eliza as his wife with dignity in a proper ceremony in the presence of family and friends. Now, they would have to marry in the middle of the night while on the run from a man who needed to live in an asylum, not a mansion.

Always one to work with what he had, Littledove asked, "Where can we get married?"

"Parson Grist can marry us. He lives down this road," said Eliza. "The church will be on the left."

Littledove urged the horse on, following the road as Eliza directed. A drizzle of rain began, and Eliza drew the hood of her cloak over her head.

What a disaster. Bringing down the *Black Death* had gone better. Littledove nudged her arm. "Milady."

"My captain," answered Eliza, snuggling against him.

Three structures emerged from the fog to become visible from the road. One was old and squat and made of fieldstone with cracking stucco. Another was a timber frame that foretold a grand and elegant steeple. Littledove stopped the carriage in front of the third building, which he assumed was the parish house.

The light in the window made him wonder what time it really was because country folk were not known for staying up late. He half expected the light to be coming from some forgotten lamp, but Parson and Mrs. Grist were quite awake when they opened the door as he helped Eliza down from the carriage.

Littledove approached them, wondering why they were answering the door in their nightshirts when no one had knocked. On a mission, he pushed aside his puzzlement.

"Evening. We come to be married," he said.

Parson Grist exchanged looks with his wife and opened the door to let them in.

"Something to warm you?" asked Mrs. Grist, eyeing Eliza.

"Yes, please, Mrs. Grist. Thank you."

Mrs. Grist cast her sight upon her slippers and disappeared into the kitchen, clutching her shawl as if someone were trying to rip it from her body.

Eliza turned to the Parson. "Parson Grist, may I please introduce Captain William Littledove. Captain Littledove, Parson Grist. Captain Littledove and I would like to be married."

"Mighty late to be running around the earth, even to get married," Parson Grist said lightly. "Wouldn't it be better to be married in the grace of daylight?"

The clock chimed eleven. Eleven o'clock at night was no time for small talk. Littledove became peeved. "We're here. You're up. You can marry us now."

Eliza looked around the room, slowing her scan over the clutter of the parson's desk. She gathered her cloak and sat on the chair by the desk. As she folded her hands on her lap, her shoulders slumped, making Littledove realize she had to be beyond exhausted. The parson's glance flitted across his desk to Eliza.

Parson Grist cleared his throat. "I am afraid I cannot marry you, Miss Strauss. I am afraid your father does not approve of your marriage to Captain Littledove."

"Her father isn't the one marrying me," said Littledove.

Eliza sprang from the chair and grabbed a rain-speckled note from the desk. Parson Grist moved to take it from her, but Littledove grabbed his hand and twisted the entire man into submission as Eliza read the note, summarizing as she read.

"Parson Grist is not misinforming us. This note is from my father. I recognized his seal. He disapproves of our marriage, as clearly stated here. And demands that we not be married under any circumstances, or there shall be consequences."

She turned to Littledove. "He must have sent a messenger on horseback across the field. The messenger would get here sooner than we could in a carriage on the road. No wonder Parson and Mrs. Grist are awake."

So those details had not been lost on her. Littledove released the parson's hand and watched him shrink away from him. "That doesn't explain why you can't marry us."

"I, well, I, well, a marriage is not merely between two individuals, no. But between two families. Yes. And their communities. Yes. If one family is not in agreement, then at least that should be resolved before any marriage takes place."

"Where's that in the Bible?" Littledove demanded.

"Families who quarrel can have detrimental effects on—"

"Nay," said Littledove as he squinted out the window and stepped forward with such force the parson stumbled back and fell into the chair by his desk, where he clutched its arms with white-knuckled hands. The kitchen door creaked open, and Mrs. Grist's eye peered through the crack.

"There's only one consequence here," said Littledove to Parson Grist. "Plain as day, it is. Strauss is paying for your new church. That, out there, is his church, not yours. It'll never be yours because he owns you. Make sure that doesn't land you in Hell, Pastor. Come on, Eliza. Let's go. There's nothing for us here. Which way did he turn?"

Parson Grist was still clinging to his chair for life. "Turn? Turn? Who?"

"Strauss's man. Left or right?"

"Left. I think. That way." He pointed randomly.

Littledove stepped out into the rain with Eliza and slammed the door of the parish house behind him as if shutting a gate to Hell. He pulled Eliza to the carriage because she looked as if she could not move on her own and almost lifted her onto the seat. By now, the autumn rain was falling in sharp, cold pellets.

"Eliza, what's to the left? What else is on this road?"

Eliza's eyes widened slowly. "He's sent the messenger down the road! My father—he's ostracizing me from my family, the house, and now the parsonage! I will disappear as if I had never been born. Even Sarah and Jelly who died who knows where at sea are recorded in the parish books. Everyone shall turn us down! We shall not be able to get married!"

"I'll be damned if that happens. What's across the river?"

"Across— Oh, wait! Yes. Parson Miles is across the river. We do not frequent there. Perhaps Father will not expect us to go there. We can try them. There is a bridge about a mile back."

Littledove turned the carriage. They had hope now, but the way the night was unrolling put all prospects in doubt. He and Eliza would be married tonight. He knew Strauss was determined to make Eliza feel like a— a—. What an insult to Eliza, a woman with more virtue than most had soul.

And to himself, he couldn't help feeling. He was finally beginning to understand that a gentleman was more than just a person who knew how to eat with a hundred forks, but someone who could do right under difficult circumstances. Littledove set his jaw and drove the horse, not quickly but with even more determination. He would do this right.

By the time they crossed the bridge, the rain was coming down in sheets and they were soaked. The hood of the rented carriage did not prevent water from flying in through the carriage opening, and it leaked where it could have kept them dry. In the mist that rose from the river, the church and parish house were nearly invisible, and they almost missed the turn to it. Littledove took the moment when he helped Eliza down from the carriage to count the number of churches in the vicinity (one) and to check how many windows in the parish house had lights (none). By now the time was well past midnight.

He pounded on the door with his fist to be heard over the rain. When nothing within the house stirred, he pounded on the door again. He stepped back in the rain to see a light flicker in an upstairs room, and a great many minutes later, a man cracked open the front door. He appeared to be appropriately disheveled for someone in the middle of a good sleep.

"We're here to get married," said Littledove.

Parson Miles looked over Littledove and Eliza. "At this hour?"

"Right now," said Littledove.

"Well, come in, come in, then. Have a seat. I'll get my wife."

Parson Miles waved at some chairs in the room and made his way up stairs that creaked each time he set a foot on a step. Littledove sat Eliza in a chair and pulled her cloak around her because the room was chilly. He kissed her on the forehead and then on her lips, both moist with rain.

"Milady."

"My captain."

"Why's he need his wife to marry us?"

Eliza put her hand over his cheek and smiled. "Some men feel their wives are indispensable."

Littledove grinned. "Imagine that."

They listened to the murmur of a conversation without being able to make out the words. Mrs. Miles preceded Parson Miles down the stairs, trying to cover herself with a shawl.

"Come, child," Mrs. Miles said to Eliza. "Help me get a pot of coffee going. We cannot marry anyone before we have coffee."

Eliza rose from the chair and followed Mrs. Miles into the kitchen. Littledove moved to follow her, but Parson Miles stepped forward and said, "Please sit down, sir. The ladies will bring us coffee in a moment. Tell me your name because I have to at least know that to marry you." And thus began a conversation between the men.

In the kitchen, Eliza sat quietly while Mrs. Miles stoked the fire in the stove and assembled a pot of coffee. The kitchen felt pleasantly warm after the wet ride in the carriage.

"Now, what inspires you to get married in the middle of this night, dear?" Mrs. Miles asked.

Eliza spoke as neutrally as she could, although she could feel her anger rising. "It would be in accordance with good morality if we married, seeing that we are both far from our homes and must stay together."

As the kitchen warmed up, she slipped off her gloves and cloak. Her high couture evening dress was so wet and muddy she looked as if she had been digging up potatoes in the rain.

Mrs. Miles turned to face her after setting the coffee pot on the stove. Her eyes roamed over the dress. Eliza became aware of the sapphire earrings and necklace Mary had lent her because she could not reveal that her jewelry was hidden in her petticoat. Mrs. Miles slipped into a kitchen chair to wait for the coffee to finish percolating.

"Are you one of the Strauss girls, dear?"

"Yes. Captain Littledove and I have come to be married. Against my father's wishes, I am afraid," Eliza added, unable to keep the story to herself. She regretted not having told her father that she would always be a Strauss sister, no matter what he said. He did not have the power to take that away from her.

Mrs. Miles' eyes rolled up as she thought. "Captain Littledove ... Any relationship to the captain ... with the pirates?"

"The very gentleman," Eliza said proudly.

"Forgive me, dear. I am not used to having such well-known people in my house. All the same, people in distress all bear a common humility. And why does your father disapprove of Captain Littledove?"

"He wants me to marry a man whom I have never loved."

"And you love Captain Littledove?"

"Yes. Very dearly."

"And he loves you?"

"Yes, he does."

Mrs. Grist gently cleared her throat. "I don't wish to be indelicate, but I must ask you direct. Are you marrying because you are with child?"

Eliza immediately thought of Mary. "No! Of course not! Captain Littledove is a gentleman. He would never ... He has never ... No. He is a gentleman. That is not the issue."

"Then what is the issue that you come running here at this hour, insisting on being married, dear? I imagine a girl with your resources should have a proper wedding with miles of bridesmaids and such. I ask out of curiosity, not to judge you."

"My father has disowned me. I have nothing now except this man I love. Please understand, we have always intended to marry. We have been secretly engaged for some time now. Our announcement to marry is what started"—Eliza fluttered her hands—"this. All this."

Thoughts of Mary began to agitate her. "What do you think people will say when they see I have spent the night with a man to whom I am not married? We certainly love each other, but I would be ruined. Already you think I am with child because I have come here with him at this late hour, as if that is the only explanation."

"Yes, yes. I see. I see quite clearly. Those thoughts about this situation shall never leave this kitchen. Forgive me for having thought them. Did you speak with Parson Grist? He is not in town? I know Mrs. Grist's mother is not in good health."

Eliza clenched her jaw with a tension that made her head quiver. "I am afraid Parson Grist has fallen from God's grace into the soft pillows of my father's money. My father is funding his new church. He would not marry us because my father objected. He knows my father would just as soon burn down what is built of his new church with the devil's flames if he went against him. That is why we have come here. So I will not turn into a woman of ill repute when the sun rises." *Forgive me, Mary,* Eliza begged silently.

"I suspect the sun shall rise, and you will continue to be a righteous woman, Miss Strauss. Circumstances always vary with each person, and no one can judge who does not partake in the same circumstances. Have no fear. My husband shall marry you and Captain Littledove, and you shall leave here with your husband," said Mrs. Miles, putting her arm around Eliza.

Circumstances vary with the person. In that saying, Eliza took comfort for Mary.

Mrs. Miles left her alone in the kitchen to go into the front room. She returned moments later with Littledove and the parson, now dressed in his clerical clothes.

Littledove rubbed his hands together. He thrusted his thumb in the parson's direction. "He's going to marry us. Right now!"

Indeed, I am," said the parson after exchanging smiles with his wife who nodded to him. Just as quickly, the parson entered a purified air of solemnity. "Please stand side by side, both of you. Thank you. We're gathered here today in the presence of God to bless the union of Miss Elizabeth Anne Strauss and Captain William Littledove in Holy Matrimony. This holy bond, established by God, is not to be entered into unadvisedly or lightly, but reverently and soberly."

The parson raised his eyes to Eliza and Littledove. They looked at one another and nodded.

The moment arriveth swiftly, thought Eliza, filling with apprehension that her father would barge through the door and disrupt their marriage. She glanced at Littledove, who nervously wiped his nose before straightening himself and releasing a crooked grin at her.

The parson turned to Littledove and prompted in a whisper, "Rings?"

Littledove jolted. "Rings? Rings?" He looked around the kitchen, exasperated. "Ah ... Didn't get a chance to get 'em. We can do that later, right? We don't need rings to get married, right? I mean, not like we're marrying the rings."

The parson's wife turned away to hide her smile at Littledove's abundance of jitters while the parson calmly confirmed, "We may certainly proceed without the rings. They are symbolic, not necessary."

Littledove almost buckled from relief. He straightened himself again as Parson Miles guided him through the vows.

"I, William Littledove, take thee, Eliza, ah, Elizabeth Strauss, ah, Anne Strauss, to be my wedded wife, to have and to cherish, from this day forward, for better for worse, for richer for or poorer, in sickness and in health, till death do us part, according to God's holy ordinance, and thereto I plight thee my troth."

Littledove spoke with a seriousness that Eliza thought rivaled the parson's. She almost laughed out loud when he bungled her name, knowing he was thinking that the parson might not marry them if he could not say her name correctly.

But the parson was used to nervous grooms and brides, and he nonchalantly turned to Eliza and guided her through her vows. As she recited them, she took in how Littledove's face relaxed then tightened with suppressed joy when she completed reciting the vows.

The parson concluded the ceremony neatly. "By the power vested in me by God, I now pronounce you man and wife. Blessed be!"

Eliza stood motionless beside Littledove, barely believing that they were married after so much rain and mucky trials and tribulations. Eliza looked at Mrs. Miles, noting for the first time that she was still in her nightgown.

"Well!" said Mrs. Miles into their stark silence. "I think we should celebrate by having breakfast!"

"You may kiss your wife now," said Parson Miles as he put down his Bible and handed his wife the basket of eggs on the counter.

Eliza closed her eyes with relief as Littledove took the parson's suggestion to heart. He kissed her heartily on the lips but with a shy reservation she did not expect. She imagined Littledove's imagination was running full blast. Certainly, hers was.

On the carriage ride to Edith's Bay after being wed, Littledove realized he was as homeless as Eliza. The *Bessie* now belonged to a museum. His new ship, the *Madrigal*, as Eliza named her, was not yet ready for launch. People assumed he did not value home because he was always traveling, but he was really like a snail who traveled with his home. He longed to move into the captain's quarters of the *Madrigal* and bless it as home with a glass of port in the company of his wife, the blessing of his life.

In a short time, he turned his inability to control last night's events into an inward agitation. He was used to having vile things said about him, to being cursed at, to going without sleep, to being cold and wet, to not having and making do. Eliza was not, and he did not ever want her to think that deprivation and humiliation were part of being his wife.

He wanted to protect her from all the things in the universe that caused discomfort, knowing full well he could not and that she had already experienced many, some more perilous than the aftermath of pirates. Afraid to wake her with his need for her affection, he kissed her cloak hood instead of her and found solace in her weight against his body.

His thoughts eventually turned to what to do when they got to Edith's Bay. They could go to the Hareys' house and be inundated with questions about why they eloped. He did not want to visit them until he saw how Eliza was coping. She was too tired now to cope. He was not even certain he could recount the story without cursing Eliza's father in front of Eliza and Mrs. Harey.

The sun was rising when they arrived in Edith's Bay, the worst time to find a hotel room because no one had yet left. After being turned away at two inns, Littledove headed to Mrs. Beeve's Boardinghouse for Gentlemen with Eliza. At least they could wait in the front parlor with cups of Mrs. Beeve's coffee until the inns cleared out.

The moment Littledove opened the front door and the bell on it jingled, Mrs. Beeve came into the front room, bouncing on tiny footsteps, wispy, silver hair escaping from her bun in a haze. She wore a prim, plaid dress under a bib apron with blue flowers. No matter what hour anyone arrived, she was up to greet and help guests get settled. As far as Littledove knew, Mrs. Beeve never slept.

"Captain Littledove! Why! I thought I'd never see you again. I heard you were carrying gold, and pirates went after you. How are you?"

"I's real good, real good. Thanks. I see you're also shipshape. Mrs. Beeve, I'd like you to meet—"

Littledove stopped speaking because Mrs. Beeve began inflating with indignation at a rate that alarmed him. Her chest puffed out. Her thin, white brows feathered across her forehead, and her frown stretched her soft cheeks into hard planes. One hand slapped on her hip as she shook her finger at him with the other.

"Captain Littledove! Shame on you! You well know I do not allow women in my boardinghouse. For that, you can go to the tavern down the street. My establishment is beyond reproach, and I do not put up with this kind of thing!"

"No, Mrs. Beeve. We just need to—" began Littledove.

"Men always think they can get away with anything because they're men! And I thought you were a better person."

Littledove had never been convinced someone could die from embarrassment until now, but he felt himself burning and withering as Mrs. Beeve implied that Eliza was ... was ... well, not his wife. Or that, after so many years of patronage, he would bring a woman of ill repute into her boardinghouse. Or that he ever had. And why was it so difficult for people to believe he was married?

Over his helpless gasping for words, Eliza's even voice prevailed. "Mrs. Beeve, I wholeheartedly understand and encourage your position on this matter. I can certainly see you are a morally upright woman by running your boardinghouse as you do. Captain Littledove has forgotten to explain that I am his wife. I hope it puts you at ease, even if you cannot allow us to spend a few hours sitting in your parlor until a hotel room becomes available."

"Wife?" Mrs. Beeve inspected Eliza. She turned to Littledove. "You got married?"

"Aah ... yes. This is my wi—"

"Now why'd you leave that out? " Mrs. Beeve elbowed him out of the way. "Almost had me insulting your poor wife. Come along, Mrs. Littledove. I dint think you looked like one o' them bad women, but one's got to be careful in this business. If not, they come with all kinds and swear up and down they're just cousins. Now, I don't often do this, but on occasion, I let captains and their wives spend the night here—when they are properly married, that is."

"Why, thank you, Mrs. Beeve, especially after all the traveling we have done."

Littledove rubbed his face before he lifted the luggage and tagged behind Eliza and Mrs. Beeve. Down the hall, Mrs. Beeve opened the door to one of her better rooms.

"You can use my private bath so you don't run into the gentlemen," Mrs. Beeve said to Eliza. "The captain can use the regular baths."

"We are very grateful, Mrs. Beeve. Thank you very much for accommodating us under these circumstances."

And that was that. They had a place to stay. Littledove shook his head. How was it that even when women spoke plain English, words seemed to come out with altered meanings? Showed him what he knew about women.

The following day, Littledove rose early and left Eliza sleeping in the room. He returned an hour later with a basket of buttered buns, two boiled duck eggs, ham, cheese, plums, and a small bouquet of flowers.

Eliza was already out of bed, looking tired but fully dressed and brushing her hair by the washstand. Littledove abandoned the basket of goods on the table and took the brush from her. She had gorgeous hair, rich and brown with sea-like undulations. He held her hair in both hands for a moment to appreciate its weight before spreading it over her shoulders.

Having had a ponytail for so many years, he knew exactly how to brush long hair, detangling the ends first with flicks and making his way to the crown, a few inches at a time. Then came the fun part, brushing directly from the crown to the tips and enjoying the dense, fullness of Eliza's hair.

He held the brush as he would hold a key to a kingdom, knowing he was the only man whom she would allow to brush her hair. In some way, he felt he had never before been invited into a kingdom with this level of intense intimacy.

The breakfast—their third of the day after the Mrs. Miles' and Mrs. Beeve's—was the first meal they were having alone. When Eliza automatically put her napkin on her lap, he slipped his napkin into his collar and spread it over the front of his shirt as he recently learned was required to be a gentleman. Somewhere in the marriage vows, he knew he had committed to always using a napkin and utensils properly. And to not swearing in front of Eliza.

As they ate, he considered what to do. They had not yet celebrated their marriage in any way, seeing that they arrived so tired and upset and displaced. Like most seamen, he had the ability to fall into a bed and be asleep within minutes, but he woke up an hour later feeling Eliza's body quivering with sorrow in the morning sun.

A woman in that state of mind could not be asked for anything. He wrapped his arms around her to comfort her until she eventually fell asleep again, all the while ranting in his head at her father, a man who singlehandedly ruined what should have been one of the most wonderful days of their lives and almost destroyed Eliza in the process. The lobcock!

When Eliza removed her napkin from her lap and placed it on the table, Littledove lost no time in lifting her and carrying her to the bed. At first, she gasped in surprise and then squealed with delight at finding herself suspended in the air. On the bed, she settled into a profusion of nervous giggles.

"My captain," Eliza said after she quieted. She stroked his cheek and tickled his nose with the tip of his ponytail.

She seemed in good spirits as she rested against his chest, and he held her as she once held him after he'd been stabbed, because he did not think her injuries were any less threatening to her wellbeing. He could still feel the density of sorrow shadowing her, as it had shadowed her when she accepted that Sarah and Jelly were gone.

"Milady, how are you today?" he asked as he twisted her hair around his finger.

"I am well," she said brightly, then rested her cheek against his chest.

"Eliza, you gave up everything to be with me. I thought you'd only give up living in a big house and servants. Never thought you'd have to give up your birthright and your family. Me—I's never had to lose something that big. I's born without a family, if you get my meaning. I don't even know if I'm worth what you gave up. If I'd known, I'd never have—"

Eliza put her fingers over his lips and shook her head. She remained silent until she kissed him.

"You did not know, Will, but I did. I did not know exactly what the price was, but I knew it would be terrible. Any price my father sets is always terrible. He studies people's weaknesses. I have never seen him set a price that does not make a person double over in agony."

"But all you got for all that's me, and I don't see me able to make that up to you."

"Will, please understand. You hardly mattered in my father's eyes. He did it because I would not do what he wanted. I could have married any other man in the world, and he would have felt the same if that man was not Harold Bartook. He does not play for inheritance or family. Those are trinkets to him. He plays for souls."

Eliza nuzzled into his neck and released a tender laugh. "Will, you are the one good thing to come from all of this. Do not diminish yourself. You have your own value, just as Mary and Amelia have. You are not measurable in sisters any more than they are measurable in captains. You did not cause my wounds, and with you, I shall heal and learn to live with them."

"Milady, you are braver than I'll ever be."

Eliza traced his smile with her fingers.

"I know. I know. I smile crooked. Used to practice smiling right when I's a boy. And I could do it too, in front of a mirror. But when I smiled for real, it always came out crooked. The girls used to make fun of me."

"I cannot imagine girls making fun of you."

"Milady! You do it all the time!" He raised his head and kissed Eliza. "Do I kiss crooked?"

"You kiss perfectly, my captain," said Eliza, returning his kiss.

"I got something for you. Here. Pull this here." Littledove pointed to the knot on a blue satin ribbon sticking out of his shirt pocket. "Go ahead, pull it."

Eliza pulled on the ribbon until something slipped out of his pocket and jerked the ribbon taut. She gasped at the two gold rings that swung from it. Littledove cut the ribbon with the knife on his belt, and the rings fell into Eliza's palm. He took the smaller of the two.

"Now, how's that go? With this ring, I thee marry," he said as he slipped it onto her finger. "Something like that. You know what I mean."

Eliza took the other ring and slipped it on his. "With this ring, I thee wed, Will."

"Mrs. Littledove, will you please undo my tie?"

Eliza did not stop at the tie but continued until his shirt was unbuttoned. He rolled Eliza on her back and kissed her the same way he had kissed her at the shore where she once lived. Eliza raised her hips to press against his hips. Littledove grinned more crookedly than ever, glad to see his wife was as full of imagination as he was.

Chapter Eighteen

REAPING REWARDS

Littledove was smiling as if he owned the world when Captain Harey opened his front door. Without hesitation, Captain Harey grabbed his hand and shook it until every bone in his body rattled.

"Well, well, Littledove! That's the look of success if I've seen it. When's the date? Are we going to be invited? Never mind. We'll show up anyway. Mrs. Harey! It's Captain Littledove!"

Mrs. Harey came running to the door, clapping her hands. She threw her arms around Littledove but pulled back slightly when she looked over his shoulder.

Littledove remembered that the last time they had spoken he said he was going to propose. He pulled Eliza forward with his arm around her shoulders.

"Mrs. Harey, Captain Harey, I want you to meet Mrs. Eliza Littledove, my wife."

"Mrs. Littledove!" gasped Mrs. Harey as she hugged Eliza. "Why, I am delighted! So delighted! Come right in! Have you had dinner? We were just about to sit down."

"What a question," said Captain Harey. "Littledove always shows up in time for dinner. Mrs. Littledove, be aware your husband still calibrates his clocks by meals. He keeps a chronometer in his stomach."

Captain Harey lowered his head and chuckled as he led everyone into the parlor to wait for Emma to add extra settings to the table. Everyone laughed and hugged, but as the laughter settled down, the unanswered question pressed an awkward silence into room.

"We eloped," Eliza finally said.

"So, you wanted to avoid the hassles and frustrations of planning a wedding," said Mrs. Harey, although her extremely polite tone did not convince Littledove she was thinking along those lines.

"My father disowned me."

"For marrying Littledove?" shouted Captain Harey. He shot to his feet, shaking his fist.

"Because I would not do what he wanted me to do, which, I suppose, included marrying Captain Littledove. However, a good husband supersedes an angry father."

"Oh, you poor dear," said Mrs. Harey, releasing her true sentiments.

Littledove leaned toward Captain Harey and whispered, "Was horrible."

"What was that, Captain Littledove?" asked Mrs. Harey.

"Ah, said it worked out fine. We're married." He swatted the air with disgust he could not hide.

"When did you get married?" asked Captain Harey.

"Littledove twisted his wedding band. "A few days ago? Maybe more."

"Have you celebrated at all?" said Mrs. Harey.

"Aye! We've been celebrating, all right." Littledove grinned and flashed his wedding band.

Eliza held up her hand to display her wedding band, all the while blushing wildly because everyone was bound to know what Littledove most likely meant. Mrs. Harey looked down and smiled to herself.

"Well then, perhaps you can celebrate again," said Captain Harey. "Captain Ellsworth is in town. He's always asking about you, Littledove. In fact, he's asked Mrs. Harey and me to sup with him, I believe sometime in two weeks. Perhaps you can join us and inform him yourself how you're doing and introduce your new bride."

"Be good to see him again, don't you think, Mrs. Littledove?" asked Littledove, who was still getting accustomed to addressing Eliza in public as Mrs. Littledove as if they had just met five minutes ago. Did people think being ludicrously formal made other people forget what married people did?

"Where are you honeymooning?" asked Mrs. Harey.

Littledove looked at Eliza, uncertain what to say. They were not exactly honeymooning. At best, they were recuperating from being on the run.

"Ah, Mrs. Beeve's letting us stay with her. We didn't have time to plan for a honeymoon. You know how quick elopement goes."

Mrs. Harey sat up and glared at Littledove. "You and Mrs. Littledove are staying at Mrs. Beeve's boardinghouse? For gentlemen?"

"We were planning to just stay a few hours till we could get us a proper hotel room, and then—"

"Captain Littledove, you simply cannot stay with Mrs. Littledove at Mrs. Beeve's. Mrs. Beeve's is a gentleman's boardinghouse. That is most unsuitable. How long before your ship is ready?"

"Four weeks, five days—"

"Then, you shall stay here with us," concluded Mrs. Harey in some bizarre leap of logic that left him befuddled, although he liked the idea.

Captain Harey rested his elbow on the mantel and began muttering. "Pain in the aft. Thought a wife would take him off our hands … "

Mrs. Harey tittered as Captain Harey's stern grumbles slowly evolved into chuckles. By the time his chuckles turned into a full-blown belly laugh with tears, Mrs. Harey abandoned her moderate manner and began laughing wholeheartedly.

Captain Harey brought himself under control and said, "Welcome to the family, my dear Mrs. Littledove. About time your husband got married. He's been owing us a daughter-in-law for some time."

Bless the Hareys, thought Littledove as he watched Eliza burst into the biggest, most sincere smile he had seen since she first set eyes on him at her father's house … mansion … tin castle.

Under Mrs. Harey's tutelage, Eliza began learning to sew while Littledove ran around Edith's Bay lining up cargo to transport and hiring a crew. To Eliza's surprise, sewing proved not nearly as complicated as the precision of seamstresses made it appear. Of course, she was working from an extremely simple pattern Mrs. Harey gave her. To her greater surprise, the first dress she made fitted her almost perfectly.

"I thought dresses always had to be fitted!" Eliza said, recalling the hours seamstresses spent fitting her and her sisters.

"I shall tell you my secret," said Mrs. Harey. "Do you remember the dress you threw out when you first came here? Well, I rescued it and made patterns from it because I was curious to why it draped so nicely. This pattern came from that dress. Small wonder it fits you perfectly. And I've drafted copies of the pattern for you. I'll show you how to vary it."

"How ingenious, Mrs. Harey! Prying secrets from all those seams."

Mrs. Harey had indeed simplified the original dress pattern. Gone went the plethora of trims, although most of the extra yardage in the skirt remained. The bodice, once shaped with labor-intensive pleats and tucks, was now shaped more efficiently with darts. The high couture sleeves and necklines remained, and the simplicity of the resulting dress made it more likely to survive a sea journey.

The afternoon culminated when Mrs. Harey presented her with a handful of patterns for men's shirts and trousers for her to make when she was at sea, if not before, and said, "For a wedding gift, Captain Harey and I shall give you a sewing machine. We can go select it tomorrow."

A few days later, Eliza considered how to adorn her new, rather plain dress for the dinner with the Ellsworths. She spread out on the bed the collection of jewelry she once kept in her petticoat and immediately realized she could not wear jewelry that Littledove could not afford.

She stared at the collection, including the sapphire necklace and earrings she borrowed from Mary. All the pieces seemed misplaced in her new life, and she wished she had left them with Mary, who still had use for them. Once a form of delight, they were now not more than beautiful forms of currency she had to curate. Well, at least they were valuable and might come in handy in a pinch. She thought of Mary bemoaning her missing sapphire set.

Eliza put away the jewelry and drew out a silk collar she had knitted. Against the dark blue dress, it acquired startling, multi-colored, jewel-like qualities. It would do, she decided.

She was still contemplating the collar against the plain dress when Mrs. Harey came into the room holding an envelope. Eliza almost pounced on Mrs. Harey when she saw Mary's handwriting on the envelope. Abandoning her thoughts about the collar and dress, she clutched the letter to her chest and closed her eyes as angst twisted within her. When she opened her eyes, Mrs. Harey was no longer standing next to her and the door to the room was closed.

Eliza wiped her tears and struggled to focus on the envelope. So much of her hopes and fears were in it. She took her time unsealing it to preserve its precious qualities. When she pulled out the letter and unfolded its many pages, she became keenly aware it could say anything, anything at all, and she was not prepared for anything.

My Dearest, Dearest Eliza, my Love and Sister,

I sincerely hope this letter finds you well. I have sent it to your Mrs. Abraham Harey as the envelope you left for me under my pillow recommended. I suppose if it does not reach you, then you shall never know. I hope it does not fall into false hands. Forward go I all the same because I must. I simply must, as you must endure the contents of this letter. Please forgive me for communicating all this in a letter rather than in person, but you, of all persons, will understand the circumstances.

First and foremost, Amelia and I want you to know that you are still our beloved and adored sister, no matter what has transpired, and we love you with all our hearts and souls and are incomplete without you. Please carry this in your Sacred Heart always. We hope you will find it within yourself to continue to love us with the same ferocity as we shall always Love You.

Mrs. Miles and her husband the Parson paid a visit as your Captain Littledove requested that they do. She told us you and Captain Littledove were happily married the night you left the house. Father was so angry he made them leave, but we still managed to have a conversation while waiting for their carriage. Parson Miles said he would be happy to officiate if you want to reaffirm your vows in a ceremony that we can all attend and that would give us all cause to celebrate properly and joyously, as you both deserve. He offered, even if he was a bit unsettled because of Father. Amelia and I are looking forward to that event. I asked Parson Miles to pay Parson Grist a visit and insist that he note in his parish book that Miss Elizabeth Strauss was married to Captain William Littledove at their parish. I believe he has the authority and conviction to bend Parson Grist to this task. I know this will be important to you, although anyone studying the Family Genealogy in the future will surely find it most curious.

*I do not know whether you are sailing with Captain Littledove or waiting for him to return from sea. Perhaps you are still enjoying your honeymoon. If I do not hear from you, I shall try to visit Mrs. Harey at this address in due time to find out where you are and how you are doing. We truly have great desires to see you again, seeing that our parting was so violent and incomplete. Several things have happened at home since you left under those terrible circumstances that shall remain unmentioned. Most of them are not pleasant to recount, but recount them to you I feel verily obligated. Please forgive me the harshness of the news, for I do not know how else to mention these things delicately. First, I am sorry to say Father was fatally wounded by a gunshot a few days after you left. Not one **suspect** comes to mind. He has been laid to rest in the Family Cemetery alongside Mother, Sarah, and Jelly in a private ceremony. Oh! How rapidly Our Family decreases! How rapidly our gravestones have multiplied in such a short time! Mr. **Harold** poses that poachers were responsible, but it is **difficult to prove** because Father was by himself.*

I hope I am not being cross after delivering such news to you and certainly understand if you take a moment to catch your breath. Still, I must mention that on Father's desk I found a draft of a new will. It excluded you but was not finished, as he took it upon himself to make other adjustments as well. Amelia and I shall not dispute the one that is registered, which includes you, despite what Simon is wanting Amelia to do. We agreed to burn the latest one to prevent confusion, lest it become the inspiration of malicious intentions in others. I hope that brings you some peace of mind. Fear not, we shall always look after one another.

*Father insisted in the will that **Amelia's** inheritance is to be managed by Simon, something which greatly upsets her, and she said caused her to take a misstep and fall down a flight of stairs after expressing her disagreement to Simon. As an unfortunate result, she has* *many bruises and lost the baby. This incident caused me great fright of the kind you cannot imagine. I have painful fears she shall never see a penny of it, and we may need to provide for her. We have determined this year's apple harvest will not be as good as last year's. I went on the **b**eaten path across the orchard and noticed many apples are ruined this year.*

More misfortune came in the form of Richard breaking our engagement, which upset me so greatly that a doctor had to visit me to alleviate such conditions that were causing me so much angst. I am now recuperating after spending a week with terrible fevers and delusions. I was convinced I would not survive.

Mr. Harold terminated the partnership Bartook Investments had with Father. He gave as cause that in the presence of muddled leadership, Bartook Investments could not make wise business contracts with the company. Perhaps you may understand this better than I, but Mr. Harold said he leaves happy with what he needed. He sends you his regards and wishes you happiness in your marriage. Very sincerely, I believe, for Mr. Harold has always sincerely admired you, if not loved you.

*Also in his will, Father left a board in charge of the company with instructions to find someone to manage it. I plan to attend the first meeting and imagine I shall have to learn a thing or two about business so that we are not swindled, as according to the current will, we three, or five as we used to be, are the owners unless there is a boy grandchild at the time of his death, which there is not. According to the registered will, we shall all receive an equal share of the profits each year. That profit shall go directly to Amelia, which greatly comforts her. Simon is furious and wants to challenge the management of the company as he claims Father promised to make such arrangements for him to run the company when he sold his company to him. However, attorneys have told him his case is fruitless because no one could present a contract with the conditions. The more Simon wants Amelia to do a thing, the more she resists, and the more bruised she becomes. Amelia desperately **n**eeds to **r**ecover her health. **A**lone, I feel. Perhaps Captain Littledove, who has traveled the world, can recommend a place for her to recuperate her health, **l**est she become more ill through circumstance and **d**ie. Please let us know when you can receive her. She will need help traveling away from her house. I believe your Captain Littledove is just the person to assist in such an endeavor, seeing that he has already battled pirates so successfully and fearlessly.*

I regret the reception Captain Littledove received when he came to visit and hope both of you shall return to see us under better circumstances. We have much to discuss, including what to do with the house (one-third yours) because Amelia cannot live here, and I do not wish to live here anymore, as nothing holds me here, although I do not want to give up the family graveyard. I am feeling that I would like to be cremated when my time comes. That way anyone can pick me up and carry me elsewhere without a fuss. If God does not object, that is. I shall consult with Parson Grist. I cannot presume to know what you will want to do, but I do not see you living here either, as you have always had the character of a sprite, although I am certain Captain Littledove's new boat can be moored in the bay.

I sent a letter to Mr. van der Joost telling him that my sister's husband, who defeated the Black Death, purchased one of his ships, and he sent back a note to say he added several bottles of top-quality single malt, whatever that is, and Champagne to the captain's suite to help him celebrate his marriage and success. He was especially grateful that Captain Littledove rid the world of Black Death pirates, as they were making his clientele quite nervous. He also says he shall not be able to attend the upcoming dinner at the Captain's Club, although he very much regrets it because it would provide an opportunity for him to meet Captain Littledove. My writing this probably ruins the surprise, but I think it is better that you know many important people are gratefully relieved with what Captain Littledove has done.

I miss you dearly, most especially now that I am alone in a house that holds only memories, many of which are not pleasant. We very much want to become better acquainted with your Captain Littledove, seeing that he seems to care so much for you. I must admit I was a little envious that you were so the apple of his eye when he was here. While I was devastated when Richard abandoned our engagement, especially under the circumstances, I can now admit it was a mixed blessing. I wish you here to comfort me because I am still very sad and a little angry. The Folly has no magic when I go to it alone. Please, please write back as quickly as you can. Amelia cannot write to you despite her desires because we want to preserve her plan to recuperate a secret. Know that we shall all be ill at ease until we hear from you.

Much Love and Adoration, Mary and Amelia, Sincerely by proxy

Eliza reread the letter several times. Each time, something different became more important than everything else. She could see her sisters! How had she lost faith in her sisters that she believed they could be mandated to not welcome her? Such was the power of her father's voice—that he could speak and convince everyone of something that could not be possible was truly imminent.

And they wanted to welcome them as husband and wife! They could have a wedding celebration! She had her inheritance! She could visit home! Her name would be in the parish book, even if only indirectly as a reference.

Then the darker parts of the letter made their way into the forefront of her mind. Most disturbing were the messages that were clear to anyone who knew the circumstances. Amelia did not fall down the stairs. Simon beat her until she lost the baby. Being bruised was why Simon would not allow her to leave the house, among other horrible reasons. Amelia needed to go somewhere Simon could not find her, which meant on a ship in the middle of the sea, at least for some time. Possibly she would have to live somewhere far away from Edith's Bay. Mary would have to manage her money from the company.

Eliza could not help but be relieved Richard bailed out of the marriage with Mary, although she was angry that he had abandoned his responsibilities to her sister. A man who welcomed all fruits with the same greed would never find singular joy in any wife he had. Whatever their father promised Richard could not come to fruition now that he was dead, and Richard no longer had any use for Mary. To him, Mary must have been an unwanted dowry, not a wife. Eliza sighed, deeply relieved Mary did not die from inciting a miscarriage.

Finally, Eliza read only the words whose first letter was slightly bolded. The code was not sophisticated, but a casual reader might mistake bolded letters as anomalies of ink or nib or a peculiarity of handwriting and miss the messages: **S**uspect **H**arold **d**ifficult **t**o **p**rove **A**melia's **b**eaten **n**eeds **r**ecover **A**lone **l**est **d**ie

Eliza made a quick calculation. Yes, they would go back and bring Amelia with them even if they had to delay the *Madrigal*'s first voyage by a few days. She knew Littledove would find a way to get her out of Simon's house. He would not sail and leave Amelia if he knew she was in danger.

Eliza's thoughts finally rested fully on the point that Mary suspected Harold of having killed their father. Mary's suggesting such a thing was unimaginable if she did not feel strongly about its truth. Perhaps her father had not offered Harold anything but tried to take something away from him.

Perhaps Harold was not the milquetoast everyone thought he was. After all, Littledove killed a man, and Eliza never once held it against him. Circumstances varied with the person. In truth, she could not bring herself to wonder about what the circumstances might have been. She was too relieved to be away from the manipulations. Having married Littledove still did not prevent her from fearing her father's vengeance.

Eliza rested her elbows on her knees and her head on her palms. Her father was no less ruthless than Benedict Pascal, only more sophisticated. He could pillage a life from behind a desk. She hesitated to give any pirate credit for anything. They took and destroyed much more than they had given or left behind. She used to think they had given her strength, but now she realized the strength had always been within her, dormant and ready to come forth, blooming as needed.

She would always be grateful to have ratcheted the strength to walk away from their father so she, her sisters, and the men who did not love them could also now be free. She allowed this truth to percolate through her before she gave the *Black Death* pirates this credit: Had they not attacked, she might have gone home and married Harold and to this day remained trapped in her father's snares with her sisters.

All these thoughts brought Eliza before her father's specter. She was not ready to cope with the shameful, massive relief her father's death made her feel. He was one half of her, although she never felt that anything in her was like him. He almost ruined Mary's life and nearly killed Amelia with marriages that suited only him. He was willing to sacrifice his children to augment what he mistook as power.

Eliza could not free herself from the shame that she could not mourn for him. More devastating, she could not imagine she ever could.

She folded the letter and slipped it back into its envelope, both adorned with pale pink roses. The ocean rocked the dead in her waves and rested them in her womb. She never ceased finding comfort in the thought that Sarah and Jelly were in the ocean's womb. Her father would be buried in soil that provided another degree of separation she would welcome when she was on the sea. She found herself hoping the soil got into his clothes and made him itch for all eternity until he became raw and begged for mercy.

Littledove knocked at the door, more gently than was usual for someone with his exuberance. He stepped into the room and sat beside Eliza, pulling her to himself.

"Milady, Mrs. Harey said she thought you're upset."

Littledove, she knew, always felt responsible for everything that went wrong, even if he were only a spectator at a tragedy. She clutched the letter, realizing it had the power to absolve him of some of the guilt he still felt for eloping with her. Eliza smiled at the unwitting generosity in Mary's letter.

"Will, I am not upset. I am overwhelmed. Please read this so you may rejoice."

Rejoice. Was her father's death included in that sentiment? She luxuriated in a sense of release, wondering how she had lived a life that continuously held her under threat. Eliza handed the letter to Littledove and held him in her arms as he read it.

Chapter Nineteen

RECEIVING PROMOTION

Mary's letter was still on Eliza's mind a few hours later as she put up her hair in preparation to dine with the Ellsworths. She wished she'd had time to take a nap because the day already felt long with all the sewing and the impact of Mary's letter, and the evening was yet to begin.

As she put on her simple dress, she thought about how so much of her life had been restricted by what she wore, how she wore it, when she wore it, how well she carried and moved in the attire. She was taught to walk, to sit, to stand in ways that best showed off her dresses without much regard for who was inside any of the dresses.

Her attire was made phenomenal so she could command the attention of the men her father permitted into the parlors without her needing to exert her person. She knew Littledove fell in love with her while she wore a dirty dress with rips and her hair was in a messy braid, but she still could not undo her apprehension about the consequences of severe plainness in an evening dress.

Littledove swept into the room, asking if she was ready, and fell silent mid-sentence as he stood by the doorway and stared at her. Eliza nervously touched the points of the lace collar one more time, although Emma starched it to be certain none of the delicate points curled up. Perhaps the dress did need a piece of jewelry. How could she pull that off without betraying Littledove?

Littledove looked down and shook his head before breaking out his lopsided, lustful grin. "Aye! I sure as the dickens married a beauty. You ready, milady?"

Eliza took a moment to allow relief to flow through her before she reached for her gauziest pale gray shawl that looked silver against her dark blue dress. Littledove draped it gingerly over her shoulders, barely touching her.

Apparently, he had taken to heart Captain Harey's earlier warning to never touch a wife when she was freshly made up or she would feel disheveled for the entire evening and hold him responsible. But Eliza stretched her neck and kissed him, pressing her wide skirts against him, as if her dress were impermeable to wrinkles because she felt impermeable to everything.

Littledove did not understand the propriety that mandated wives to sit on one bench of a carriage and husbands sit across them on the other bench. Did people think married people had no self-restraint?

He compensated himself by admiring how lovely Eliza looked, her gentle roundness imbued with subtle sensuality. Perhaps men arranged to sit across women in a carriage to better ogle their graces. Littledove caught Eliza's eye and smiled. She smiled back slyly, and he wondered what about himself was amusing her.

Everyone startled when Captain Harey banged the handle of his cane on the roof of the carriage and started pulling out envelopes from his coat pocket. Through the trap door on the carriage roof, he called, "Captain's Club!"

He fumbled with the envelopes as he explained, "Good heavens. I almost forgot about these. Didn't I ask you to remind me, Mrs. Harey? If I don't deliver these papers, Michaels said he would revoke my membership. I'll just be a moment. If you'll allow me."

Mrs. Harey sighed as the carriage pulled into the circular, cobbled driveway of the Edith's Bay Captain's Club, a downright impressive structure with a dome like the one on the Pantheon dominating its architecture. Littledove knew the massive granite structure was buttressed with the dues of captains and donations from wealthy industrialists who either sold ship wares or needed their goods transported all over the world.

He sank into his seat, wanting to become invisible. Just about every captain of a tall ship in Edith's Bay applied to become a member as soon as he could afford the dues. It even had a reciprocating membership policy with other naval clubs around the world.

All that encompassing welcome being advertised, everyone also understood that the current members carefully monitored the club's exclusivity by voting on the appropriateness of new members to mingle in its lofty atmosphere. The ship had to be of a certain size, and the income had to match the ship. Being a captain did not guarantee membership, Littledove knew firsthand, recalling with a pinch his disastrous behavior at the graduation dinner that permanently ousted him from membership.

"Do you want to accompany Captain Harey?" Eliza asked him. "You have not been to the Captain's Club since we returned."

"Ah, nay. Not a member. Never bothered," said Littledove. Even now, he wanted to die when he thought of Admiral Stoop hearing about the incident in his grave. He looked out the window opposite the club entrance, as if something fascinating boded there.

A little while later, a footman knocked on the carriage door and said, "Captain Harey sends word that he shall be delayed by a few minutes and to please forgive him. He shall be back shortly."

Mrs. Harey looked at the watch pinned to her bodice. "I hope he will not be in there forever and make us late." By way of conversation she added, "How much longer until the *Madrigal* will be ready, did you say?"

"Two weeks, four days. Mrs. Littledove and I ran out yesterday to see her. She is a beauty. A real beauty!"

"Mrs. Littledove, I am never certain whether Captain Littledove is speaking about you or his ship—"

The footman knocked on the carriage door again. "Captain Harey is experiencing an unexpected delay and invites you to please come inside where you may wait in comfort while he resolves the difficulties."

"Thank you," said Mrs. Harey as she gathered her skirts to step out of the carriage.

"Ah, no!" said Littledove and added when he saw Eliza's incredulous stare, "I mean, I'll wait here. You ladies go on in."

Mrs. Harey signaled the footman to close the door. She lowered her head and looked at Littledove from the top of her eyes.

"You real good know I can't go in there!" Littledove whispered in a hiss.

Eliza crossed the carriage to sit by him. "And why can you not go into the Captain's Club, Captain Littledove?"

"Not a member. Never applied." He wanted to strangle Mrs. Harey for having forgotten.

Mrs. Harey placed her hand over his. "Captain Littledove, that incident happened many, many years ago. Much has changed since then. I shall personally guarantee you safe passage if you are with me and Captain Harey. You know Captain Harey will not permit any lack of respect toward you. Why, I doubt the officers will even recognize you. Besides, if we do not go in there, he'll be there all night, and we'll be late. Come, let us go now. Come along, help us out of the carriage like a gentleman."

He looked at Eliza, recalling how brilliantly she had rescued his career on the USS *Vesuvius*.

Eliza pressed her cheek against his shoulder. "I think everything shall turn out fine, Captain Littledove. Whatever happened long ago probably does not matter today. People do not have long memories, and you have become very successful. Besides, I have never seen the place. Come, let us go. I do not think you have anything to fear."

Littledove wondered how much worse things could get. Eliza, gracious creature that she was, hadn't mortified him by asking what the "event" was. Feeling cornered, he opened the carriage door and stepped out. His stomach churned as he helped Mrs. Harey and Eliza descend. He felt about the same as he had when he had gone on deck to wait for the pirates to slash his throat.

Outside the doors of the establishment, Eliza smoothed his lapels and collar. "My captain, you are in no way less than anyone else here. Remember, you are the only captain who defeated the *Black Death* pirates, for which all others are grateful. Walk in there with the same confidence as you walk the decks of your ship, for you are just as valiant as they are—if not more."

Eliza smiled with such brightness and confidence that Littledove pushed back his shoulders to live up to her opinion of him. In they went.

Under the massive dome, he kept his eyes on a neutral distance and continued to hope no one would recognize him. At least no one else was in the reception area. However composed he presented himself, he continued to pray for death. If anyone sneered openly, he would feel so humiliated he swore he would never again dock in Edith's Bay.

"Captain and Mrs. Littledove and Mrs. Harey," Mrs. Harey informed the desk attendant. "Captain Harey is delivering documents to Captain Michaels. We have been invited to wait while he does."

"Yes, madam. Please come this way." The attendant walked them to two oak doors as massive as the ones in Eliza's father's house. Two footmen opened the doors, and the attendant preceded them into a crowded room. Littledove put on a stoic face as he looked around nervously.

In a piercing voice that cut through the din, the attendant announced, "Ladies and gentlemen, Captain William Littledove."

Immediately, applause and cries of "Hip! Hip! Hurray! Hip! Hip! Hurray for Littledove!" deafened him.

Bewildered, he froze in place and blanched. On cue, Captain Harey came up behind him while the cheering continued and patted him on one shoulder. "Don't worry. It's good. We're here to celebrate your defeat of the *Black Death* and to open membership to you."

"What?" he said, too dazed to understand speech. He turned to Eliza of the sly smiles.

"We were all in cahoots! Congratulations, my captain." Eliza stroked his arm.

"Aah …"

Captain Harey slipped his hand over Littledove's elbow and guided him through the cheering crowd to the far side of the room, where a table and a podium stood. Captain Harey positioned him at the podium.

"Just stand here and play along. You'll be fine. I promise. It won't be difficult. Look sharp, look sharp," Captain Harey whispered and left.

The president of the Captain's Club, the retired Captain Michaels, stepped up to the table beside the podium. "Captain William Littledove, thank you for coming tonight. And thank you for tolerating so much trickery on our behalf to get you here. We all admit it would have been easier to have sent you an invitation, but what would be the fun in that?"

Chuckles rippled across the audience. Littledove let his sight dart across the room. He could not get his bearings.

Captain Michaels continued. "I would now like to satisfy your curiosity as to why we have asked you to come here. As president of the Edith's Bay Captain's Club and on behalf of its members, I wish to present to you a certificate for outstanding achievement and courage in the sinking of the *Black Death* and for delivering her captain to stand trial in the courts of Edith's Bay. The entire community of seafarers and their families are supremely grateful for what you have done. We shall be honored if you will please accept this small acknowledgement from us."

To the sound of applause, Captain Michaels handed him an enormous, red leather folder. Littledove cracked it open to glance at the award. It was written in indecipherable calligraphy but looked impressive all the same.

"Aye, thank you. Appreciate this," he said with a stiff nod.

Beginning to trust that he was not there to be ridiculed, he rolled his shoulders and stood as if he were about to set course and sail. When the applause died down, Captain Michaels pulled out a little card from his pocket.

"For the same accomplishment, we wish to present you with a lifetime membership to the Edith's Bay Captain's Club, with all the privileges it entitles, an award that has been granted to only five other captains since the institution's inception in 1811."

Littledove took the card with great delicacy, as if it might disintegrate into fairy dust when he touched it. "Ah, yes. Thank you. Appreciate this too. Aye."

"Speech! Speech!" several members called out, causing another thunderous round of applause.

Littledove went back to feeling stricken. Eloquence was not his best characteristic. He was used to getting things done with one-line commands. But Captain Michaels had already stepped away and left him to deliver whatever speech he could muster.

"Aaaah. Aye. Aah, thank you. Yes, thank you." He took a few nervous squints at the audience and stole another moment to compose himself. He cleared his throat and a moment later began speaking in the best commanding voice he could muster.

"Thank you. I'm real sure you all know no one gets to blow up a brigantine alone. And that makes me think you'ren't thanking enough people. Because for every me, there was twenty-six other men on the *Bessie* doing what they were supposed to do, taking all the risks I took. And for them, we all got to be real grateful, even if they's not here right now, because nothing would have come out the way it did without them. Their names need to be listed somewhere here so their service won't be forgot, because when they got to shore, they just wandered off to other jobs like they never done something useful on the *Bessie*. We all owe them our gratitude—me the most. Aye."

Murmurs rippled through the audience and slowly evolved into applause. After the applause died down, Littledove realized they expected him to continue speaking.

"Aye. All right. I also want to thank Captain Ellsworth of the USS *Vesuvius* and his crew for finding us and towing the *Bessie* back. I know he's probably getting a lot of ribbing for catching us instead of the *Black Death* because that was what he was heading out to do, but without Captain Ellsworth and his crew, chances're real good we'd'ave died at sea. Everything's real important in everything that happens, and we real appreciate being towed back."

Littledove saluted Captain Ellsworth, causing the naval captains to stand and salute. The audience applauded again, more vigorously than ever.

"Also, but not least—fact, not one little bit least—we—me, especially—owe everything to Mrs. Littledove, who kept me alive with boiled handkerchiefs and kitchen towels for bandages, broths she cooked up and made me eat. She even talked the one hen the pirates didn't take with them into laying eggs and didn't tell me she was giving them all to me because she thought I needed them more than her. All this between working the bilge pump to keep the *Bessie* afloat after storms and burying at sea them's left on the deck. She did this all by herself after losing two of her sisters because I couldn't even sit up."

A low murmur swept across the room.

"My wife—she says she did it because she didn't know what to do unless I told her—but if truth be told, she did it because she's a brave and decent person. They say behind every good man there's an even better woman. I'm here to tell you there's no bigger truth than that. Ah, that's it. Thanks."

Littledove stepped back when the audience rose to a standing ovation. With the sweep of one hand, he redirected the ovation to Eliza and then to Captain Ellsworth.

The recognition of the crowd was as good as being forgiven with a lifetime membership to the Edith's Bay Captain's Club. He slipped his fingertips into his jacket to touch the card and reassure himself it was still in his pocket.

When the round of applause died down, a cocktail hour seamlessly began. Littledove longed for a shot of whiskey to steady himself, but he would not permit himself the indulgence. He did not want the faintest scent of inebriation to make people reminisce about his past behavior, especially when they began surrounding him to express congratulations and engage in small talk, something he felt required more wits than he had available at the moment.

Eliza was having no difficulties finding interesting things to discuss with strangers as she stood beside him until she floated away holding a glass of sherry with someone who offered to give her a tour of the building. Like a natural seafarer, Eliza always wandered off, but Littledove sensed she would always wander back to him.

Captain Harey, whom Littledove had not seen since being abandoned at the podium, came up and slapped him on the arm. "So, I take it you were surprised?"

"You old devil!" Littledove took his hand and pumped it. "I'll be thanking you the same someday, just you wait."

"Let's just hope it doesn't happen because I need to go after more damn pirates. You should know the vote went almost unanimous in your favor." Captain Harey's eyes twinkled as he tipped his head toward a man in the distance.

Littledove looked sideways. "Horace objected?"

Captain Harey chuckled. "He still despises you."

"He's still mad I booted him to second place on the Master's exam? He's the one who accused me of cheating."

"He threatened not to come to the dinner when it passed in spite of him, but he was moved by a higher power."

"What, God told him he had to come?"

"Mrs. Horace told him if he did not attend she would never speak to him again." Captain Harvey lowered his voice. "Their daughter, son-in-law, and the two grandchildren were on the *Andrea*."

The severity of this news soured Littledove. He looked at Captain Horace, contemplating giving him condolences, but Horace turned his back to him when he saw him. Littledove could not bring himself to hold the gesture against Horace. It was petty, at best, for a man who had recently lost so much.

"May I say I am very sorry to hear about your losses, Mrs. Horace," Eliza was saying to a woman wearing a mourning gown.

Eliza and Mrs. Horace bowed their heads in a private conversation that lasted a few minutes while Littledove wondered whether anyone was aware of Eliza's losses. For all intents and purposes, Eliza should have gotten married in a mourning gown.

He was not even sure anyone knew how she lost her family in two horrific events. Even if she regained some of her family, she still underwent the losses as if she might never see any of her sisters again. At least they were making plans to have a small marriage celebration. Eliza had already compiled list of invitees, which, not surprisingly, did not include Pastor Grist.

When Littledove looked up again, Eliza was heading toward him, arm in arm with Mrs. Horace. Littledove prayed for death. Eliza could not know the woman's husband despised him with a passion. Such sentiments were not imprinted on any dress of any color.

"Mrs. Horace, may I please present to you my husband, Captain William Littledove of the *Madrigal*, previously of the *Bessie*. Captain Littledove, Mrs. Lillian Horace, wife of Captain Horace of the *Nine Stars*," said Eliza, already having discerned how to correctly introduce a captain.

Littledove bowed before Mrs. Horace curtsied. Mrs. Harey had recently told him in no uncertain terms that he had to bow immediately after being introduced, not after a lady curtsied to him. Mrs. Harey had been so insistent he was tempted to bow to any woman within a yard of him.

He copied the way Eliza handled the black dress by saying, "I's real sorry about your losses, Mrs. Horace."

"Thank you, Captain Littledove. I am pleased others shall not have to suffer similar losses in the future. We are all grateful for your service. It was of military quality. Thank you."

"Welcome, ma'am."

Mrs. Horace strolled away, looking undisturbed and very individuated from her husband's sentiments about him. Wives of captains were bundles of extreme strengths, he concluded. Life at sea with men of the sea did not coddle anyone, not even the uninitiated. He looked for Eliza and found her in conversation with someone else.

Captain Ellsworth came up to him, reaching out to shake his hand, and Littledove said, "So, this is what a military man calls a light supper?"

"Let me just say it took military maneuvers to plan this in such short time. But you deserve it, Littledove."

"This was your idea?"

"A job well done. You should have been a military man. Navy got bamboozled because the *Black Death* put up regular white sails when they docked. We were also looking for a galleon, not a brigantine. Found out later they often docked right in Edith's Bay, registered proper and all. Wolf disguised as lamb! Probably docked next to your ship, for all we know. Made fools of all of us."

"Aye. Them black sails got confusing in the distance. Couldn't figure out what it was until she gained a lot on us. Didn't help that no one who saw the ship survived. Could be that was their intention all along in killing people. Man like Pascal'll never make sense to me," said Littledove, feeling himself choking with memories of the massacre on his ship. He changed the subject. "You know where I can find a steward like the one you got? He seemed pretty good."

"A steward? On a cargo ship? Whatever for, Littledove?"

"My wife. She's used to eating better."

"Yes, quite a fine woman you've married there. Very charming, but don't be deceived. She has the backbone of a captain. You may want to find her a job on your ship. Admiral Stoop's wife became his purser, if I recall. A woman like Mrs. Littledove might take over your job if she gets bored. I'm curious. Is she by chance one of the Strauss sisters?"

Before Littledove could answer, Captain Ellsworth held out his arm and stopped a man from walking past them. "Captain Crockett, Captain Littledove is looking for a steward. You know of anyone?"

Captain Crockett began rattling off the names of stewards while Littledove wrote their names down along with the names of places to advertise for them. When Crockett and Ellsworth walked away, Littledove slipped into a shadow and looked up at the impressive granite dome.

He wondered if with time he would feel as much at ease in the Captain's Club as he felt at Mrs. Beeve's boardinghouse, where there was never as much posturing or pomposity. He knew Eliza would never become a creature of Mrs. Beeve's. She was clearly at home in the Captain's Club's highly social flora. And now that he was a member, they could stay at the club's accommodations. Good thing he had etiquette. He'd be needing it.

He tucked the list of stewards into his pocket next to the Edith's Bay Captain's Club membership card. They seemed to go together. Afraid to admit how greatly he valued the card, Littledove chose to think the membership had already come in handy because he could never get a list of stewards at Mrs. Beeve's.

He could not help feeling he was doing well so far. He had yet to bungle—at least not blatantly. He looked at Eliza, who was wandering back from across the room. He so wanted to find a way of expressing his gratitude for her presence in his life.

She returned his look, eyes full of tenderness, and mouthed, *My captain.*

Milady, he mouthed back, feeling pleasantly triumphant.

Historical Note
Addressing People During the Victorian Era

Victorians had a gift for social complexity that today we deem unnecessarily formal and overwhelming. The higher and more educated the social class, the more rigid and complex were its social traditions. Eliza, an upperclassman woman, would have been familiar with these protocols; Littledove, from the merchant class, not so much.

People in the lower classes, such as tradespeople, servants, and farmers, addressed one another more or less as we do today. First names were acceptable in mixed company, although men commonly used surnames instead of first. Children addressed elders as Mr., Mrs., or Miss Surname. Employees and employers would address one another by surname.

In contrast, people in the upper classes seldom referred to anyone by first name, except immediate family members and very close friends, and only when alone. The upper classes used these distinctions partly to distinguish themselves from other classes.

For upper-class Victorians, addressing someone in public was a complex endeavor by which one's social class and relationship to the person being addressed could be assessed. "Public" was defined as more than two people present. For example, if a married couple was having a conversation and their five-year-old walked into the room, they were then in public. In some houses, the presence of servants constituted being in public, while in others not so much because servants were meant to be invisible.

The mode of address depended as much on the social context as on the personal relationship. In an informal public setting, such as at tennis game, men from the upper classes addressed one another other by their surnames without the title of mister. A man could call the same man Smith during a tennis game, Mr. Smith in a business setting, or John if they were close friends or brothers and they were in private. Being on familiar terms did not soften the discipline of addressing someone in public.

Upper-class women frequently used first names in informal settings where men were not present. If the company was mixed, the use of first names depended on whether the women were on familiar terms with the men, and the men usually added a Miss or Mr. to the first names, as in Mr. Henry or Miss Mary. More often, men would address a woman as Miss Surname. For example, "I am most honored to make your acquaintance, Miss Smith." Usually, if one person was called Mr. or Miss Surname, everyone else also shifted to calling everyone Mr. or Miss Surname.

In public, married persons were always addressed by surname, even by their spouses. For example, Mr. Smith might say to his wife in front of their family, "Good morning, my dear Mrs. Smith." To do otherwise was considered extremely rude to the spouse. In (very) private, a husband could address his wife by her first name ("I am very happy you do not have a headache tonight, Jane."). Parents could also call their adult children by first names when in private.

Male children were addressed formally as Master First name, as in "Master Teddy." Female children were addressed formally as Miss First name, as in "Miss Sarah." Otherwise, children were addressed by their first names. Servants were required to add Master or Miss to the child's first name. Depending on how long the servant had been at the house, the tradition of calling a child Master or Miss First name might persist into the child's adulthood.

Male servants were addressed by their surnames without titles like Mister, as in "Jeeves, let's have some light here." Female servants were usually called by their first names only or Miss First Name, even if they were married. The exception was the cook and sometimes the head housekeeper, who was usually called Mrs. Surname, even if she was not married, because Mrs. was considered the greatest title to which an American Victorian woman could aspire, just as marriage was expected to be her greatest accomplishment.

GLOSSARY OF NAUTICAL TERMS AND SWEAR WORDS

Addlepate: a person who is confused or muddled in an eccentric manner

boatswain: (pronounced bo'sun) a ship's officer in charge of equipment and crew

bunter: a low-class prostitute

clarion: a long trumpet known for its clear, shrill tones; typically depicted as played by angels

cock bawd: a pimp

forecastle: (pronounced fo'c'sle) the area under the deck in the front of a ship, traditionally used as the crew's living quarters

hardtack: a very hard, flat cracker that tends to not go stale quickly and needs to be softened with a liquid before becoming edible; typically carried on long sailing voyages instead of bread. Recipe:

4-5 cups flour

2 cups water

3 teaspoons salt

Set oven to 375 F degrees. Mix all ingredients together into a dry dough. Roll the dough into a rectangle about 1/2 inch thick. Place rectangle on an ungreased cookie sheet. Cut the dough into 3×3 inch squares and with a fork, poke holes into each square. Bake for 30 minutes per side. Cover with cheese cloth and let dry and harden for several days at room temperature until it has the consistency of a brick (Yes, really). Break into squares and store it in an airtight container. To eat, soak in water or milk, or ladle stew over it and wait for the hardtack to soften before eating it.

hen frigate: a ship carrying women, especially a captain's wife

lobcock: a flaccid penis

purser: an officer on a ship who keeps the accounts, especially the head steward

ratl'ns: the pronunciation for "ratlines," ropes tied into squares that sailors use to climb to the crow's nest or top of sails

wear around: a technique of turning the stern (back) of the vessel through the wind to change the ship's direction

READING GROUP QUESTIONS

1. What does Eliza expect Littledove to be, and what does she realize about him?

2. What does Littledove assume Eliza is, and what does he discover about her?

3. What qualities does Littledove have that make people want to give him opportunities?

4. What holds Littledove back? What assumptions do you make about yourself that hold you back?

5. How significant was getting kicked out of the Captain's Club to Littledove? Have you had a similar experience?

6. Littledove kills one man in self-defense, shoots one man in the knee, and punches Eliza's father. Is Littledove really a gentleman? What *is* a gentleman?

7. What do Eliza and Littledove have in common that compensates for their differences?

8. Do Eliza's values change? What experiences have you had that changed what you value?

9. At the folly, Eliza claims that true wealth is the ability to select one's forms of deprivation. Do you agree? Does this adage apply to any level of wealth?

10. Do you think Eliza breaks some pattern in her family that helps liberate her sisters?

11. What experience have you had that has unleashed strengths in yourself that you didn't know you had?

BIBLIOGRAPHY

Star of India 2001 Sail Training and Seamanship Manual. Maritime Museum of San Diego. (Available free on the Internet)

1811 Dictionary in the Vulgar Tongue–A Dictionary of Buckish Slang, University Wit, and Pickpocket Eloquence. Compiled by Captain Francis Grose. (Available free on the Internet.)

The Erotic Muse. Ed Gray. ©1992 Board of Trustees of the University of Illinois. Illini Books Edition.

ALSO BY ISABEL TUTAINE

Song of the Wooden Sparrow

In Isabel Tutaine's debut novel, two outcasts find unexpected connection in 1894 Maine. Dr. Leah Maays returns from Ghana widowed and faces a community hostile to female physicians. When she meets Duncan Shay, a man ostracized for his criminal past, their unlikely friendship blossoms into something deeper. Both must decide if they're willing to risk rejection to find belonging in this tale of redemption and defying society's limitations.

www.ingramcontent.com/pod-product-compliance
Lightning Source LLC
Chambersburg PA
CBHW040903010826
48978CB00013BB/1128